CHASIN' IT

BY

TONY LINDSAY

CHASIN' IT

BY TONY LINDSAY

Urban Books
7 Greene Avenue
Amityville, NY 11701

ISBN 09743636-7-7

First Printing July 2004

10 9 8 7 6 5 4 3 2 1

Acknowledgements

I would like to thank my agent, Audra Barrett. You sold the work when others said it wouldn't see the light of day. I'd also like to thank my editor, Martha Weber, who pressed out the literary wrinkles.

Much Love

Prologue

He was thirteen years old, wearing a pair of sky blue shorts he'd sewn himself. They were as close to a pair of culottes as he would dare. The shirt was also a Terri original. It had three buttons down the back. For his birthday Madear said he could wear whatever he wanted.

He was on the sidewalk in front of Madear's house, bare-footed and jumping double dutch. Linda and Brenda, the twin girls with buckteeth who always made him play the father when they played house, no matter how much he protested— "You're the only boy that plays house with us. You have to be the daddy."—were turning the rope. Jackie, the only girl on the block who had more Barbie dolls than him, and Sharon, the first person to call him a faggot to his face, were on the side singing and keeping score. The song they sang kept track of how good the jump was. The further along in the song he jumped, the better his score.

"Miss Mary Mack, Mack, Mack, all dressed in black, black, black, with silver buttons, buttons, buttons all down her back, back, back. She asked her mother, mother, mother for fifteen cents, cents, cents to see the elephant, elephant, elephant jump over the fence, fence, fence. She jumped so high, high, high she touched the sky, sky, sky and she didn't come down, down, down 'til the fourth of July, ly, ly."

They were on the sixth chorus; none of the girls had made it past the fourth. Normally the twins would miss a beat while turning, causing him to mess up, but this day they were flowing smoothly. They wanted to see how far he could go. It was already established he could jump double dutch better than any girl on their block or any block in the neighborhood. It was one of those days when they wanted him to show off. And show off he did.

He was jumping, turning, spinning and grinning, first with both feet then with one foot; then he switched to the other foot, then both feet as one, then he touched the ground, spun around and spelled his name out loud.

"T. E. R. R. I. Terri! I touched the ground! I spun around! I jumped so high I touched the sky! Now spell my name out loud!"

All the girls joined in. "T.E.R.R.I, Terri! T.E.R.R.I, Terri! T.E.R.R.I., Terri!"

Chapter One
September 1993

It wasn't much of a morning, as mornings go. No bright sun, no clear blue sky. The sky was covered with thick, gray clouds, and a heavy mist claimed the streets. Terri Parish woke to this morning in the back seat of an abandoned Chrysler New Yorker.

When he blinked his eyes open and saw the gloomy sky, he smiled because he thought it was evening. He wanted to sleep through the day. The smile left his face when he saw the *Chicago Sun-Times* delivery truck turn the corner. Newspaper trucks meant morning—early morning. Terri Parish didn't want morning; morning would give way to a whole day.

He fumbled around on the floor of the abandoned Chrysler and found the liter of Richards Wild Irish Rose red wine. At one time he awoke to Dom Perignon and fluffy, satin-covered pillows—not anymore. He uncapped the liter, turned it up, and gulped.

He remained slumped in the back seat of the Chrysler. He had a problem, a big problem, a hundred-and-thirty-five-thousand-dollar problem. That was the amount of money in the white plastic garbage bag that lay on the floor between his feet.

The night before he had hit the lick of a lifetime: every ho's dream, a dope-drunk trick with cash. The problem was the trick was royalty. He was the third highest in command of the city's largest street gang. Terri would be one dead hooker if he didn't use his brain.

A fool could see an opportunity, but a survivor figured out how to take it. Terri Parish considered himself a survivor at the very least. He'd grown up in Chicago and over his recent lean years he'd learned the rules of the city's streets. Stealing from royalty meant death, and he was not ready to die. He removed his shoulder-length wig and began scratching his scalp through his own thick hair. When he took the money he knew it was a dangerous, but it was also an opportunity, a chance of a lifetime.

1

Taking the money was his only real chance of leaving the city. Trying to save the money wasn't working for him. He had to have a lump sum of cash all at once. The previous night's trick provided it. For two years he'd tried unsuccessfully to save enough money to leave. He couldn't accumulate more than a hundred dollars without spending it on crack cocaine. He couldn't save and get high, and over the past two years getting high had taken priority over leaving and everything else.

His addiction to crack cocaine kept him broke and in Chicago. The night before was different; the cocaine rocks returned all they had taken from him with interest. He just had to be vengeful enough to take the chance.

He turned the liter of Richards red wine up again. Getting drunk wouldn't help his predicament and he knew it, but it would help him accept the fact that it was morning and wasn't a thing he could do about it. He'd have to make it through the day.

Life was a challenge, and a girl working the streets had to have balls. Taking chances was part of his life. Every time he got in the car with a trick, he was taking a chance. Sex in cars was a dangerous trade with few rewards. Only a fool didn't look for licks, and he was no fool. The trick slipped and he took him. Royalty or not, Terri felt he had to take him. Only a fool would pass up a hundred and thirty-five grand, and his Madear didn't raise him as a fool.

That night, life had given him a chance to stand, and stand he did. From the moment he woke he felt a change coming. Terri got an early start. Early for him was about 10:30 A.M. He'd risen early because he'd rested well the day before. No crack cocaine, only sleeping and eating. There were days his body required rest and nourishment. His body could no longer drug and date non-stop. At twenty-eight he knew when to rest.

After the day of rest he woke the next morning refreshed. He showered, trimmed, douched, plucked, picked, lotioned, powdered, brushed, combed, and tucked all morning. When he was satisfied that he was truly one fine, naked black girl he began to dress.

His plan was to go downtown and catch the lunch trade. If a girl was smart and quick, the lunch trade could keep one fed and high for two days. A girl had to be dressed, and Terri had the clothes. True, his wardrobe was not as extensive as in the past, with most of the valuable pieces being sold or traded for crack cocaine, but he could still manage to put a nice outfit together.

He pulled a black mini-skirt from the shallow closet, along with a red, skin-tight nylon T-shirt. The T-shirt had one purpose: to show the world he was becoming a real woman. His small, firm breasts and protruding nipples caught all eyes in this T-shirt.

The black leather mini-skirt was equally tight, and unlike some queens he required no butt padding. He had an ass—a gorgeous, half-basketball-sized ass, an ass that belonged in leather. "You got a girl's booty," was what his first lover Payton told him.

Yes, he had a gorgeous ass and great legs. His legs were second only to Tina Turner's. In his club days she was his act. He went to Vegas doing Tina. At eighteen he was the headliner at the Baton Club, Chicago's premier drag club. He did so well he earned a brief spot on *Oprah*. He won the title of Gay Ms. Chicago the same year. One of the judges told him it was his legs that made the difference.

He chose black fishnet hose to accent his fine legs that day. Nets to catch, and he was out to catch.

His first choice for hair was his own. He decided against it when he discovered he had no pressing oil. Three wigs took space on his dresser. He tried the blond Tina Turner wig; it was too much for downtown. The Anita Baker was too short. It allowed the naps from his kitchen to show. He settled with the Cher.

The shoes were easy; red pumps with short spike heels. If he owned a power outfit, this was it. His makeup was slight, a little eyebrow pencil and lipstick. *"You can't hide ugly, and there is little sense in covering up beauty,"* was Madear's advice about makeup. It stuck with him.

Mirrors were never his enemy when he was rested. His skin remained tight and clear; bags only appeared after two or three sleepless nights. Good skin ran in his family; the Parishes didn't crack 'til after sixty. He felt good, and it felt like a good day. Money was on the way.

He thought about straightening out the single-room-with-private-bath apartment he rented at the Cedar Park Arms transient hotel before he left, but the windup clock read 11:45 A.M., time to go. He closed the door on the mess and hoped Sally, the ancient white maid, forgave him.

Sally's fat and equally ancient husband worked the hotel desk during the day. He was a disgusting, toothless, old white man who chewed tobacco, and since he had no teeth, the tobacco juice dripped from the corners of his mouth.

Twice Terri was short on his rent and allowed the fat mush of a man to suck his budding breasts. It wasn't as unpleasant as Terri expected. Actually, it felt kind of good to have his little breast gummed. Life was full of surprises. He told the mush not to have Sally clean his room that day. He blew him a kiss and pranced out the door.

With hair flowing, skin glowing, ass tight and titties right, Terri stepped out to State Street Parkway, smiling in the September afternoon sun. The north loop neighborhood was always busy. Bars, boutiques, specialty food stores and restaurants speckled the street. It was a yuppie heaven except for the Cedar Park Arms transient hotel. No yuppies lived there; they ignored the occupants until carnal desire and/or intoxication took them over.

All types of people walked the busy State Street Parkway in the sun's cheerful glow: homeless, rich, hustlers, whores, police, servicemen, businessmen and doctors. Terri no longer worked the white trade in the area because nine out of ten times they were cops. Vice cops changed more than the hoes who worked the strip, and they paid tricks to tell them who was hoeing. The safety of the ghetto was a mile away.

When Terri was broke and needed to get high he would venture to the Cabrini-Green housing projects, but not today. Today was downtown trade only. He hadn't made it to the corner of the block before a black Chevy Blazer pulled alongside him. The Blazer slowed. Terri's normal routine would be to stop then give the driver a big smile if he was a young black man.

The young black men who could afford to drive new Blazers around the area were usually the cocaine dealers, the 'rock boys'. A couple of the rock boys knew him, and they knew he would show them a good time.

Terri didn't stop. He told himself downtown trade only; no neighborhood shit today. He wouldn't cheapen himself like that, not today. Today he wouldn't be called faggot for a hit of cocaine. Today he wouldn't have sex in an alley like a dog. Today he wouldn't look in the face of a young boy who regretted being with him. A horny, young punk with cocaine rocks to trade for a blowjob. Not today. Today, downtown trade only.

The sun lost its cheer as the Blazer paced him. It became only bright light—bright light that revealed the deep scuffs in Terri's red pumps; bright light that exposed the run down the center of his tight, red nylon T-shirt; bright light that showed the fallen hem of his leather mini-skirt; bright light that displayed the rips in his black fishnets; bright light that told him maybe downtown was too far to go.

He stopped and looked at his reflection in the window of Walgreens pharmacy. He had to smile because his reflection looked good. Damn good. The red T-shirt was bright in the sunlight, the leather was clinging and his smile was inspiring.

Fuck the Blazer, he thought with confidence, and he restarted his walk.

He was headed downtown to horny businessmen looking for an afternoon quickie, a lunchtime thrill; married, respectable businessmen who would cum quick; businessmen who used rubbers; men who didn't blame him or beat him because they desired him; men who appreciated his skill and paid him well for it.

He quickened his pace. He wasn't going to stop, nor was he going to look at the Blazer. The tinted window rolled down and the slightest aroma of smoked cocaine escaped. He slowed a bit but continued, determined.

"What's up, Terri baby? Damn, you looking good, girl. I ain't seen you looking that good since Statesville."

That stopped him. Whoever was in the Blazer knew him from the joint. In the joint he was Queen Bitch. He turned and saw the reddish-yellow grinning face of Mo-red.

* * * * *

Terri Parish had never wanted to return to Chicago. He had served five years in Statesville Penitentiary for forgery and credit fraud. All during his time served he swore to never return to the city. The only reason he returned was to help Madear during her last days.

His best friend, Charles 'Charlene' Bowman, was doing hair in Birmingham, Alabama and making a killing. He wrote Terri letters describing how plentiful and relaxed life was in the South. Charlene Bowman had been Mo-red's ho in the joint.

Terri never met a man as hateful and abusive as Mo-red. He gorilla pimped Charlene, made him conform to his wants by beating him. He forced himself on Charlene whenever he wanted. He beat him whenever he wanted and sold him to whomever he wanted for whatever he wanted.

6

Mo-red was royalty, a chief in one of Chicago's largest street gangs. He could provide for Charlene when he wanted. He could get the heroin Charlene's addiction required. Terri assumed that Mo-red was the lesser of two evils for Charlene.

It was after one of Mo-red's fierce beatings when the friendship between Terri and Charlene formed. Charlene was crouched in the middle of the community shower stall, bleeding heavily from his nose and slashes across his back. He was dressed in a red-and-black bikini bottom. The other inmates stepped over him and continued their morning showers.

Terri cursed them all and went to Charlene's aid. He wrapped Charlene's torso in a towel and helped him from the floor. Terri took him to his cell and away from Mo-red.

Charlene, even though badly beaten, was afraid to go to the infirmary, where the nurse would report the attack. He feared getting Mo-red into trouble. Charlene wanted to return to Mo-red's house. Terri insisted he stay with him awhile. Throughout the morning Terri cleaned and tended to Charlene's wounds. He became big sister to a needy younger sister.

They tried to talk about anything but Mo-red. They talked about fine guards, jealous queens, greatly endowed cons and the outside. On the outside both were queens—twenty-four hours a day, seven days a week in drag. Neither of them was a 'joint-made faggot.' For each, becoming a real woman was paramount.

Originally from Chicago's south side, both had moved to the north side of the city, and at one time they lived less than two blocks away from each other on Melrose Street. They discovered they shared some of the same trade clients on the outside. It appeared the same police sergeant had paid both their rents on the outside.

They performed at some of the same clubs only at different times. Terri had done his shows prior to Charlene becoming active in show life. Terri noticed Charlene didn't say that he had heard of him, but Terri knew he must have. A queen's fame lasts longer than the queen does.

For two years before the beating, Terri seldom spoke to Charlene, who stood five feet eleven inches, weighing every bit of two hundred pounds, and paraded around the joint in cut-off blue jeans and halter tops. He dyed his hair weekly, from pastels to blond. He wore gaudy costume jewelry, smacked his chewing gum and used blue eye shadow and pink rouge on his tan skin. The polish on his fingernails and toenails seldom matched. Based on appearance alone, Terri guessed they would have little to talk about. Their first conversation started badly.

"Are you a nurse or somethin'?"

Terri watched Charlene sitting in the only chair in the cell—his director's chair. Terri would have preferred him to sit on the bunk or the rug. Terri relied on the director's chair. He didn't want Charlene's blood staining the yellow bands of the chair.

Terri spent hours staring at the bright, cheerful yellow of the chair, which was different than the yellow directional lines painted on the prison floor. Terri detested the urine-stain yellow of the directional lines. The chair's yellow was butter yellow, a sunny day in June yellow, Madear's fluffy scrambled eggs yellow.

Terri didn't want the chair stained, but he did not redirect Charlene to the rug or the bunk. Instead he sucked his teeth and reached under the bed for the first aid kit. "No, I'm not a nurse. I merely saw you needed some help."

Standing behind Charlene, Terri gently pushed his back forward, guiding him to a bent position in the director's chair.

"I didn't ask you for your help, so I don't owe you shit."

Terri ignored Charlene's ungrateful words and twisted the seal open on the brown plastic bottle. He poured the liquid across Charlene's wounds.

"Ouch! Ain't you got somethin' that don't sting?"

"This usually doesn't sting." Terri continued pouring the hydrogen peroxide despite Charlene's protests.

"Well, it's stingin' today, Ms. High and Mighty."

Terri saw Charlene squirming and wondered if it really did sting. "Please be still." Terri tore some gauze from the roll in his first aid kit.

"Ms. High and Mighty? Why would you call me that?"

"That's you. Ms. Queen Bitch, Ms. I-fuck-the-guards, Ms. Vegas showgirl, Ms. I-got-my-own-cell, Ms. Snooty Ass."

Charlene's hostile tone shocked Terri. He had no idea Charlene viewed him in such a light. Terri stopped tending the wounds.

"Look, maybe this was a mistake. If you don't want my help I can stop."

"I didn't say I didn't wantcha help. I was just wonderin' why the Queen Bitch would help me."

Terri noticed that Charlene asked the question with his head lowered; the hostility was gone from his voice. Terri decided not to explain why he was helping Charlene because he didn't know why. He placed pieces of the gauze lightly across Charlene's wounds, allowing them to absorb the blood.

"My name is Terri."

"That's your name, but you is the Queen Bitch. Ain't no other hoes livin' as good as you in this joint."

"Living good? I don't believe any of us are living well. We're locked up in here like animals."

"Yeah, but you the animal with the most. You's the Queen Bitch, like it or not, and every ho knows it. Shit, we sucking off four times the mens you sucking and getting four times less than what you got."

"I don't have anything to do with that. Madear, my grandmother, once told me the value of one's work should be reflected in the price."

It wasn't his fault, Terri concluded. He wasn't the one prancing around the prison with lime green hair and mismatched nail polish.

"What does that mean? Why do you say shit like that? That's that snooty, high and mighty shit. The value! Fuck the value! You's a ho just like the rest of us. You just got lucky."

"You're right." There was no sense in upsetting Charlene; he'd been through enough. True, Terri was lucky, but his poise had a lot to do with the luck.

Terri peeled the blood-filled gauze from Charlene's back and replaced it with fresh strips.

"I know I'm right. And you ain't got to worry about my blood. I tested negative."

Terri hadn't thought of the danger of Charlene's blood until he mentioned it. "I'm not worried. There's a chip of tile in your shoulder. This might hurt." Terri grabbed the chip with his eyebrow tweezers and pulled it free.

Charlene nearly jumped from the chair. "Shit! Might hurt? You knew damn well that was gonna hurt. How bad is my back?"

"It should heal without bad scars," Terri lied. The scars would heal horribly.

Terri peeled the remaining gauze strips from Charlene's back and sprayed the wounds with antiseptic. He covered them with large gauze patches and taped them in place. That was all he could do.

"You lucky you didn't get Mo-red when you was trying to pull him from me, or this would be you."

"What?" Terri's tone reflected the indignation, offense and disgust he felt. He snapped the first aid kit closed. Mo-red was a barbarian, an animal, a red gorilla. Nothing about him appealed to Terri. One emotion alone was present in Terri's mind where Mo-red was concerned: fear. He slid the kit under the bunk and sat on the bed facing Charlene.

"I know you was after him a while back," Charlene said.

10

"Baby, the last thing I need is a pimp in the joint. True, when I first got here I thought I would need protection. I have never been a fighter and I have absolutely no size. I figured I would be raped and killed the first night if I didn't find a protector, but it wasn't like that for me. Like you said, I got lucky.

"The first couple of weeks no one said too much of anything to me. Charlene, I was so scared I couldn't sleep or eat waiting for it to happen, waiting to be raped and beat to death. My cellmate at the time was an old guy named Hank. Every time he walked in the cell I jumped damn near to the ceiling. Then he told me I had a guardian no one wanted to mess with. I asked him who it was; he said he couldn't say, but he told me I was safe and I could relax.

"Charlene, that made it worse. I owed somebody and didn't know who it was. Then they moved me to this cell by myself and the guards started *visiting* me. No, child, Mo-red is all yours."

Mo-red walked past Terri's house repeatedly and did not enter. Terri ignored him and continued talking to Charlene. After Mo-red was out of sight, Charlene asked, "Ain't you scared of him?"

"No. I'm not scared, because he has you. If you were gone, I'd be scared. I don't think I could handle it."

"What do you mean?"

"How he beats and sells you." No sooner than the words left his mouth Terri regretted them. He saw Charlene's eyes downcast. He was putting himself above Charlene, being Ms. High and Mighty, but he knew he could have easily been in Charlene's shoes. It could have been his back sliced raw.

"He ain't beatin' the real me," Terri heard Charlene whisper. "He's only beatin' the outside me. The real Charlene is safe on the inside. He cain't get to her. I learned a long time ago there is two of me." Charlene's eyes were still on the floor.

"Two of you?"

11

"Yeah, the one that can take whatever a motherfucker like Mo-red puts out, and the other one—the one nobody can touch unless I let them, the pretty one, the soft one inside. Don't you have two selves?"

Terri saw the eyes of a child looking up at him. "No," Terri answered, looking at the red stains in the yellow bands of the director's chair instead of into the wounded eyes.

"Ain't nobody ever split you in two?"

"No."

"My uncle split me when I was eight years old. I used to hate him for it, but now I'm glad he did it, because she's safe on the inside. Nobody can touch her unless I let them."

Terri couldn't hear the defiance Charlene tried to put in his words. He knew Charlene wanted to sound tough, but all he heard was the child.

"When you were eight?" Terri turned his head and looked into the corridor. He didn't want Charlene to see the tears that were welling in his eyes. He didn't want Charlene to think he pitied him, but he did. Charlene was scarred long before Mo-red took the wire coat hanger to his back.

"That's when it started. My uncle—my grandmother's son, my father's brother—was my first."

"Did you ever tell?"

"Who, Ms. High and Mighty? Who was I supposed to tell? My grandmother who was happy he came over and brought her a bottle of gin? Naw, wasn't nobody to tell. After he got me used to it I didn't mind it too bad, but I started hiding from him because I knew it was wrong.

"My grandmother lived in an old frame house. She had an old coal bin on the side. It was blocked off from the basement, but it was just enough room left for me. I hid in there every time he came over, and he never found me. That's where I hide my other self. I can go there so good sometimes I can see the spider webs in the dark corners. I can hear my grandmother's radio, and I can even hear my uncle driving off cursing because he couldn't find me."

That night alone in his cell, after Charlene returned to Mo-red, Terri decided Charlene would be his friend. Terri had no 'girlfriends' in the joint and it was the same on the outside. It wasn't that he didn't want girlfriends; he just saw no need for them. Friendships in the past always proved to be more trouble than what they were worth. Some queen was always screaming about Terri wanted his man, or trying to tell Terri how to behave, or setting him up with some financially strapped and ugly date. Charlene was different.

Charlene needed guidance. He was fifty pounds overweight, illiterate, addicted to heroin, and he let Mo-red treat him like a dog. Terri decided to work on the weight first. He put him on a vegetable and fruit diet, and over months the pounds dissolved.

Charlene's wardrobe basically consisted of cut-off jeans and halter-tops. Terri had Charlene pick out some material from Joann's fabric catalog. He made Charlene four dresses, and all were three sizes too small before the weight loss. Terri was happy with Charlene's physical changes, but there was more work to be done.

He started him out reading Donald Goines' *Whoreson*, then he slipped in Maya Angelou's *I Know Why the Caged Bird Sings*. He followed that with Gloria Naylor's *The Women of Brewster Place* and when Charlene was begging for more, Terri fed him his personal favorite, Toni Morrison's *Sula*.

Six months passed and both Terri and Charlene were pleased with the changes. Mo-red was not. Two days prior to Charlene's release, he came to Terri's cell, sweating and in tears.

"He won't give me a blow. He told me to snort the fuckin' books. I need that blow, Terri. I need it bad. My sick is on."

Charlene's pacing made Terri edgy.

13

"Why wouldn't he give it to you?" Terri asked, sitting up in the bunk.

"Because I wouldn't lick his unwashed asshole."

Terri attempted to hide the disgust he felt. Mo-red was truly a heathen.

"What will happen if you don't get it?"

"I get sick, sicker."

Terri had never seen Charlene or anyone else sick from withdrawal. He'd only heard that they got flu-like symptoms and muscle cramps. Compared to licking Mo-red's dirty asshole, that seemed minor. Charlene stopped pacing and stood in front of him.

"Will you die?" Terri asked.

"Yes. No, I'll just wish I was dead."

Terri made room on the bunk and Charlene sat next to him.

"Then what?" Terri held Charlene's hand; it was moist.

"I don't know. I ain't never went that far." Terri allowed Charlene to pull his hand away, stand and resume pacing.

"Do you want to go that far?" Terri remained sitting.

"Not today. He's got a fresh batch in. I can smell it in the house. He put a dime bag in his asshole and told me to lick it. I did it before, but I just didn't want to do it today. I'm outta here in two days—you know that and he knows that. I gotta get a blow, Terri. You gotta help me."

"Me? What can I do?"

"Mexican Mickey got some shit from Mo-red, but he won't fuck me for it. He's scared of Mo-red. He'll fuck you, Terri, and give you two bags. He told me he would. He's in the shower. I'll go with you." Charlene knelt in front of him with pleading eyes.

Charlene was trembling, his nose was running, and small beads of sweat were forming on his forehead. Terri didn't want Charlene to suffer.

"Mickey's kind of cute," Terri said with pseudo interest and a small smile.

14

He didn't think Mickey was cute. Mickey had tattoos covering eighty percent of his body, and his nipples were pierced, but his little sister needed him and Terri was confident he could satisfy Mickey in less than five minutes.

"You'll do it?"

Terri felt Charlene squeezing his kneecaps.

"Yes."

Mickey was in the shower, but so were Mo-red and six of his soldiers. They raped Terri and beat and raped Charlene. Terri didn't get a chance to say goodbye to his little sister. Charlene was released directly from the infirmary.

After that, Terri gave into Mo-red out of fear. As with Charlene, Mo-red gorilla pimped Terri. Terri never gave Mo-red a reason to beat him. Whatever Mo-red asked, he did. At meals he'd sit beneath the table and suck Mo-red while he ate. At night Terri massaged his back until he fell asleep. He sucked and sexed whomever for whatever Mo-red wanted, but the beatings still came.

Mo-red would beat him because it rained; beat him because the movie was canceled; beat him because a trick complained; beat him because his parole was denied; beat him because the toilet overflowed; and beat him because he wasn't a real woman.

Terri never told; he took the beatings in silence. His only relief came when the beatings were so severe he'd have to go to the infirmary. *Ain't nobody ever split you in two?* Yes, was Terri's answer after Mo-red dislocated his shoulder and broke three ribs.

Four years before Mo-red, Terri was Queen Bitch. He could pick and choose who he wanted in the joint. He was one of the few queens who tricked with the guards. The guards had freedom. They could have real women, but a dressed up Terri was what many of them preferred.

Terri was a star. He'd done Vegas and appeared on *Oprah*. He was a celebrity, and sex with Terri was an event. He made

15

fantasy real. When he closed the drapes made from prison linen across the bars, started the slow, spinning light and played Minnie Riperton's "Adventures in Paradise," even the unimaginative fell under his spell of dance and seduction. When a man entered Terri's house he was king for his time and he paid well for the imperial treatment.

Terri received a cassette player with over two hundred tapes, a battery-operated color TV, a Crock-Pot, a small crystal lamp, a Chinese vase, a Persian rug and one director's chair. Terri referred to the guards as patrons of the arts. The gifts he most appreciated were the clothes: African gowns, evening gowns from Italy, and French undergarments. If the clothes remained in the packaging of the shops where they originated, extra attention was given to that patron. Marshall Field's and Saks packaging were his favorite.

Mo-red took it all and dared the guards to object. He beat Terri in front of them and told them Terri was his property. If they wanted Terri they had to pay him. The guards begged Terri to let them help. Terri refused because in his mind inmates controlled death in the joint. His life behind prison walls was in Mo-red's hands.

Mo-red was everywhere. He moved into Terri's house and mind at the same time. He was intrusive in both. He was too big for the house. He broke the yellow director's chair, knocked over the crystal lamp, crumbled the Persian rug, cracked the vase and fouled the air.

Mo-red demanded Terri's complete attention in the house. Terri could not take his eyes off of Mo-red unless Mo-red said so. He'd sit for hours staring at Mo-red, responding to whatever Mo-red said or did. He watched Mo-red read. He watched him look at television. He watched him masturbate. He watched him defecate. When he was allowed to close his eyes, all he saw was Mo-red.

Terri tried to follow Charlene's example and keep his inside self safe and untouched. In thought, he saw himself safe in his childhood bedroom, the one he had seen in the Sears and Roebuck catalog, the one for which he cried and begged Madear. In his childhood bedroom he tried to keep Mo-red away from the soft Terri, but he couldn't. Mo-red was in every part of his mind.

Charlene's secret letters provided the fresh air Terri needed. The day Terri decided on suicide was also the day the first letter came. One of his patrons smuggled the letter to him in the shower. Terri held a shank knife in one hand and the letter in the other. Charlene's letter won. He read the letter while Mo-red slept. After he read the letter he ate it.

The letters turned Birmingham into a land of milk and honey. Charlene wrote of slow, sweet men with lots of money; clear, bright, sunny days and star-filled nights; peach cobblers; well hung country boys; fried okra; cheating husbands with spare houses; fresh chicken; gay policemen; hand-churned custard; and a doctor who did the change dirt cheap. That was Birmingham—a new place, a place without Mo-red. A place Terri could only dream about when Mo-red slept. He could think of nothing worse than Mo-red in Birmingham.

Under Mo-red's rule Terri went from Queen Bitch to hag, fucking whomever Mo-red said, for whatever they gave Mo-red. Terri no longer pranced the yard. He simply walked. He no longer dressed. He wore standard-issue clothing unless Mo-red ordered him to dress. He was just doing his time and praying for the breaths of fresh air Charlene sent.

It was three days before Terri's release date when he received the first letter from his mother, Diane. She hadn't written in five years. She wrote to tell him that Madear was dying and she could no longer care for her. Diane was marrying a doctor with eight children and God wanted her to take care of them.

She and the doctor would pick him up when he was released so he could do the Christian thing and take care of

Madear. It was all set up. The state would pay him a caretaker's salary and he could stay rent-free with Madear.

Terri cried for himself and Madear when he read the letter. She was his mother, his Madear, more than the selfish, stank slut who wrote the letter. Diane didn't raise her own son and now she was going to raise a doctor's eight. To hell with her. Madear needed him. He needed Birmingham. Chicago had him. He had to go back.

After the tears he got dressed, really dressed, in silk and leather. He left Mo-red and didn't return. He spent his last three days under the protection of his patrons.

* * * * *

"Oh, so you don't know a nigga now, huh?"

Terri stood still on the sidewalk, allowing passersby to walk between him and Mo-red's Blazer.

"I know who you look like, but that man is locked up for another five years," Terri answered.

"Yeah, well even a bad nigga can play good. Come on over here, Terri, with your fine ass. Girl, you look good in that leather skirt. You always did like silk and leather. Come on over here."

Terri knew better. This was trouble, big time trouble. If he got in the Blazer, he wouldn't see downtown today. If he didn't get in the Blazer, he might never see downtown or anyplace. He stared into Mo-red's smiling face and remembered a crazy man, a man crazy enough to kill Terri for rejecting him. Playing along was Terri's only choice.

Terri approached the Blazer. Mo-red opened the door. Terri hopped in, smiling and praying. He closed the door.

Chapter Two
Madear

Madear was the only person in the world for whom Terri would return to Chicago. When he returned he saw Madear was dying. He saw it in her brown eyes circled in gray. He saw death in the warm eyes that cared for him when others didn't. He saw death in the knowing eyes that never judged him. He saw death in the wise eyes that tried to teach him to value himself first. He saw death in the only eyes that cried when he was sentenced to five years. He hadn't wanted to see Madear's eyes through bars or two-inch thick safety glass.

Terri forbade her to visit him in Statesville, but he wished he hadn't. He needed to see those eyes after the prison gates closed on him and locked out the free world. It wasn't until he came home and was looking into her eyes that he ever thought about how much that must have hurt her.

It was always Terri and Madear against everybody else. He denied her a chance to fight with him. He saw it in her eyes; she missed him and needed him. He told her he was sorry and promised to make her better.

Caring for her was not a chore. He did it with love. His mother, Diane, moved out of Madear's house the day he moved in and never offered a moment's worth of help. That was fine with Terri. He wanted Madear all to himself. He had five years to make up.

When he arrived she was bedridden and barely talking. He didn't feed her the broth and diabetic shakes Diane had left behind. He found Madear's teeth, cleaned them and served her the food she raised him on: greens, pork chops, fried corn, sweet potatoes, broiled chicken, stewed oxtails and an occasional shot of Old Grand Dad. Within a month she was fussing about his cooking and lack of housecleaning.

The second month they tackled the walker in the house. By the end of the month Madear was shuffling step by step around the block. They talked for hours; or rather she talked for hours. Terri listened. He would ask a question and she would answer with history—family history, most of which was unknown to him. She seemed determined that he should know what she'd experienced and why.

He never asked her about her sickness; she never asked him about prison. They talked mostly about her past, seldom about the present, and some about the future. She thought Birmingham was a good idea and was looking forward to going with him. There was little left in Chicago for her either.

"At one time, T.T., this city had promise. A Negro with a brain could make something happen. I was never a dumb woman. I educated myself. I learned how to talk by listening close to white people. I couldn't stand a dumb-sounding nigger. Always speak clear, T.T. Sounding common is just that—common. There is a language, English, and niggers are not speaking it. If you speak what niggers speak, the white man will treat you like a nigger.

"Your mother's father was a dumb nigger. He didn't want shit but a whiskey bottle and some coochie. I left his drunk ass in Ohio, with your mother in my stomach. Lying son of a gun told me he was bank robber. That man couldn't steal doo-doo out a baby's diaper. His aspirations did not go beyond emptying a whiskey bottle. He stayed drunk, broke and inside me. The truth be spoke, I did not mind him being inside of me at all, not one bit. To coin a phrase, he made my love come down.

"I told the ignorant man he was my first. Now keep in mind I met him in a whorehouse. He believed I was a virgin, and I believed he was a bank robber. We were both stupid.

"I bought this house on my own in 1945, a year after your mother was born. There were no dumb women buying property back then, T.T., only clever women. This city has always respected money. It will give one a chance if one gets the money. I bought this house from Lady Diane, a whore from Maine that told everyone she was from England.

"She didn't want any colored men with her girls, not even the colored ones. She said colored men were too big and they loosened a girl's grip. When a colored man found his way to her establishment, he always had to show her his privates. If it was longer than a new pencil or fatter than a breakfast biscuit, she sent him away un-serviced.

"The neighborhood was turning colored so fast she was turning away more business than she was taking in. Then she did what she taught me never to do. She panicked and made a decision out of fear. She sold me this house for seven hundred dollars cash.

"I turned it into the finest colored brothel in the city. Men paid ten dollars for my girls, T.T., and that wasn't a small amount. Most colored girls were lucky to get two dollars for they services. I kept the prices Diane established and raised them a dollar a year. White men and colored men paid my price and received the best sexual experience in the city.

"I didn't have any lazy girls working here. They were paid to be the best, and I made sure they were. I watched each one of them. At times I would sit in the rooms and orchestrate. I told them what they was doing wrong and what they *had* to do right.

"I lost girls that I had trained to customers. Men married my girls, T. T., and more than one fool fell in love in my brothel. I didn't allow love. I could care less if it was lesbian love between the girls or a customer totally infatuated. I didn't allow love. When a customer began cooing over a girl, I insisted he switch girls. Nine out of ten times that would work. The lesbian love proved difficult.

"The girls were together throughout the course of the day. Of course one expects bonding, but a entire day of hugging and snuggling—unacceptable. I only had to experience one love-struck lesbian to realize I wasn't having it in my brothel.

"Spanish Marie cut up three of my most attractive girls and two of my best customers fighting over old, very black, tired, about to be retired Fran. No, no. No love. I trained them to be businesswomen and ladies. That's why the gentlemen took them out of here. I taught them the things that were important: how to watch your money and act like a lady. The same as Lady Diane trained me.

"I met her on the train from Ohio to Chicago. I was hiding in the diner car, where the colored porter, who I traded pussy for fare, told me to stay. There was only to be one meal served on the run, so I would be fine until the morning. I was sitting in the car crying because I had no idea were I was going to stay once I arrived in Chicago.

"Lady Diane was passing through the dark car and heard me sobbing. We began talking and I told her everything. She told me I was selling my goods too cheap.

"The value one puts in one's work should always be reflected in price. She asked did I only give a train ride worth of pussy. I told her no, I fucked him silly. She said, 'Well, I suggest renegotiations are in order. Let's see if we can get you sleeping quarters, shall we?'

"When she finished with that porter I was riding first class next to her. I followed her like a hungry alley cat to this house. When I saw it, I knew one day it was going to be mine.

"She let me work a few customers until I started showing with your mother. Once I started showing I did the laundry. When I got too far along for laundry, she put me on the books. She taught me how to balance accounts and pay bills. In two weeks I took over the ordering of supplies and payroll. She told me I was a natural bookkeeper.

"After your mother was born I worked a few customers, but mostly I kept the books and ran the house. Once Lady Diane saw I was capable of running things she started traveling. Upon each return the colored population in the neighborhood had grown. Frustrated, she asked me if I wanted to buy the house. Her brothel in Maine was doing well and she was thinking of opening another. I could go with her if I wanted, or buy this

23

one. She inquired how much I thought it was worth. I couldn't give her an answer—not one I could afford. I told her what I had and she accepted it. I became the owner."

After her sickness Madear talked to Terri in spurts, not pausing for a reply. When she finished she fell asleep. When she woke, she picked up right where she left off. When she was able to get around with the aid of only a cane, Terri suggested her two favorite things: shopping and the theater.

When Terri was a child Madear wouldn't give him money for the movies. Instead she took him to the theaters and small playhouses across the city. Musicals were her favorite. She and Terri both marveled at the costumes, the energy, and the showmanship.

The theater, Madear told Terri, was real acting. Picture shows was practice. Actors—true actors—didn't cut and start over. Life did not allow cuts, and neither did the stage.

The theater was magic for Terri. On a small stage a world was created. People became who and what they wanted. A man could become a wolf, a nun could fly, toys came to life. Anything was possible under those magic lights. At ten years old his mind was made up. He would live his life under magic lights.

For his fifteenth birthday Madear took him to see *The Wiz*. After the play he clicked his heels, danced, sang and twirled on the busy corner of State and Madison. Nine-thirty at night, a fifteen-year-old boy dressed in skin-tight hip hugger jeans and a yellow, sleeveless sweater, singing like Diana Ross while clicking his heels, attracted critical attention. The shouts of "faggot" and "sissy boy" ended his performance. He quietly boarded the bus with tears in his eyes when it arrived.

He sat next to the window, content with crying. He expected Madear to hug him and tell him those boys were stupid and mean and he should pay no attention to them. Instead she slapped him twice. She told him to never ever allow anyone to steal his joy. Joy was precious, and only a fool let others take it. The good feeling was his alone and only he was responsible for it.

Life, she told him, was mostly bad, and only a fool gave away the little joy that came. If singing and acting like Diana Ross made him feel good, he would be a fool if he let anyone stop him from doing it. Then she kissed him and the conversation was over. That was how it was with Madear; she got his attention then gave him what he needed. Words were minimal back then.

They never spoke about her dying. Terri tried to put it out of his mind. Madear was getting around fine and enjoying their weekly outings. He took her to every Black play in the city and to a couple of gay productions on the north side. They shopped at the Water Tower and Orland Park malls. He spent all the caretaker's salary on keeping her happy. Terri believed people didn't die when they were happy.

He was soaping her back in the tub when she made what turned out to be one of her last requests.

"You know what a couple of girls like us need, T.T.?" Madear asked, pulling the loofah from the brass towel rack that was anchored on the wall beside the tub.

"No, Madear, what?" Madear only used Ivory soap despite Terri's many suggestions and recommendations for scented and herbal soaps. Terri slid the family size bar across her shoulders.

"We need to get us some." Madear dipped the loofah in the warm tub water.

"Some?"

He'd braided Madear's thick, white hair earlier into two French braids, parted down the middle. He avoided getting it wet since Madear refused to have it pressed. She didn't want it dyed or pressed, simply braided.

"Yes, some."

"Some what, Madear?"

"Some stuff, boy. Don't make me spell it out for you. I want a man—a young man with one longer than a new pencil and fatter than a breakfast biscuit. I've been thinking about it lately. I might not get into that heaven those colored preachers you've been watching on the television talk about, so I might as well get me a little more pleasure before it's over. With a little—well, maybe a lot of lubrication—I should be able to slide one in.

"I have been looking in your magazines and I saw a company that will send a man directly to us. I figure that's what we need. We'll go downtown, stay at one of the five-star hotels and order us two. What do you think about that?" The seriousness in Madear's tone told Terri she wasn't joking.

"I haven't been in that kind of a mood, Madear, but if that's what you want, I'll get it for you." He wasn't comfortable with the thought of Madear having sex. He never thought of Madear and men. He knew she'd had her share, but he never thought of her actually performing the act.

Terri sat on the side of the tub looking at Madear's large, sagging breasts, noticing the white hairs growing out of her chin and on her chest. He rinsed the suds from the wrinkled skin on her back and decided that sex would be too much for her to handle. Just the thought of her lying spread eagle with a young stud humping into her disturbed him. After all, she was his grandmother.

"If you haven't been in that kind of a mood, why do you have the magazines?"

"I like keeping abreast." He would firmly tell her no and that would put an end to it.

"Abreast? No, you're horny and you just don't know it. Your subconscious is controlling your actions. You're horny and you don't want to be. It's okay. I got the solution. You're lucky to have such a cosmopolitan grandmother, one that reads and watches public television.

26

"You're experiencing Post Traumatic Stress Syndrome. It's common after life-threatening experiences. The key is getting right back into the swing of life. And T.T., the men pictured in the advertisement seemed more than capable of getting us both back into the swing."

"Madear!"

Terri would have to talk her out of it. She was thinking of doing it for him. She wanted him to get back in the swing.

"It's the truth! You should see how full their underwear looks."

"Madear!" Maybe she wasn't thinking about it for him.

"Oh, I guess you limit yourself to the articles alone?"

"No, I read the ads." Terri took the loofah from her and rinsed her back again.

"And have you seen the one I'm speaking of?"

"Possibly."

"Let me help you with your recall. It has four men and they're all hung like mules. Okay? Ring a bell?"

"Yes, Madear, I have seen that ad." *What could it hurt?* Terri thought.

"Good. Call them. I saw another advertisement in the magazine for a clinic right here in the city. They offer the hormone treatment and implants. Are you still planning on getting breasts? Do you think they can perk mines up?" Madear scooped up her sagging breasts. "We could go together."

"What hotel you want to stay in Madear?" Terri asked, ignoring both her questions and making a mental note to keep his magazines out of the main bathroom.

"The one in the Water Tower." Madear released her breasts, splashing the water.

"How young a man do you want, Madear?"

"Order me one you would like. No, maybe not. You like them kinda yellow, like that boy next door. You didn't think I knew about that, did you? You and that Payton. That boy took you to his prom. Told his daddy he couldn't find a girl, so he was going with his buddy. I thank God you didn't wear a dress. That would have killed his stupid daddy, but that purple tux wasn't too far off. Do you ever hear from him?"

"No, Madear, I think he got married." Was there anything she didn't remember?

"Married? That boy ain't married. That boy loves you. Watch what I say. He'll be back. I know love when I see it. He didn't like you wearing dresses, did he?"

"I don't think so."

"Loved you like you was, huh?"

"I don't know, Madear. When do you want to go to the hotel?"

Terri did not want to think of Payton. Payton, who didn't like Terri's girl's booty or girl's eyes, but married a girl. Payton, who called him a whore when he told him about the white football coach who gave him thirty dollars for letting him suck his thang. Payton, who wrote him a letter in his senior year telling him that he was no longer gay. Payton, who wrote that sticking his thang in women was more natural than sticking it in men. Payton, who broke his heart with a letter.

"T.T., tonight, and I'm the one that changes the subject when we talk, not you. I want a dark one. A real dark one with muscles like that one boy you had, the one that scared you. What was his name? Jessie. I saw a man this morning in a music video that reminded me of him.

"Jessie was a keeper, but he was too dark for you. Blue-black. You don't see colored folks that dark anymore. I want him dark like Jessie, but I want mine ugly. Jessie was a little too pretty for me. Get me an ugly one, mule ugly. Like your mother's father. A dark, ugly man will lay down with any old thing. Get me one like that."

"Yes, Madear." He would order her the mule she wanted, but not one for himself.

The next morning he joined Madear in her suite where she was being served breakfast in bed by the mule she had requested. She smiled, said "Thank you, T.T.," and died.

Terri refused to feel guilty about her death. He gave her what she wanted. He tried to fill her last days with joy. He did his best. Happy people did die.

At the funeral while his mother cried and openly mourned Madear's passing, he sat peacefully in the back of the church in a black, light wool Evan Picone two-piece suit with veil, smiling and thinking of Madear's last night. He had done the right thing.

He didn't go to the burial. He'd had his fill of his mother. He went to the house and began to pack. The last state check was ten dollars more than a first class one-way ticket to Birmingham. Diane could have the house. All he wanted was his freedom.

The doorbell rang. It was his new father, his mother's husband, the doctor. Dr. Albert Goody. He was alone. Terri opened the door.

"Can I come in?" Dr. Goody asked with apprehension while standing in the doorway.

"Sure, where is your wife?" Terri opened the door wide and stepped aside for Dr. Goody.

"She's not coming. I was sent," he said, closing the door behind him. He stood stiffly in front of the closed door. "Your mother sent me to tell you that you are going to have to find someplace else to live."

Terri expected this from his mother. All his life he could only remember her taking, never giving. She was a street-walking whore who cared about no one but herself. She dropped him off on Madear the week he was born and never looked back. No Christmas presents, no love, nothing that showed she was his mother. If Madear hadn't told him, Terri wouldn't have known who his mother was. He dreaded her as a child because her visits always made Madear cry.

The worst whipping Madear gave him was when he refused to let his mother in the house. He was thirteen years old. It was a frigid winter night and she was banging on the front door, demanding to be let in. Terri was lying on the couch, warm under one of Madear's handmade quilts. He was cozy and could think of no reason to walk across the cold floorboards to the door. He ignored the banging. The noise woke Madear, who let her in. Madear looked to the couch and saw Terri was wide awake. Her stern, furious gaze forced him to cover his head with the quilt.

The next morning Madear beat him with a razor strap. She told him that no grandson of hers would leave his mother out in the cold, and if he ever did it again, she promised him death. He believed she would beat him again, but he knew she wouldn't kill him.

Despite the whips on his butt, he still could not think of a reason to let her in. Diane simply was not worth it, and nothing had changed as far as he was concerned. His mother was a bitch, a bitch who wasn't worth cold floorboards or staying in Chicago to argue with over Madear's house. Selling the house was expected.

"Do you understand, Terri?"

"There is no problem, Dr. Goody."

"I don't think it's fair, Terri, but it's not my decision. Your mother is a determined woman."

"That's one word for her."

Dr. Goody stood silent for a moment, obviously uncomfortable. He wasn't a short man, but the excess weight did shorten his stature. His huge stomach caused his upper torso to slump. His weight, along with being forced to do an uncomfortable task, dwarfed him in Terri's eyes. Terri pitied the man who stood in front of him with head hung low.

Men ruled by women always confused Terri. Couldn't they spot a bitch before they married her? Or did the men, through some form of weakness, breed the bitchiness? Some of his best tricks had been men with ball-busting bitches for wives. Pleasing them was simple. They all wanted a docile, obedient, praising, sex toy.

"She wants you out today, Terri." His words sounded apologetic.

"I was just packing, Dr. Goody."

"Really, Terri?"

"Yes, Doctor. I know your wife better than you."

"Perhaps. I never told your mother, but I've seen a couple of your shows. I saw you at the Baton years ago and I saw you at Victor Victoria."

"A fan?"

"No. Well, yeah, sorta. I saw you in Vegas too. You did Tina Turner."

"Really! You come on in here and have a seat. You can talk to me while I'm packing. I'm going to need a lift to Midway anyhow. Come on in."

Terri grabbed Dr. Goody's huge, sweaty palm and led him up the stairs to his bedroom. Terri felt the slight resistance in Dr. Goody's arm but he ignored it and pulled him. He would give Diane the house, but he was going to take something.

"I, I, I . . . I shouldn't sit in here, Terri."

"This is where I'm packing, Dr. Goody. Relax. I won't bite you, despite what my mother has told you. Now tell me about when you saw me in Vegas." Terri pointed to the corner of the bed, offering Dr. Goody a seat.

The room hadn't changed since Terri was a child. Despite age fading and wearing out the colors and material, it was the same room he had cried to get.

Madear had bought him the queen-sized canopy bed for his tenth birthday. He begged her for it when he saw it in the Sears and Roebuck catalog. She bought it but refused to buy him the pink-and-white comforter or the white canopy cover.

Terri refused to eat until she gave in. When it was all over, the room was identical to the one the little white girl had in the catalog, from the pink carpet on the floor to the white dressers, mirrored vanity and the eight white stuffed teddy bears. The room was the first thing Terri could remember demanding. He suspected it was one of Madear's few times giving in to someone's demands. Maybe that was why she kept it as it was. Whatever the reason, he was glad she did. The room was his beginning. He could remember little before and everything after it.

"Oh, Terri, it was a damn good show. You looked just like Tina. You moved so much like her. I've seen Tina Turner perform. I know what I'm talking about." He sat timidly on the bed.

Terri hadn't thought of having a man since he left Statesville. Mo-red curbed that desire. He couldn't think of sex without thinking of Mo-red, and he wanted to forget Mo-red. He woke up night after night in pain from the memory of Mo-red's beatings. He could feel Mo-red's hands around his neck and his foot on his face. He could still taste his unwashed thang in his mouth. Whenever he sat alone, a vision of Mo-red appeared in the room, ordering him on his knees. Terri smelled him in the kitchen and outside by the garbage. He saw him in the shadows and in the mornings on the shower wall. He heard Mo-red calling through the radio and the television: "Bitch, come here. Bitch, come here! You hear me calling you, bitch?" Yes, he heard him and saw him. He saw his face in the dishwater; in the smoke of a cigarette; in the frost of a window. He appeared anywhere. Terri was still Mo-red's hag three months after he left Mo-red.

Dr. Goody said he saw him in Vegas. He wasn't a hag in Vegas. He wanted and needed to hear about Vegas.

"Did you like the show, Dr. Goody?" Terri stood a distance from him, waiting for the reply.

"Like it? Terri, it was marvelous."

Marvelous? Did he say marvelous? Terri stepped closer.

32

"You were so good, Terri. Like I said, I seen you a couple of times before, but in Vegas . . . mmm, girl, you stole the show."

Girl? Did Dr. Goody say girl?

"I don't know much about performing, but I think it's all in the moves, and you moved just like Tina. I felt like Tina was on that stage. It was magic."

Magic.

"Magic? Now that's a bit much, Dr. Goody."

"No, not at all. A good performer brings magic to the stage, Terri. The best are able to get outside of themselves and reach. And girl, you reached."

Outside of yourself? Reach? Girl?

"Believe it or not, I got to reach sometimes myself. Doctors got to have a little magic too."

"I suppose you do."

Terri thought about giving Dr. Goody a show. After all, he was a fan. Just a small performance. It would be a test—a small test to see if he could still reach.

"You know, Dr. Goody, you're right. It's all in the moves. Anybody can look like a star, but only the gifted can move like one. I studied Tina. I watched hours and hours of her tapes."

"It showed, Terri. It really did."

Terri opened the top drawer of his vanity and removed his panties. He laid them on the bed next to Dr. Goody. Terri saw him look at them then look away. The suitcase was on the floor of the closet in front of which Dr. Goody was sitting.

Terri opened the closet and bent over near Dr. Goody, purposely exposing the top of his black nylons, which were held up by silver garter straps. When he saw Dr. Goody was about to turn away Terri bent further, displaying the sheer black lace panties that allowed Dr. Goody to view his perfect, half-basketball ass.

Terri heard Dr. Goody take a quiet breath. He smiled from ear to ear. He swung the suitcase from the floor to the bed.

"Open that for me, please, Dr. Goody."

"Ca-ca-ca-call me Al-Al-Albert."

"Okay, Albert."

Terri gave him a smile he'd forgotten he had then returned to the closet, pulling out blouses and scarves. He caused them to glide across Dr. Goody's face before he packed them in the suitcase.

"Oh, excuse me, Albert. Here, look at this one. Tell me what you think about it. You might remember it. I wore it in Vegas."

Terri held up a sheer gold leotard. It was new, and he had never worn it in Vegas. He had told that lie to keep the conversation going.

"I could only wear this on stage, but I love it so much. It's so soft, and it clings heavenly. It's only for stage. I haven't worn it in years. I wonder if it still fits." Terri caressed the leotard and held it against himself. "What do you think, Albert? Do you think I could still fit it?"

"I don't see why ya couldn't."

"You're so nice, but I know I've gained since Vegas. Feel." Terri put Dr. Goody's fat, club-like hand on his waist. "Right there, Albert. Feel that bulge. That will show, don't you think?"

"Na-na-naw. That's nothing."

When Terri felt Dr. Goody gripping his waist, he maneuvered an off-balance fall that landed him in Albert's lap. The doctor didn't utter a word.

"Do you really think this will fit me, Albert?" Terri asked, squirming his half-basketball into a comfortable position.

"Yeah, Terri, I know it will fit you."

Terri felt Albert's heavy breath on the back of his neck.

"Oh, Albert, look at me sitting in your lap like a child. I get so into my clothes sometimes I forget myself."

Terri stood when he felt Albert's thang throbbing against his butt. The show was in the tease.

34

"Albert, would you do me a favor? It's so silly, but it would help me a lot. I'm thinking about going back on the stage, but I'm concerned about my body. Could I . . . could I try this on for you? Please? It won't take long, I promise. Since you've seen me perform before, you could tell me if I've lost it. Just a short dance, Albert, please?"

From the corner of his eye Terri observed Albert sitting with both hands in his lap, trying to cover his rise.

"If you think it will help you, sure, I'll watch you dance."

"Really? Thank you! You're a doll. Now wait here." Terri sashayed to the bathroom and gently pulled the door, leaving it open an inch—not open enough to see inside, but enough space for Albert to try to peep in.

In the bathroom, doubt appeared in the soapy water as the image of Mo-red calling him a silly ho and telling him that nobody wanted his tired ass. He stepped away from the basin and closed his eyes. He reached for Vegas: the magic lights, the applause, the overwhelming desire of the crowd. He was there. On the stage, he felt the heat of the lights. He smelled his French perfume. He saw his adoring fans. He reached to them and they reached back. They trampled Mo-red reaching for Terri's hand. He undressed in the bathroom to the applause of thousands of encouraging fans. They wanted him.

He douched with the soapy water, now free of Mo-red's reflection. He lubricated himself with a mixture of Vaseline and strawberry-scented shampoo. He slid on the skin-tight top and the fans roared their approval.

When he entered the bedroom, Dr. Goody had pulled the shades and dimmed the lights and returned to his seat on the bed, an anxious fan.

Terri smiled. "Are you ready, Albert?"

"Yes."

"Should I cut on the radio?"

"I already hear the music."

Did he really? Well if he didn't, he soon would. Terri was sure of that.

"Take off your jacket, Albert, and relax. Remember, you said you would be honest. Now, it's been awhile, so don't be too critical. Okay?"

Terri purposely stayed out of Albert's line of vision, only allowing him brief glimpses. He lingered behind the bathroom door, the closet door and the tall dresser.

"I, I, I'm ready, Terri."

"Are you now?"

The dance began. When Terri was satisfied that Albert's eyes were fixed on his petite body, he started with belly dancing sways to find the beat. Once found, he elongated the sways into spiral circles. His hips led. With thighs together, he was hiding his first rise in months.

Terri became a snake. Hands gripping his thighs, shoulders leading, he stood, bringing motion to the letter S. He jerked as if struck by a whip, and his hips regained the lead. His hands went down to his ankles. He slowly opened his legs and slid into a full split. He brought one leg up and placed it behind his head. From Albert he heard, "Sweet Jesus."

He stood from the floor, found a faster beat and gave Albert the view from the back. Terri moved his half-basketball with seductive precision. He caused it to quiver, shake, pulsate, stop and quiver again. He moved each cheek independently to the same beat then he took it into circles—big circles, small circles, tiny circles. When he began to make it smack, he heard new words from Albert.

"Damn, damn, hot damn!"

Terri put his circling half-basketball within Albert's reach. He expected the chubby hands; he didn't expect the lips or the tongue that found their way under the leotard. Terri continued to circle as Albert continued to probe.

Terri's knees began to weaken. He was no longer circling. He was pushing back into Albert's face. He felt an orgasm coming and he wanted it.

"Don't stop, Albert! Please don't stop. Lick me good, big man!" He said it with a little more bass than he intended.

Terri was swept up by Albert, who laid him facedown in the bed he had cried to get. He felt Albert unsnapping his leotard and burying his face between his butt cheeks. Albert's tongue went from between cheeks to booty hole with the force of a hungry man. If this was Albert's first time licking a booty then Terri was a Catholic virgin selling her coochie on Easter Sunday.

"Oh you fat, long, thick-tongue-having motherfucker! Watch out!"

The cheering fans, the magic lights and Albert's experienced tongue did it. Terri released his first orgasm in months. The lights flickered, the crowd of fans was spinning, and Terri lost his breath.

He found himself chewing on the bed sheet. He thought of the smile Madear had while the mule was serving her breakfast. She was right; he did need some. He took a bow and waved goodbye to his fans. *See you next time.*

He rolled over and pulled Albert up to him.

"Come up here and let Mama take care of you like you know she can."

Terri grinned and laughed all through the ride to Midway Airport. He laughed so much his jaws hurt. Albert had every Richard Pryor and Red Foxx tape ever made. Terri had heard the tapes before, but never in the frame of mind he was in then. Terri was free to go, and he was going.

He was about to start his life over, and the only baggage he was carrying were the Fendi bags that held his clothes. For the first time since he left Statesville, he felt Mo-red was behind him. He felt strong enough to close that chapter of his life.

Albert turned down the volume of the tape player.

"Terri, I had a great time with you this afternoon. Do you really have to leave Chicago?"

"Oh yeah, it's a must."

Terri looked out the passenger window of Dr. Goody's Lincoln Town Car. It was a beautiful afternoon. The turquoise sky was clear, and only strands of thin clouds were present.

"If I had a place for you to stay, would you?"

"Why would I stay? It's time for fresh experiences."

"I don't know . . . for me?"

"Albert, you don't really want me to stay for you. We had a good—no, great afternoon. You helped me get over something and I'm grateful, but it would take a lot more than gratitude to keep me from Birmingham."

"How about an apartment and three thousand dollars a month allowance?"

"Albert, that's sweet, but really, baby, I got to go to Birmingham. It's a fresh start for me. It's freedom. If you had ever been locked up, you would understand how important starting over is. I want a fresh everything. I'm not rejecting you, because Lord knows you know how to work that *thang*. But I want something more, something new. Can you understand?"

"Yes, I do. I don't like it, but I understand. Here." Albert pulled an envelope from his pocket and handed it to Terri.

"What's this?"

"It's bribe money your mother sent. She's planning on selling the house. I wasn't supposed to give it to you unless you refused to leave. It's five grand. Your share will probably be more, but that's all your mother is willing to give you now."

"She is such a bitch. I wish you the best with her, Albert. When I get settled in Birmingham I'll send *you* my address. Maybe you'll come and see me."

"I would like that, Terri. I really would."

Chapter Three
A Mule

Dr. Goody dropped Terri at the airport two hours before his flight. He was dressed in a plain white oversized T-shirt, a pair of Levi jeans and a pair of pink ladies' Nikes. His hair was in a ponytail. He was struggling through the airport with three large Fendi suitcases and a Fendi backpack. He didn't notice the attendant approaching him.

"You need some help, dude?"

Terri saw nothing but muscles. Either this guy just got out of the joint or he lived in the gym. He called Terri dude, so Terri didn't think he could be flirting. Terri did need help. He thanked the attendant and accepted his assistance.

The attendant picked up the suitcases with ease and loaded them on his cart. Terri told him he was going to the Southwest terminal. The attendant said fine and led him through Midway Airport.

This guy was Madear's type: black as tar and mule ugly. He helped Terri load his bags on the conveyer belt and directed him to the Southwest Airlines waiting area. When Terri tipped the mule he noticed him grinning. Terri gave a cautious smile and told him goodbye. Terri figured the mule had noticed that he wasn't really a dude. Maybe the pink Nikes or the lavender nail polish was a clue for him.

It's funny how good sex builds one's confidence. A couple of hours ago he wouldn't have cared about being noticed by a man. Good sex was truly wonderful. He felt attractive and it felt good. When he was younger, around twenty, trips to the airport always resulted in meeting a new man. Not only gay men found him attractive in those days, a lot of "straight men" valued his poise.

Dr. Goody was partly right. The moves were important, but attitude was paramount. One had to feel feminine and know that deep inside a lady was there—not just a woman but a lady, a soft, caring soul that could mother the world. Feminine ways were always part of his make-up. Femininity attracts masculinity. That he knew.

That was what had come between him and his first love, Payton. Payton didn't like his feminine ways or his desire to become a lady. He didn't see the power in femininity, the value of softness. Maybe Payton did love him as Madear said, but he didn't love what he wanted to be. When Payton left his life, Terri found that many other men found his femininity attractive and were willing to offer more than pretty old dresses.

Terri smiled when he heard real women complaining about a shortage of men. Men were plentiful in his life then, and they were generous. He never met the cheap bastards he heard women complaining about. Maybe if they'd had a Madear like his, the cheap bastards wouldn't exist for them either.

Once, a stray cat gave birth to a litter of kittens under Madear's porch. Out of all the kittens one caught Terri's attention. The kitten was pure white with one brown paw. She was the first one to leave from under the porch and the only one to scratch him. She didn't hurry to the feeding bowl when he brought it, but he always had a treat for her.

Madear asked him why he gave that kitten more. He didn't know why. She told him that kitten was the pick of the litter and she knew it. She expected to be treated better, and life would treat her that way. It was the same with people. "When you expect the best, you get it. Always be the pick of the litter," she told him.

Terri sat in the waiting area smiling. A new life was less than three hours and forty-five minutes away. Twenty-six was a good age to be starting over. He wouldn't make the mistakes of a teenager or young adult. Fast cash would not tempt him in Birmingham. No bad checks written under the name of Clair Jones, no false lines of credit for Clair, no new cars for Clair. Clair died when the judge sentenced Terrance Parish to seven years.

It was just an idea. He filled out a credit application with information he believed banks would prefer. Clair Jones was a recent graduate from the University of Chicago. She secured her first job with Saks as a buyer earning $35,000 a year. She had $75,000 in U.S. savings bonds and lived rent-free with her parents. She was a single, white female with no children. American Express accepted her, Visa accepted her, Carson accepted her, Lord and Taylor accepted her, GMAC accepted her and Citibank gave her a checking account.

Terri maxed out all the credit cards and never paid one note on Clair's little red Corvette. Instead he paid five years to the State of Illinois. No, he would not make the mistakes of youth. He was starting over.

Terri had an urge to buy a pack of Newports, but he decided against it. Smoking was an old habit; he would leave it in Chicago. He pulled an apple from his Fendi backpack and bit into it. Of course it was sweet. Everything would be sweet from now on. He was making decisions for himself, taking control of his destiny.

He felt a heavy tap on his shoulder. He turned and saw the mule.

"Hey, I'm off and you got a couple hours before your flight. You want to go get something to eat?"

Hell, motherfucking no! was what Terri wanted to say. *Get your ugly ass far, far, away from me!* is what he wanted to scream. His answer, however, was more civilized.

"No, baby, that's okay. I've been waiting a long time for this. Sitting here is no problem." Terri smiled.

He had nothing against dark men. One of his first loves was dark, but Jessie was fine. This black mule was pure ugly. His eyes were out of line—one was higher than the other—and there was no space between his nostrils and his big, pink upper lip. Terri tried not to stare at his forehead, which could not have been an inch high.

"Can I sit with you?"

No! Go away you ugly, foolish mule! Terri toyed with saying.

"Sure, baby, sit on down." Terri put the Fendi backpack on the floor.

The attendant sat and asked, "Where you going?"

"Birmingham!" Terri couldn't help but answer with excitement.

"Why?"

None of your fuckin' business, you hideous bastard. Please go away! Terri thought.

"I'm going to start my life over."

"It's warmer there."

"Yeah, I know. I'm getting out before the hawk comes."

"It ain't that bad. I like the cold."

"You can keep it, baby. How long have you worked here?"

That was a mistake. No more questions. Send him away, Terri told himself.

"About two months. I just got out of Indiana State Prison."

A fucking con. Get him away but do it nicely, Terri decided.

"Why are you staying around here?" Terri asked.

"Money. I'm rich and I'm gettin' richer every day."

Rich? A rich mule. No, more like a lying bastard, Terri confirmed.

"Nigga, please. If you're rich why you working here?"

"I got rich here."

"How rich are you?"

"Rich enough to know you just got out of Statesville a short while ago."

That shocked Terri.

"Who are you?" Terri asked, standing.

"Relax, baby. I ain't nobody. Just a nigga working in the airport."

"Don't play with me." Terri was pulling his bag from the floor.

"Relax. My brother was in Statesville three years ago. He sent me the prison paper. You was in it, all dressed up and shit. He sent me the paper because he wrote a article or something. I kept your picture and put it on my wall. Girl, I fucked you more times than God knows. I don't mean you no harm."

Terri remembered the photograph. It was from a Halloween party. It took him four weeks to prepare for the party. He was without a doubt the queen of the ball. It was before Mo-red.

"You remembered me from a photograph?" Terri sat back down. Flattery was a weakness.

"Oh yeah."

Terri heard the lust in the attendant's answer.

"But I'm not dressed now."

"Don't make a difference. I ain't gon' never forget your face."

I'll try my best to forget yours, Terri thought.

"Well thank you for the compliment, baby. I'm glad I made your time easier. Don't tell your woman about it." Terri gave him a smile that suggested it was time for goodbye.

"Ain't got no woman. I got too much money for a bitch. I cain't trust no ho."

Against all his better judgment Terri asked, "Where did you get so much money?"

"I work at the airport. I got cocaine coming and going to over twenty states. I buy low and sell high. You can call me a broker. I figured the shit out after I got this job."

It was a good plan, but Terri doubted the mule's ability to keep it going; he obviously talked too much. "You are throwing bricks at the joint, baby."

The mule wasn't the first ex-convict Terri knew whose behavior would attract the attention of the authorities. Some people never learned, but the mule wasn't Terri's problem. If he was dumb enough to remain illegal after the joint, more power to him.

"So what? It don't matter because I'm rich."

45

"Being rich is not being free. There is nothing like freedom. How rich are you?" Terri wanted to hear his dollar value for freedom.

"I'm rich enough to buy you some titties, rich enough to put you in a two-seater Benz, rich enough to come across a black diamond mink last week that's about your size. That's how rich I am, baby."

Terri blinked his eyes. The mule was pretty damn rich or told damn good lies. How did he know Terri wanted titties? For that matter, how did he know Terri wanted a two-seater Benz and a black diamond mink? Terri laughed when he realized most drag queens would want these things. It was a line. The mule was using a good line—a damn good line. Terri summed him up as a bus station pimp in the airport, selling pie in the sky.

"And why would you buy me all those wonderful things?"

"That's how I would treat cha if you was mine."

"I'm too old for you, baby."

"Money ain't got no age."

"But I do. I like older men, baby."

"I'm twenty-five. You cain't be much older than that."

"I'm going to Birmingham, baby."

One of Madear's warnings entered his mind: *"When you doing well, T.T., sweet shit always appears. It's sweet, but it's still shit. It's got to be sweet to make you stop, but it's shit all the same. Watch out for sweet shit, T.T."*

"I tell you what—" The mule reached into his uniform jacket and pulled out a banded stack of hundred dollar bills. "This is ten grand. It's yours if you stay with me for a week."

Now that's sweet shit, Terri thought while counting the bills. The mule's ten plus the five Diane had given him made fifteen grand.

"You'll give me this for a week? No strings attached?"

"I don't know what you mean by strings. I do wanna fuck."

46

Terri chuckled. "Sex won't be a problem, baby. Not for ten grand. It's just that when the week is over, you know I'm leaving."

"If you want to, but I think you'll want to stay. Look, I know what you are and you know what I am. We know a lil' about each other and that's a good start. For me it will be like a fantasy coming to life. I never thought I would meet you, but I did. I dreamed about being with you so long, I guess it had to become real. I'll always treat you like a treasure because you are."

Terri couldn't remember the last time a man rapped to him. It felt good. Life was looking up.

"If I don't stay, we're not going to have a problem, are we?"

"None."

"Damn, this is some shit. You're crazy," Terri said, holding the bundled stack.

"Yeah, but I'm rich."

"Sure of yourself, huh?"

"Got to be."

"What's your name?"

"Clyde Parks."

Terri looked into Clyde's face to see if he could find any attractive feature. He saw none. Clyde's attraction was his money.

"This is the deal, Clyde. I'm going to take this money to Western Union and wire it to my daddy. I'm going to wire a note with it, giving him your address and your legal name and telling him if he doesn't hear from me in a week, he's to call the police. We got a deal?"

"Fo' sho'."

Terri wired the money and the note to the only daddy he had, Dr. Albert Goody. He wanted Clyde to think that he had somebody who cared about him. Somebody who would miss him in case Clyde turned out to be a maniac.

What Clyde called a car was a Nissan Pathfinder, a sports utility vehicle. The showroom sticker was still in the window. It stood out proudly in the full airport parking lot.

"Is it yours or do you sell cars part time?" Terri asked, smiling.

"Oh no, it's mine. I bought it yesterday, but I was thinking about taking it back fo' that Maxima. I might just keep this and get the Maxima."

"Oh, you got it like that, huh?"

Terri cut his eyes in Clyde's direction, hoping the bright sun in the parking lot might change Clyde's appearance. It didn't.

"Yeah, I wasn't lyin'." Terri saw a smile appear on Clyde's lumpy face. "Let's go shoppin'."

"Shopping?" Terri asked with a hint of challenge in his voice.

Shopping was close to a religion with Terri. He did it only with loved ones or rich ones. If he was broke he would not shop. He would rather do without than buy less than the best. High-end retail stores and boutiques were where he practiced faith. The thought of shopping in a discount store made him cringe. He majored in tailoring/dressmaking in high school. If he had to, he would make his own rather than shop down.

Shopping for himself with another's money, however, placed Terri in an ecstatic frame of mind. He became very agreeable, pleasing, doting, cute, cuddly and cunning. He smiled more men out of money than an IRS tax lien. Once it was established they had money and they were willing to spend it, Terri initiated a sensual experience that would have made Josephine Baker blush.

"Yeah, shoppin'," the mule said.

Terri sat back in the seat. "Any particular store you have in mind?"

"Wherever you want to go."

"I wired my money to my daddy."

48

"It's on me."

"Okay," Terri answered as perky as any California valley girl. "There is a group of small boutiques on North Michigan. Are you familiar with the area?"

"You mean down there by Gucci?"

"Yes!" Terri snapped the affirmation from his mouth. He placed his head on the mule's muscular shoulder, took one of the mule's hands into the palms of his own small, dainty hands and asked quietly, "Do you shop there often?"

"Naw, but it looks like I'ma start."

Terri was pleased with the answer and kissed him on the cheek. "Only if you want to."

"It's where you wanna go, right?" Clyde made it sound as if the world were his to offer. Terri liked his bravado.

"Yes, Clyde, it's where I want to go."

Terri left his head on Clyde's shoulder and dropped one hand to the inside of his thigh, tracing the inseam of his uniform pants. With the other hand he continued to hold Clyde's hand and kissed his fingertips.

"But if you don't want to take me I'll understand. After all, you just met me."

Terri guessed that getting money from Clyde would be easy for one reason: Clyde wanted him more than he wanted Clyde, and Clyde wasn't trying to hide it. Clyde was ugly, and Terri was certain he was accustomed to paying for affection. Terri began mapping out the week in his mind as Clyde drove.

The first night there would be no real sex—just a little oral stimulation to let him know he was in the company of a professional. If Clyde worked the following day Terri could postpone intercourse a little longer; if not, he might have to give him a little in the afternoon, after more shopping, of course.

If he worked, Terri would prepare a dinner Clyde would tell his mother about. After he fed him, he would give him a bath and full body massage, along with a serious hand job.

That should put him out for the night. He would keep Clyde wanting as long as possible.

There were too many ifs. Terri couldn't plan without knowing Clyde's schedule. "Do you work tomorrow or do I have you for the whole day?"

"Monday through Friday, 7:00 A.M. to 3:00 P.M. I don't work overtime."

"Good. Save the overtime for me."

The first night and Tuesday night were covered. Wednesday would be as far as Terri would push it. When Clyde came home Wednesday, Terri would be sexually demanding. He would attack Clyde as soon as he walked in the door and drain him into the night.

Thursday morning would be the same. Terri might stop him from going to work. Friday night maybe a movie and a little oral sex in the theater to get him excited for home. Friday night he would build Clyde's ego, tell him he was the best lover in the world.

Saturday morning, more shopping, then that night the switch would start. He would remain sexually demanding, drain him again and demand more, act unsatisfied when Clyde was unable to perform.

Terri would wake up Sunday morning complaining about Saturday night, drain him again and continue to act unsatisfied. No man wants a lover he can't satisfy.

Sunday morning, Mr. Clyde Parks would find a demanding, selfish bitch in his house, one he would be happy to get rid of. Terri's skill would come into play, causing not anger but insecurity. An angry man wouldn't allow Terri to leave with all his new things; an insecure man might buy more.

The Gucci valet was at the door of the Pathfinder. "Oh no, Clyde. Gucci last, the Water Tower first. Okay?" Terri offered a timid smile, barely showing the tips of his pearly white teeth.

"Whatever you want, baby."

50

Gucci was fine for purses and accessories, but Terri was after clothes. Clyde parked the Pathfinder in the underground lot of the Water Tower Mall. He reached into his jacket and handed Terri a stack of hundreds half the size of the first. Clyde leaned his seat back and lit a joint. It was obvious he wasn't going in. Terri had been planning on giving him a kiss on the elevator.

"You're not going in?"

Terri seldom shopped alone. He didn't like shopping alone. He didn't like the looks he got purchasing ladies' clothes when he wasn't in drag. He was dressed for travel, not shopping. Shopping required more than lavender nail polish and pink Nikes. If he had on a bra maybe he could pull it off.

He wanted someone to talk to, someone to laugh with and to whisper with. He wanted someone on his side against the onlookers, the gapers, the eyes that said *Look at that sissy buying ladies' clothes.*

"No, not this time, baby. Maybe next time."

Terri heard the finality in Clyde's tone. He didn't know Clyde. He didn't know if Clyde was gay. A lot of men in prison had sex with men but they were not gay in the outside world. Was Clyde in that category?

"Why not?" Terri gave up the smiling and the cooing. He wanted an answer.

"I ain't into shoppin', awight?"

Terri could put two plus two together. Clyde was in the closet. Terri looked at the money in his hand. It was only for a week; it really didn't matter. He would shop fast and talk to Madear in his mind.

"Okay, fine. See you in a little while." Terri gave him a light kiss on the lips.

When Terri entered the mall, excitement took over. He couldn't stop grinning as he rode the escalators up to the fifth floor. He had five thousand dollars to spend on himself. The mall was close to empty and that pleased him more. The Water

Tower Mall was by far his favorite. The ceilings were high, the walkways were large and the lighting was bright and cheerful.

The stores were all high-end retail: Field's, Lord and Taylor, White Hall and many smaller boutiques. Shoes would be first. When he entered the Italian shoe boutique the lone sales clerk who greeted him made him more relaxed. The clerk didn't have on pink Nikes, nor were his nails covered in lavender polish, but they could have been.

"Hey, girl."

His warm greeting brought a smile from Terri. "Hey yourself. What's on sale, girlfriend?" Terri didn't know the slender black man from Adam, but as Madear often told him, birds of a feather flock together.

"Nothing you want, sugar. Believe me. And by the looks of that bundle in your hand, you don't care!"

Terri watched the clerk snap his fingers twice above his head and start laughing. Terri was still holding the money Clyde gave him. He'd forgotten to put it in his pocket.

"Girl, I left my bag in the truck. The man I'm with sorta rushed me."

"Did he give you that bundle?"

The clerk was standing close enough to Terri to count the cash.

"Yeeeas!" Terri whispered through his grin.

"Ohweee! He got a friend?" the clerk asked, almost touching the bundle.

"Girl, I don't know. I just met him," Terri said, fanning the bills.

"Bitch, you're lying!"

Terri heard no malice in the *bitch* phrase.

"It's the truth, girl, but I tell you what—you give me your number, and after I find out what's what, I'll give you a call."

Terri gave the clerk a once-over; he wore a pair of beige Levi Dockers, tight—Terri guessed they were two sizes too small—a plain, white Jill Sanders cotton shirt, and Gucci loafers with no socks. He had style. Terri really would try to hook him up.

"Girl, I ain't got no damn phone." Terri sensed the clerk's sad, angry regret, but as suddenly as the clerk said the words his eyes lit brightly and he said, "But you can call me here! I work every day but Sunday."

"Okay. I'll call you here, but I'm getting ready to spend enough money to get your phone cut back on!" Terri sat in the yellow leather armchair and crossed his legs.

"Ohweee! Child, I hope so. I could use a blessing. What do you want to see first, *Ms. Thing*?" The clerk asked, placing his hand on Terri's shoulder.

"Do you all still size here?" Terri asked nonchalantly, looking down at his nails, knowing full well the implications of the question. The shop sized for custom-made imported shoes.

"Yes we do, girlfriend!"

Terri could see the clerk was one of those people whose emotions always showed. His expectation was obvious.

"Very well, then. Bring out the new line of Manolo Blahnik."

"Ohweee! I knew you was gonna ask for them! Baby girl, you go. I get twenty percent on them! Who else?" the clerk asked, doing a half spin.

"Well, do you carry Bruno Magli and Prada?"

"Oh! Hell, yes. Take off them Nikes, baby, and make yourself at home. I'll be right back. Bitch, I knew you knew how to shop when you walked in!"

The clerk sashayed to the back. Terri slowly unlaced his Nikes and thought about his day.

Madear was buried, Dr. Goody proved good, and a rich, ugly mule gave him fifteen thousand dollars. This was a day he would remember. He enjoyed a fast pace. The months he spent with Madear were slow and steady. Prison was slow—too damn slow. For the first time in years he felt a little like his old self.

He lost more than five years in prison—a lot more. He lost parts of himself. Dr. Goody brought back a piece and Clyde's attraction brought back another. Terri knew other parts were missing, but they were gone so long he couldn't label them. He couldn't identify what exactly was missing, but he knew he wasn't whole.

He didn't think about himself much when he was with Madear. They stayed busy with day-to-day life, but now Madear was gone. He was left with himself. He began to regret not taking that flight to Birmingham. A fresh start was what he was chasing, not an ugly mule's money. When would he learn? he asked himself. Fast cash; he'd chased it most of his life.

The vigor Terri required for shopping was gone. He bought a pair of red Prada pumps with a spiked heel, a pair of black Bruno Magli loafers, and one pair of tan Manolo Blahnik flats. He gave the clerk Dr. Goody's address for shipping then gave him a hug and a promise to call once he found out if Clyde had any generous friends.

He rode the glass elevator to the lower level. His shoulders felt as if someone was leaning on them; he let them slump. Shopping for the day was over. He should have been on a plane to Birmingham. He went into the men's room on the lower level to wash his face. He couldn't greet Clyde in this mood. Clyde bought a cheerful, happy Terri for a week, not a sad, weighed-down Terri. He heard Madear in his mind: *"A customer is entitled to what he pays for."*

Terri splashed his face with cold water and dabbed it dry with a paper towel. He pasted a smile on his face. "Hey, sugar!" He rehearsed his greeting for Clyde in the mirror.

Clyde was wiping the city dust from the Pathfinder when Terri approached him with his rehearsed greeting.

"Hey, sugar!" Terri said with as much sweetness and allure as he could muster.

"Hey yourself. You're finished already?"

"It wasn't much fun alone. Here's your change."

CHASIN' IT

Terri gave him the change to establish trust. Although the mule knew the relationship was based on money, Terri didn't want to appear greedy. *"Graditude gets you more than attitude,"* Madear would say.

"Thank you." Terri noted the surprise in Clyde's answer. "Hungry?"

"No, I'm ready to see your place."

Terri needed to settle down, maybe get a little something to drink and relax. He was getting depressed. He told himself he would change after prison, no more chasing fast money, but there he was, chasing it.

Terri grabbed Clyde's pack of Kools off the dashboard and lit one. He noticed the bright, sunny day was gone; the evening sun was covered with thick, gray storm clouds. "Do you mind if we stop first and get some wine or something?"

"No, not at all, but don't expect too much from my place. It's only me, and I ain't no fancy brother."

Terri expected Clyde to live either on the west side of the city or the south side. He didn't expect downtown. Clyde rented a two-bedroom apartment in Doral Plaza, a high-rise on Michigan Avenue.

The apartment was barely furnished. Two wicker chairs, a black leather sofa and a compact stereo system occupied the front room. One bedroom held a card table with a triple-beam scale and one chair. The other bedroom had only a futon and piles of clothing on the floor.

"You know, there are manufacturers of dressers."

"Yeah, but I ain't got around to buying one."

Terri noticed each bedroom had its own bathroom. The kitchen had the basics—a gas stove, a refrigerator, a sink and no table. Terri guessed they came with the rental. There were no dirty dishes in the sink. Terri spotted a box of paper plates and plastics utensils. He laughed.

"A true bachelor," he said to Clyde, who was showing him through the apartment.

"Yeah, I guess. I don't like washing dishes. I got some in the cabinet."

Terri opened the dish cabinet. What Clyde called *some* was two plates and a two jelly jars for drinking.

"Don't do much entertaining, do you?"

"Nope." Clyde took him in his arms. "You can fix it up for me."

Clyde's kiss was rough, awkward and frantic. He forced his tongue through Terri's teeth and into his mouth. He groped at Terri's butt and slobbered down his cheek. His embrace was unbearably tight. Terri envisioned himself as a tube of toothpaste being squeezed with the cap on. He twisted his head free of the kiss.

"Wait a minute, baby. I want you too, but let's shower and slow down a bit. We got time." Clyde's thick arms encompassed Terri's waist.

"We gonna shower together?" Clyde asked.

"Not this time. I'll met you in your bedroom." When Clyde released him, Terri walked away, switching his butt and accenting his natural stride with a snap at the end of each step. He felt Clyde's eyes on him.

"You like my booty?" he asked without turning around.

"Yeah, girl, you got a helluva ass!"

Terri grabbed the smaller of his suitcases and went into the bathroom attached to the bedroom with the table, chair and triple-beam scale. After the shower he slid into a black teddy trimmed in purple frills with purple panties. The panties were to remain on. No real sex the first day. Terri didn't bother to lubricate.

When he walked into Clyde's bedroom he gasped. Clyde was lying naked across the futon. He was stroking and oiling a thang big enough to fill a large plastic water tumbler. Terri hoped that Clyde wasn't a rapist; his earlier plan was out the window. There was no way he was going to have repeated sex with Clyde. His thang was too big.

56

Once a day would be enough, and once Clyde got in, that would be it. No ins and outs. Clyde's thang was big enough to cause damage. No wonder he didn't have a woman. Neither a queen nor real fish would want that monster tearing into them day after day. Terri would have to rethink his plan.

"It ain't as bad as it looks. Once it's inside you'll love it," Clyde said, smiling.

Clyde wanted intercourse, eliminating the teasing oral sex Terri had in mind. He laid next to Clyde on the futon and tried to quickly rethink his plan. Clyde's lustful groping and squeezing indicated the high level of his desire. Maybe if Terri worked him fast, Clyde would reach a quick orgasm.

Lying next to and looking directly at Clyde's monster, Terri decided against trying to rush Clyde. He was too big to play with; the work would have to be slow and steady. Terri was about to slide out of his panties when Clyde directed him to keep them on. Terri closed his eyes and lay facedown on the futon. Clyde slid a pillow under Terri's stomach.

"Girl, I never thought I would have you for real."

Clyde kissed him on the back of his neck before he mounted him. Terri took in several deep breaths and blew them out slowly. He relaxed every muscle in his body. Clyde was working the head of the monster in.

"I am not going to hurt you, Terri. If it hurts, let me know."

Terri didn't answer. He kept his eyes closed and waited for the pain. The head entered with little pain.

"Is that okay? Should I push in some more?"

Terri nodded. The amount of pain he had expected didn't come as Clyde slowly worked into him. Clyde had slicked up his monster good, and it glided into Terri.

"More?"

"Yes," Terri answered.

"More?"

"Yes."

"More?"

57

"Yes." Once Clyde was completely in, Terri exhaled completely, releasing all his anxious tension. He relaxed knowing he could handle the length and width of Clyde. He spread his legs and arms wide across the futon and let Clyde ride.

Terri lived in Clyde's world for eight months. Clyde pampered him. Anything Terri thought he wanted Clyde gave him: furs, diamonds, cars, vacations and money. Despite the pampering, Terri was not happy. He loved Clyde's lifestyle, but he did not love Clyde.

Clyde was true to his word. He treated Terri like a treasure and like a precious keepsake, but Terri began to feel the satin-covered restraints of the treasure chest. Clyde didn't like the theater, he didn't like concerts, he didn't like gay clubs and was too deep in the closet to take Terri to straight clubs. Clyde could go out without Terri, but Terri couldn't go out without Clyde.

When Terri told Clyde he needed some space, Clyde took him to Jamaica. When he complained of being alone in the house, Clyde bought a cat. When he complained of being bored, Clyde bought him a home theater. When he complained about not having anyone to talk to, Clyde gave parties.

The parties were worse than being alone. Clyde's friends were people who worked for him, so they all kissed his ass. All they talked about was prison, sports, selling drugs, cars, guns and the police. At times it sounded to Terri like they actually admired the police and missed prison.

Whenever Terri told Clyde he was thinking of leaving, Clyde would give him cash. Terri wired over forty thousand dollars to Dr. Goody over the eight months he was with Clyde. When Terri refused the money, Clyde took him to get his breasts. Clyde adored the budding breasts as much as Terri did.

Because of this, Terri tried again to love Clyde, but he could only reach Clyde's surface.

When he tried to really get to know Clyde, he found there was nothing to know. Clyde was only worth what he could buy. He wasn't gay; he was homophobic. Gay men not dressed as women enraged him. He couldn't stand to see two men kissing. When they made love, Terri would lay facedown in the bed with panties and bra on; Clyde entered Terri through the side of his panties. When they slept, he cuddled Terri from the back.

According to Clyde they were not a gay couple, they were just a couple. Since they were not a gay couple, they didn't go to gay clubs or gay events. Straight clubs were out because too many people knew Terri in the city and they would mistake Clyde as gay. All of Clyde's friends acted as if they believed Terri was a woman, but they knew he was a man. They had their hands out, so they played along with his fantasy.

Clyde's favorite basketball player changed with every game. He went from Lexus to Cadillac on the persuasion of the salesman. His favorite singer changed with each new hit list. His opinions were those of others. He held no true opinions on anything. He mimicked the words and thoughts of others.

He bought six Malcolm X posters and twenty T-shirts but refused to read his autobiography or watch the movie past his thug life. He said he loved rap music but would go to no concerts and never played it unless his friends were around. To Terri, Clyde was as deep as a gangster rap music video character. Terri found nothing to reach; there was no real Clyde.

Other than Terri and selling drugs, the only thing Terri felt Clyde had any real interest in was getting high. When Clyde got high he would lock himself in the room with the table, scale and chair for hours. Out of boredom and curiosity, Terri joined Clyde in the room. Clyde warned Terri that smoking cocaine was totally different than snorting it. Terri told him he could handle it.

"If you can handle it, I can handle it," Terri said with hands on his hips.

"But it's different for me. I been doing it for years; I know when to stop. I don't let it control me; I control it. I've mastered my high." Clyde sat back in the only chair in the room.

"Okay, fine. Are you going to show me how to do it or what?" Terri sat in Clyde's lap.

"Terri, I ain't sure I want you smoking this shit," Clyde said, shaking his head.

"Why? You do it damn near every day." Terri was toying with Clyde's glass bowl pipe.

"What's wrong with just tooting it, like you been doing?" Clyde pushed the pipe out of his reach.

"I want to feel what keeps you locked up in this room for hours and stops you from fucking me," Terri said with a little spite in his tone.

"Ain't nothing stopping me from fucking you." Clyde kissed him on the neck.

"It did last night. You stayed in here until time to go to work." Terri pinched the back of Clyde's hand.

"Ouch! I was weighing shit up." He shook and licked his hand.

"No you wasn't. I smelled the smoke." Terri pinched the other hand.

"Damn, that hurts. Stop it. Awight, if you want to try it, fine, but if I see you cain't handle it, I'ma cut you off."

"And who's supposed to cut you off?"

"Nobody. I got my high mastered."

When Terri first exhaled the smoke from Clyde's glass bowl pipe, he knew he was in trouble. Nothing had ever cleared his mind so completely and put him at so much peace. *Tranquil* was the only word to describe it. The problem was it only lasted for a few minutes. To hold the feeling he had to fill his lungs again and again.

The first night lasted for two days. When Terri left the room he swore to himself he wouldn't smoke the drug again. Yes, it made him feel good while he was high, but when it was over all he thought about was past mistakes, prison and Mored.

Smoking cocaine depressed him, and Terri decided the high wasn't worth the low. Terri stayed in the bed for three days with muscles aching, crying for Madear.

On the third day Clyde called him into the room with one chair, a table and a scale.

"Take a hit from the dog that bit you and you'll be awight."

"No. I'll just toot a little."

"I told you smoking ain't for everybody."

"Tsst." Terri sucked his teeth at Clyde's grinning face. "You were right, okay?"

Terri covered a small makeup mirror with powdered cocaine. He snorted half of it, but the feeling wouldn't come.

"What's wrong with this stuff? I'm not high."

"It ain't the coke."

"Then what?"

"It's you. Your system wants it purer. Besides injecting it, smoking is as pure as you can get it. Tooting takes longer to get into your bloodstream. Just wait a couple of minutes. You'll feel it."

Terri waited, but the feeling that came was less intense.

"Give me the pipe."

"You sure?"

"Give me the damn pipe!"

The hours in the room turned into days as addiction claimed them both. Terri no longer cared about not loving Clyde. It no longer bothered him that he didn't go to the theater. It didn't matter that he was losing so much weight that none of his clothes fit. It didn't matter that they took no more vacations. It didn't matter that he didn't know what month it was. It didn't matter that Clyde couldn't get hard anymore. It didn't matter that Clyde lost his legitimate job. All that mattered were the chunks of cocaine Clyde brought to the room.

When Clyde lost his job at the airport, it complicated his illegitimate business. They got busted. The police raided their apartment. Both were locked in the room with one chair, a table and a scale, trying to take another hit from the cocaine pipe before the police kicked in the door. Clyde tried to tell the police that Terri was not involved in his business, but both were charged with distribution.

Sweet shit was all Terri could think during his three weeks at the county jail. His public defender, a large, white woman with blond hair and bad skin named Carla Jakes, told him the best she could do was fourteen years with a chance of parole in eight. The arresting officers reported ten kilos of cocaine. It was a double class X felony. Terri was going away.

Carla Jakes bit into a Snickers chocolate bar and suggested a private attorney. Maybe the right private attorney could pull some strings that a public defender wasn't privy to. She winked and handed him a card.

"Call this guy, tell him I referred you. It will cost you twenty grand to start. Be sure and tell him I referred you. If you don't call him, we go to trail in six months. If you call him, I won't see you again."

Terri made two calls. First he called Dr. Goody to see how much money he had.

"Of course I've got your money, Terri. It's a little over fifty grand."

"Thank God. I need you to take twenty grand to a lawyer named Peter Jakes."

"I can't take the money to him, Terri. I can't get involved like that. I will wire it to him. Is that okay?"

"Fine, Albert, just do it today."

"What about the rest of it?"

"I'll call you."

"Never made it to Birmingham, huh?"

"Not yet, Albert, but I'm working on it."

Terri's next call was to Attorney Peter Jakes.

"Yes, I'm familiar with your case. This is what we can do: thirty grand gets nine years with parole in three, fifty grand gets you free."

"Free?"

"As a bird."

"What about Clyde?"

"There's nothing I can do for him. He killed a guard last week. He's gone."

"A guard?"

"Dead as a fish. What about you—nine with three or free?"

"Free! You'll get the money tomorrow."

"Go to trial in a week. See you then."

It was like Madear told him: the city revolved around money. It was no more apparent than in the court system. Those without private attorneys were at the mercy of the system. Terri knew inmates in the county jail waiting sixteen months for trials. Either they had public defenders or they were having problems coming up with their lawyer's money. Justice might have been blind, but she could count money.

* * * * *

He sat chained to a bench with twenty others waiting to be devoured by the legal system. He was dressed in a man's blue suit, a white shirt, a pair of black wing-tipped shoes and a blue-and-gray striped tie. The last time he wore a man's suit he was sentenced to seven years.

His attorney who shipped him the clothes assured him that would not be the case. Terri had no choice but to trust his unseen attorney; he had already paid him. The lawyer's assurance over the telephone didn't stop the feeling of doom that enveloped Terri. The legal system was no friend to black males and even less of a friend to gay black males. The twenty men who were chained to the bench were black.

All Terri heard the judge saying was *fifteen to life*. He said it as easily as if he were ordering a drink: *scotch, no ice; fifteen to life; scotch, no ice; fifteen to life . . . scotch, no ice; fifteen to life.*

Terri's stomach was twisted as tight as one of Madear's dishrags. He found it difficult to breathe. He could no longer distinguish between what he imagined the judge was saying and what the judge actually said.

Bring the prisoner here or *Get all the picaninnies out of here.*

We're getting behind or *Kill all their kind.*

That's beyond the scope of this court or *Fuck it, use the rope and burn the corpse.*

This requires another read or *Make all the niggers bleed.*

Fifteen to life or *Scotch, no ice.*

Terri's tongue was beginning to swell, preventing his teeth from touching. He read about it once: Africans on slave ships who swallowed their own tongues when the misery became unbearable. Now he knew how they did it. First the tongue swells, then it's easy to swallow—as easy as a reflex.

He felt a tap on his shoulder. He turned and saw the fat face of Carla Jakes on a man's body.

"Hi. I'm P.J., Peter Jakes, your attorney. Damn, you look like shit. Relax. Here, wipe some of that sweat off your face. We're up next."

The fat lawyer handed Terri his monogrammed hankie and left.

Sweat? Terri felt as if it were blood. He had to open his mouth to breathe. When the bailiff removed the handcuffs, Terri doubted his legs would work. The bailiff allowed Terri to lean on him as he walked to the table and joined P.J.

"Hang in there, pal. We'll be out of here in two shakes of a lamb's tail," the attorney assured him.

Terri envisioned a lamb shaking his tail once and running over a hill, laughing at him. Then he heard it: *Case dismissed, insufficient evidence* or *Damn, missed. Nigga over the fence.*

Either way, Terri was out of there.

His lawyer handed him three hundred dollars, a bundle of clothes and a storage key. The remainder of his clothes had been put in storage. The jewels and cars, however, had become property of the Chicago Police Department. P.J. told him he was able to salvage three of his furs.

The money given to Terri was overpayment that had been wired to P.J. His fee was fifty thousand; someone wired fifty thousand plus three hundred more. Terri figured that was Dr. Goody's way of washing his hands of him, sending all his money.

Chapter Four
First Love

Terri stood on the corner of Twenty-eighth and California in front of the courthouse. It was cool for Fall, almost cold. If it weren't for the sun he would have needed more than a suit jacket to keep warm. He was uncertain of where to go. The lawyer told him he was free, but for some reason he still felt trapped. He blamed it on the men's clothes. He wanted out of the suit. He wanted to get butt naked, high and fucked. He hailed a cab on California Avenue.

"Hold up! Is that you, Terri?"

The cabdriver was Terri's first love, Payton. He looked bad—tired and worn out. He eyes were sunken and his yoke-yellow skin was as dry as sand. Rotting teeth weakened his once-dazzling smile. His clothes were soiled and his black, curly hair was matted. He fouled the air of the cab with body musk as strong as a rotten onion, but despite his poor appearance, Terri was happy to see Payton. His mind went back to the first time he and Payton were sexually intimate.

They were in Payton's grandmother's attic. They were supposed to be looking for her spring curtains. Rifling through the boxes, fourteen-year-old Terri could seem only to find dresses; pretty old dresses that looked about his size.

He'd done it alone before, played dress-up in his grandmother's clothes. He wanted to try on these dresses. He wanted to try on these dresses in front of Payton. He wanted to try them on for Payton. He wanted Payton to like him in the dresses.

Payton had been the boy-next-door all of Terri's life. He was the boy who fixed his bike, the boy who walked him to school, the big boy who stopped other boys from jumping on him, the boy who told the other kids that they were cousins: *"That's why we be together."*

Payton was also the boy who held Terri's hand in the show when no one was watching, the boy who kissed him flush on the mouth the night before they were in the attic. Payton was the boy for whom Terri wanted to look pretty when he tried on the old dresses.

Terri disrobed and stood naked, fidgeting with a pink-sequined, spaghetti-strap gown. He thought Payton's head was buried in one of the cardboard boxes his grandmother used for storage until he heard Payton say, "You got a booty like a girl."

Payton stepped closer. "Damn, your thang is bigger than mine and I'm older than you. Nobody on the football team's thang is bigger than mine. I thought I had the biggest one. Mines is bigger than my father's, my uncle's, my brother's and even the coach's. Damn, I ain't never seen one bigger than mine."

Terri had never seen another boy's thang up close. He didn't know and didn't care if his was big, but he was watching with great interest as Payton pulled his from his jeans.

"See. Get yours hard and let's see who's the biggest then," Payton said.

Terri didn't want his to be bigger than Payton's. He didn't want any part of him to be bigger than Payton.

"I don't want to. I just want to try on the dresses," Terri said quietly.

"Yeah, I thought you would like them. I saw you through the bathroom window last night in a bra and some panties. You want to be a girl, huh?"

Terri noticed a change in Payton's voice. He was grunting more than talking. Terri watched him as he was slowly stroking himself.

"No. I don't. I just like to play around and stuff."

"Don't lie. I seen you a couple of times wearing your grandmother's clothes. I seen you pretending. My grandma ain't never gonna miss them dresses. I might give you that one. Put it on."

Terri slipped into the gown he was fidgeting with. He didn't take his eyes from Payton's face. He wanted to see if

Payton liked him in the dress. He watched as Payton dusted off
an old mirror and set it against the chimney in the sunlight.

"Come see."

Terri couldn't stop smiling when he saw himself. The dress
was so pretty and he was pretty in it. What made him smile
more was the image he and Payton reflected together in the
mirror. Payton was head and shoulders above him. His light
complexion, Terri felt, was the perfect contrast with his own
pecan-brown skin. They looked like a couple.

"You got girl eyes when you smile," Payton told him.

Terri felt Payton pressing against him, almost embracing
him. Terri leaned back into him.

"I don't like girls, Terri. I don't like how they sound, feel
or smell. I like you, even though you got a girl booty and girl
eyes. If you take that dress off and lay down with me on them
old rugs and give me a kiss, I'll give you that dress. I want to
show you what I know how to do. If you like it, we can do it all
the time. It's what boys that like each other do."

Terri felt Payton's hand slide under the pink spaghetti-strap
gown. He felt Payton's fingers caressing his thighs.

"You want to try it?"

"Yes."

After they did what boys that liked each other did, Terri lay
crying in Payton's arms on the dusty rugs.

"I didn't mean to hurt you."

"You didn't. Not really."

"Then why are you crying?" Payton asked.

"I don't know, but I feel good. I never felt this good
before."

They became a couple; a secret couple for two years until
Payton graduated and won a science scholarship to MIT.

Terri wondered for years how he would react when he saw
Payton again. Would he spit in his face? Kick him in the balls?
Ignore him? Ask him why he wrote that he wasn't gay when he
knew he was? Ask him why he broke his heart? Tell him that

he hated him? He surely didn't expect to be happy to see him, but then again he didn't expect to be getting out of jail when he saw him, nor was he expecting Payton to look so worn.

"Hey, baby! How have you been? Get me away from here, Payton, as fast as this hack will go."

Terri jumped into the front seat of the cab. Payton pulled away from the court and lit a joint at the same time.

"I thought you was in Statesville. What you doing at the county?"

"I got out of Statesville almost a year ago. I been in the county for three weeks."

"Damn, Terri, jail is not a place to keep going to."

Terri took the joint Payton passed. "Baby, you are one hundred percent right. Wrong place, wrong time. That's all it was. What about you? I heard you were married."

"*Were* is right. I did it for two years, trying to pretend I was my father. She was a nice girl, but I wasn't what she thought I was. We moved up to Philly. I was working for Temple University and made good money, but I wasn't happy pretending. I gave her the house and left. Came back to this bitch of a city and been stuck ever since."

"Why are you driving a cab?"

Payton was an MIT graduate. Terri wasn't sure, but he believed that would qualify him for more than driving a cab. He decided not to ask Payton if he was back to being gay. It didn't really matter. Payton was an old friend and Terri was glad to see him.

"Because I can work when I want and get the money I need. Shit, I ain't trying to get rich. I'm just trying to stay high and live."

"I heard that. Where are you living?"

Terri inhaled the joint. The thought that occupied his mind was that maybe after he got Payton cleaned up he would do for a high and a good fuck.

"I got a little spot at the Cedar. Cheap rent and good drugs down that way. It's close to the loop, so I can hack then go home and sleep or whatever."

"They rent by the week?" Terri passed the joint back to Payton.

"Yeah. Shit, he'll rent a room by the hour. I heard about Madear. I'm sorry, Terri."

"Yeah, me too. Hey, I need a place to stay for a couple of days until I can get a plan together. You think they'll rent me a room?"

"You don't need a room. You're stayin' with me. Let me radio off and we'll go get a little of this and a little of that and try to bring back old times."

"Sounds good to me." Terri couldn't help it; he had to say something. "But you know I'm gay, and I don't want that to cause you no problems." Terri stared straight out the front windshield of the cab, avoiding Payton's eyes.

"I was wondering if you was gonna bring that up."

Terri heard Payton deeply inhaling the joint.

"Bring what up?" he asked in a coy tone.

"The letter."

"What letter?"

"The one I wrote you while I was away at school."

"Oh, that letter. The letter that broke my heart. The letter that made a young, gay boy feel unnatural. The letter that made me cry for three weeks. The letter I burned with all your grandmother's pretty dresses. That letter . . . it meant nothing to me."

Terri didn't turn his head. He continued to look out the front windshield. "Don't give it a second thought. I haven't."

"I was confused, Terri. Being gay and alone was hard. Being away from you was hard. Being away from home was hard. All the things I was used to were gone. It was like I was starting over. It was a new me, and the gay students were

71

treated like shit on the campus. I couldn't go through what they went through.

"The isolation, the assaults, the insults; it would have been too much for me to bear. The majority of students on that campus hated gays, and I didn't want to be hated. I needed somebody, and I couldn't take a chance of starting a secret thing like we had. I got friendly with this girl named Becky and we had sex.

"She was the first girl I had in my life. I did it, so I thought I wasn't gay. I didn't want to be gay and hated. I really thought I wasn't. I was happy and I was doing with it Becky, so I wrote you the letter."

"You married a white girl?" Terri cocked his head, looking at him.

"Yeah," Payton said, not returning Terri's gaze. "We moved to Philly after graduation. Once I got off that campus and back in a major city, I started sneaking to gay clubs. Then I got tired of sneaking. I told her and left. I came back here got a job with AT&T.

"I met this thug nigga that smoked cocaine and I got turned out. I lost my job and he left me shortly after. All I got left is the habit."

"So you're back to being gay?" Terri wasn't smiling when he asked the question. If he could, he would have burned two holes in the side of Payton's head with his eyes.

"As a blade!"

Terri didn't speak immediately. He wanted Payton to know exactly what the letter did to him. He began slowly: "The only time I questioned whether or not I was gay was when I got your letter. I didn't know the name for it. I only knew I liked boys—no, I liked you. People called me sissy before they called me my name. 'Hey, little sissy.' 'Florence, is that your little sissy grandson?' I was always a sissy. I didn't know what it was. It was me. Sissy, me. The two went hand in hand.

"When I got older—thirteen, fourteen, fifteen—it was a problem. That's when I noticed being a sissy wasn't all that good, but you made it okay. I wanted you and you wanted me. What did you say? 'It's what boys that like each other do.'

"You made my world okay. So what if it was a secret? We had each other. Then you left. I was okay with that because I knew you were coming back. We were in love. Then you sent that damn letter and my whole world changed.

"I was a sissy, something unnatural, something you didn't want to be anymore, something I still was. I never thought it was something wrong with being what I was until you sent that letter. After the tears and the burning of your grandmother's dresses, I stood naked and looked in the mirror, and without the dresses I saw a girl with a thang. I saw a boy that liked boys. I saw a sissy. And wasn't shit I could do about it.

"I never let the coach make love to me, because I was waiting for you. Yeah, he sucked me and paid me well, and yes, he begged me to let him inside me, but I was waiting for you. After that damn letter I took that hundred dollars from him and all his friends.

"They didn't have a problem being gay. The coach showed me gay restaurants, gay bars, gay bathhouses, gay inns, gay people—a lot of them. True, most of them were white, but they were gay like me, and they didn't have a problem with being gay. I wanted to be like them: gay and proud of it. They didn't hide in secret. Shit, they had damn parades. Gay Pride Day! It was a whole different world."

"What happened?"

"What do you mean what happened?" Terri couldn't hide the anger in his tone.

"Are you still part of the white Chicago gay life?"

"What are you talking about?" Terri snapped out the words.

"Do you still go to white gay clubs?"

"No. I grew up. I met a man named Jessie who showed me what I didn't want to see."

"What was that?"

"That being black and gay ain't being white and gay. They were paying me; what I thought was friendship was patronage. I learned a lot and I grew up."

"I didn't mean to hurt you with the letter, Terri. I had to grow up too. We all grow up."

"You right about that."

"Only a fool lives in the past and worries about tomorrow. Live for today, T.T." Madear's words echoed in Terri's head. He started to cuddle under Payton, but Payton's scent changed his mind. Instead he took Payton's hand into his.

They brought back old times for about a week. When Terri's three hundred dollars ran out and Payton's daily cab money proved not to be enough to support both of their addictions, old times were over. They were no longer two lovers making love and getting high. They were two addicts looking for a high.

Terri had a dealer's habit; he was used to smoking large quantities of cocaine. Clyde gave him boulders, but Payton's money brought him only pebbles.

They were standing over the dresser that served as dinner table, clothes rack and all-purpose catchall. The room Payton lived in was too small for a table. Payton dropped eight small bags of rock cocaine on the dresser.

"That's not enough, Payton. We won't be able to get high for an hour," Terri said, complaining about the drugs Payton brought in after working.

"Well, that's eighty dollars worth of shit—my whole day's pay. It's going to have to last a little longer than an hour."

"You only make eighty dollars a day?" Terri asked with disbelief and ridicule. He thought Payton was stashing some drugs away, and if not, he wanted him to feel pitiful about bringing home such a small amount.

"That's all I made today. Some days I do better, some days I do worse, but it's all we got today."

74

"Well, I want more than this. I been waiting all day for you and this is all you bring back?"

"Shit, ain't no law say you got to wait for me. You can contribute to this party."

Terri couldn't believe Payton was being defensive. "What do you mean?" Terri asked, opening one of the small plastic bags of cocaine.

"Do like the rest of them queens out there. Get your money on."

"I thought you didn't want to see me in drag."

Payton had told him if they were going to be lovers, they would have to be two male lovers, not one man pretending to be a woman. Terri had agreed only because he didn't have long-term plans for Payton.

Payton accepted poverty too easily. He was happy with a little, as long as it was enough. Enough for Terri meant enough to get more. Payton had no intentions of finding a better job or getting a bigger place. Birmingham was back on Terri's mind.

"Terri, you want more than I can give you. If you want more, you got to get it yourself. Our thing is our thing, but don't let it stop you from getting your coins. Shit, it's plenty of tricks out there, and they ain't seen you before. You're fresh meat. You could make a killin'."

"And you won't have a problem with that?" If Payton said yes, Terri knew he would be on his way to Birmingham in a week.

"None. Get yo' money on."

* * * * *

Terri got his clothes out of storage and brought Vegas to State Street Parkway. He was under the magic lights again. He strutted up and down the parkway like he was on Caesar's stage, slinging his furs, throwing his hair, showing thighs, flashing his new titties, bouncing his half-basketball ass and

75

passing out a dazzling, alluring smile to any trade whose eyes he caught.

The going rate was twenty-five for a blowjob and fifty to a hundred to fuck. Terri charged fifty for a blowjob and negotiated the price for each fuck, starting at a hundred. When he first hit the strip, he mostly tricked with white trade. White men paid better.

In the beginning some complained, but he remembered Madear's story about Lady Diane and held firm. They paid his price. It took Terri a couple days to get used to the pace of the streets and sex outside. The money was fast. What took him an hour in the past took ten minutes on the street.

His first 'date' on the streets was a young, white man in a shirt and tie, driving a black-and-gray Saab 900. Terri was standing in front of the Cedars Arms when the Saab pulled to the curb.

"Hey, cutie pie. I'm looking for a good time. Can you help me?"

"Fifty for a blowjob, a hundred fifty for a fuck, and we fuck inside. That's thirty more for the room."

"A blowjob will do just fine."

When Terri got in car, the young man already had his thang out and ready.

"Pull around the corner to the left and park in the alley," Terri instructed.

Terri slid a rubber on the stubby thang and went to work. The young man reached orgasm in less than a minute and handed Terri a crisp fifty-dollar bill. *Get the money first*, Terri reminded himself.

Terri hadn't stepped out of the alley when another car pulled to the curb. This was an older white sailor driving a Jeep.

"You datin'?" the sailor asked. "I got twenty for a blowjob."

"My blowjobs are fifty, baby." Terri smiled.

"Fifty! Fuck it. I got no time to find anyone else."

The sailor pulled in the same alley. He was not hard and ready, and complained about the rubber.

"I tell you what, sugar," Terri began. "If you trust my guarantee that I don't have AIDS, we can suck each other's thangs with no rubbers and I won't charge you."

The sailor stopped complaining, and ten minutes later reached orgasm and left.

His next date was a black man. He wanted to have sex in the car for seventy-five dollars. "Look, baby, this is not *Let's Make a Deal*. I charge a hundred for a fuck, we do it inside, and that will cost you thirty more. If you're not willing to pay, please pull off the corner," Terri said with a smile.

"Bitch, I'll take the pussy."

Terri stepped away from the car and clapped his hands twice above his head. Payton appeared from nowhere and put a .32 revolver to the driver's head. "Get your ass on down the road."

The next 'date' was another white man, older, Terri guessed about sixty. He paid Terri a hundred dollars and begged him not a wear a rubber while he sucked Terri's thang. Terri didn't expect to orgasm, but the old gentleman had skills. He emptied a good hundred dollars worth of sperm in the old man's mouth, which he swallowed.

Next was a white limousine driver. His crotch was musty. Terri tried to hold his breath and rush the man, but he wasn't to be hurried. His musk had Terri dizzy. After he released Terri told him, "If you ever come back to me smelling that bad down there, I'll bite it off." Terri got out and slammed the door shut. The next time the limo driver pulled along Terri's corner, he smelled of Irish Spring soap.

The date that ended Terri's first night on the strip was with two tipsy, young white women who walked up to him.

"I'm sorry. I don't understand," Terri said.

"We'll pay. Wait, how much do you have, Molly?"

"I told you, Maggie. I have three hundred to spend on this."
Molly was blond. Terri watched her trying to steady her
drunken swagger.

"Okay, we will pay five hundred dollars for you and a
friend to fuck us both," the redhead whispered in Terri's ear.

"It will have to be the five hundred plus thirty dollars to
pay for the room."

"Fine," the blond answered, grabbing Terri's shoulder for
balance.

Terri signaled Payton and they went into the hotel. On the
elevator Payton was looking into Terri's eyes, questioning.
Terri only smiled and looked away.

When they entered the room, Terri began to shout orders.
He wanted the money but he had his doubts about his ability to
have sex with a woman. If he was going to do it, he was going
to do it his way, and if they didn't like it, they could leave.

He didn't tell Payton because he didn't know how Payton
would react. If he stalled in the slightest, Terri might have
changed his mind.

"You—what is your name, Molly? Strip down and get on
top of the bed on all fours."

"Wait a second," Molly said.

"Shut up and strip!" Terri let the bass in his voice out.

"Payton, you get behind her and ride her good."

Payton's face was covered with objection.

"Now!" Terri screamed. Payton snapped alert and stripped.

"And you—Maggie, right? Take off them ugly-ass clothes
and come over here." Terri dropped to the tattered armchair
and slung his blond Madonna wig to the floor. "Now!"

Terri sat in the chair with Maggie's red hair bobbing up and
down as his thang grew inside her mouth. When he was hard
enough and sure he wouldn't go soft, he slung her facedown to
the cruddy carpet and slid into her vagina from the back. It was
his first time inside a woman's body. He had tried once in high
school, but was terribly unsuccessful.

To keep himself from going soft, he watched Payton's butt as he banged in and out of Molly and imagined Payton was banging into him.

Climax was taking longer than he thought. He watched twenty minutes tick off the clock before he released. Terri heard Maggie moaning and assumed she enjoyed herself. His eyes were on Payton, who was still banging Molly and appeared to be having a damn good time. Terri saw Payton's thighs quiver and knew he was almost finished. He stood, went to Payton and tongue-kissed him while he came.

The women handed Payton five hundred and thirty dollars. They stood in the doorway, red and blond hair all astray, clothes disheveled, and smiling sheepishly. They asked Payton when they should book their next appointment. Terri slammed the door in their faces, and told Payton, "Don't get used to that shit!" and never spoke of it again.

Sex and money or gifts went hand in hand for Terri. Payton started it, offering him dresses for his first time. His next lover, the swimming coach at his high school, paid him in cash. He got thirty dollars for spending his gym periods in the coach's office. It started out with Terri doing the coach's typing. It developed into the coach teaching him the art of fellatio.

Physical education was a required course at his high school. He failed it his freshman year because he simply wouldn't go. There was no way he was going to disrobe in front of thirty boys. Payton told him stories about boys whose thangs got hard in the locker room. Each story ended with the boys being beaten or raped, neither of which Terri was willing to risk. He didn't think he would get hard. His concern was his girl booty and his walk.

No matter how hard he tried not to, Terri switched. He tried walking with his back stiff, not moving his hips, not bending his knees, taking smaller steps, but nothing worked; he still switched. His butt moved from side to side and there was nothing he could do about it.

His other choice besides physical education was R.O.T.C., a military training program. He flatly refused. The uniforms were atrocious. It was obvious he was going to fail his second year of physical education until the coach intervened. He suggested that Terri do the department typing during his gym period. Terri was receiving straight A's in typing.

The coach's office was above the gym. At times Terri could watch Payton exercise with the football team. The coach left a small stack of reports and notes for Terri to type daily. The coach would seldom be in the office. Terri noticed a lot of the male teachers were distant toward him; he thought the coach was the same until the gifts started.

First was a chocolate bar with Terri's name taped to it on top of the stack of reports. Then a box of Fanny Mae assorted chocolates, followed by a box of Andre's mints from Marshall Field's. Then came the caramels from Carson Perrie Scots, and finally an illustrated book of sexual positions for male lovers.

The coach didn't ask. He walked in the office the day after he gave Terri the book and handed Terri thirty dollars. He unzipped Terri's white hip-huggers and began to suck him. Shocked but stimulated, Terri didn't protest. In his junior year after Payton's letter, the thirty-dollar half-hours grew into hundred-dollar overnights.

The coach introduced Terri to his friends and white gay life in Chicago. Everyone Terri met expected him to charge, so he did. He tried to give the money to Madear, but she told him to keep it because he was the one working for it.

"Don't ever sell it cheap, T.T. If this is what you're going to do, do it well. If it doesn't feel right to you, don't do it. Don't let them hurt your body. I know very little about male loving, but Fat Nancy does. I'll have him come over and talk to you. Everyone needs a teacher, someone that's been where you going. Fat Nancy has been there and back.

"Don't be stupid like your mother and give away what you work for. It's your body those men are going in. Yours. It's

your money, T.T. Don't allow any slick nigga to talk you out of it. Those niggas will pimp a man-girl just like they would a woman. Be smart, baby, and stay off them damn streets. Keep it inside, T.T.

"There is no sense in the world knowing what you're doing. Your mother never understood that. She didn't know the value of privacy. People can think they know what I do in this house but if they haven't been in here then that's all they doing—thinking. But when you got your ass standing out there on a corner for all the world to see, they know. Keep it inside, T.T. The pay is better inside, and I know it's safer."

On the streets men came fast. With some, all he had to do was touch them or allow them to touch him. What surprised Terri was the amount of men who paid to suck his thang, and that slowed him down. He couldn't cum in five minutes, and most of them wanted him to cum in their mouths. He began to charge extra for that. They acted unconcerned about AIDS. Terri speculated that they either had it already or they were just plain stupid.

Despite many requests, Terri wouldn't go all the way on the street. If trade wanted to go all the way they had to rent the room. He would rent them Payton's room for thirty dollars an hour. On a good day Terri brought in fifteen hundred dollars; on bad days three to four hundred, most of which he and Payton spent on cocaine and because Terri demanded it, clothes.

Payton no longer worked in the cab unless one of Terri's tricks needed a ride. He worked as Terri's security on the strip. He watched Terri with every trick. He was never further than a handclap away, and always armed with the .32 pistol.

Payton wasn't a big man anymore; the cocaine took its toll on his six feet two-inch frame. He barely weighed a hundred and fifty pounds, but he held a certain look in his eyes. People saw it when they looked at him. It wasn't a threatening look; it was simply the look of death, either his or the person he was challenging. The look said Payton didn't care whether he lived or died and would have no remorse in causing another's death to come.

As addicts they were happy; they had plenty of drugs. As lovers, they had problems. Terri no longer cried the tears of love he had shed as a teenager with Payton. He wasn't expecting it to be the same, but he was expecting it to be better than it was. He thought making money would motivate Payton to want more. It didn't.

Terri tried to get Payton interested in going to Birmingham. Payton said the South was dead. He suggested they move into a better building. Payton said the Cedar was cheap and that they wouldn't be making good money forever. Terri gave up; Payton was content.

Terri had the money he needed to leave and decided to do it. He'd also become fed up with Payton's 'two male lovers' point of view. At the end of a shift, Payton wanted Terri to wash off the streets, and that included makeup and all feminine attire.

"Leave that shit outside of here! Ain't no trade in here! Just two male lovers. Now take that shit off. Pretend time is over."

Pretend time. For three months Terri heard his work referred to as pretend time. There was nothing pretend about what he did. The men he sucked were real. The police he avoided were real. The crazies who hated queens were real. The jealous 'fish hoes' were real. The food and drugs he bought were real. The show he gave under the streetlights was real. If it weren't, trade wouldn't stop. He created, he did not pretend.

"Are those pretend shrimps you're eating, nigga? Are these pretend titties? Is that a pretend half-carat diamond stud in your fucking ear? Are those pretend caps on your front teeth? Is that pretend Samuel Adams lager you're drinking? Are those pretend Bally loafers on your feet? Tell me, nigga, what exactly is pretend? Are your feelings toward me pretend? Tell me! What is pretend? Am I pretend to you?"

If the room were larger, Terri would have paced it. Instead he stood with arms folded across his chest, rocking from leg to leg, waiting for Payton's reply. Whatever the words were, Terri was ready to pounce.

He was tired of Payton not respecting his work. He was tired of his superior gay-but-not-a-queen attitude. Payton considered himself a true gay man, in love with maleness. His love didn't involve pretending; no fantasy was required. He told Terri once that everyone knew drag queens were psychologically imbalanced. They lived in a fantasy world. They were men who didn't love their maleness or themselves. Payton honestly believed the gay community would be better off without drag queens.

"What I said was ain't no pretending in here. In here we are two male lovers. Two men! Do you have a problem understanding that? Two men, not one pretending to be a woman. No pretending in here!" Payton sat on the corner of the bed.

"I am not pretending! Out there or in here. I create a woman, I don't pretend to be one. I am making a woman. I am evolving into a woman—no, more than a woman. A lady. I am evolving into a lady." Terri stood in front of Payton, head bobbing and arms folded.

"You're a man. You got a thang between your legs. You're a man who's damn good at looking like a woman, but you're still a man. The man I love." Payton reached for Terri's crotch.

Terri stepped out of his reach.

"The thang is not there for long, baby, and I am no man. Male maybe, and only half. Males don't have breasts." Terri pulled up his yellow chiffon Chanel blouse, exposing his breasts. "These are real! These keep motherfuckers paying."

"Those ain't breasts. Ain't no milk coming out of them motherfuckers. Those are fat cells growing in the wrong place.

83

You are a man, my lover, and ain't nothing wrong with that."
Payton attempted to pull Terri's blouse down.

Terri slapped his hand away. "I am not a man. I am a lady
trapped behind this thang, and when this thang is gone, you and
everybody else in the world will know what a lady is."

"Fine, keep the shit on. I don't care. All I'm trying to say is
that you don't have to pretend with me. You feel like getting
high? I got some shit from out west. It's yellow dope, damn
good." Payton stood and tried to pull Terri into an embrace.

Terri pushed him back down to the bed.

"I don't pretend with you or out there. Don't you
understand? It's not a game. I want to be a lady. There is a lady
inside of here . . . Yellow? Did you say you got some yellow
dope? Let me see."

"It's in my jacket in the closet. Terri, I love you the way
you were born. You don't have to change for me."

Terri pulled Payton's beige leather Pelle Pelle jacket from
the closet and went through the pockets, retrieving the cocaine.
He dropped the jacket to the floor.

"I am not changing for you or anyone but myself. Where is
my pipe?"

"Under the pillow. Tell me, when you become this lady,
will you still love me?" Payton handed Terri his glass cylinder
pipe stuffed with copper Chore Boy.

"I don't love you and you don't love me. We are
comfortable with each other. If you loved me, you would love
my desire. My desire is to be a lady. You don't love that.
You're afraid of that. Let me use your lighter." Terri snatched
the lighter from Payton's shirt pocket.

"I do love you, Terri. I always have." He stood again, and
again tried to embrace Terri.

"Then why do you let me suck and fuck other men for
money?" Terri pushed him away and stuffed the pipe with the
yellow cocaine.

"My love won't limit you. If that's what you need to do, my love allows you to do it." Payton was standing with arms open.

"Nigga, please! My sucking and fucking keeps us fed and high. Love has nothing to do with it." Terri lit the pipe.

"You don't love me?"

Terri exhaled the smoke. "No."

"Then I'm leaving." Payton picked up his jacket from the floor.

Terri lit the pipe again. He exhaled a *goodbye*.

"Terri, I'm serious." Payton had the jacket on.

Terri exhaled again. "Just leave the fuckin' key."

* * * * *

Terri had enough for a plane ticket; however, he wanted a new wardrobe for Birmingham. He figured three nights on the corner would do it, but without Payton's protection the streets became a war zone. Terri was robbed, raped, beaten and arrested in his first week alone.

When he got out of jail after two days, he stayed high for another three. His second week on his own brought two more arrests and another robbery. The money he had hidden away behind the wall socket for the ticket was stolen; he knew it was Payton. His furs were stolen from his room while he was in jail. He put the wardrobe out of his mind. He was working for the ticket. He had to get out of the city.

The female whores forbid him to work the strip. Every night he stepped out, two or three of them jumped on him. They only allowed him to work days, when more police than trade were on the strip. When Payton passed him in the cab, they ignored each other.

It was his fourth week without Payton when TWA announced a special to Birmingham: one-way coach class for eighty dollars. Terri had ninety-six dollars in his bra. Instead of buying a ticket, he bought eight bags of rock cocaine. He told himself Birmingham wasn't going anywhere, but he needed to get high right then.

That was last time he ever got close to having the money. He had to get high because the real fish hoes beat him. He had to get high to stop the hunger pains. He had to get high because he couldn't go to Birmingham. He had to get high because he got out of jail. He had to get high because Payton was ignoring him. He had to get high.

The night Terri knew there was nothing left between him and Payton was when four teenage boys had him pressed against the back wall of Sammy's liquor store on Division Street. They were giving him one of the worst beatings of his adult life. Through the flurry of punches and kicks he saw Payton standing in the alley less than four paces away. He yelled for him to help. Payton smiled, displaying his newly capped but dirty teeth, shrugged his shoulders nonchalantly and turned away.

Terri broke free of the four long enough to dig his nails into the back of Payton's neck. Payton turned and kicked Terri in the groin.

"Bitch, you still a man."

Beaten, dizzy, dazed and barely able to breathe, Terri stumbled into the night traffic on Division Street. A hand grabbed the tail of his Yves St. Laurent pink velvet jacket and pulled him out of the path of the number 70 Division Street bus.

"Damn, ho, you gots to be mo' careful." The hand was attached to a boy not more than fifteen years old. The boy turned up a forty-ounce bottle of Olde English malt liquor.

"Thank you," Terri whispered once he caught his wind.

"Ain't no problem. You get high?"

Terri thought he heard the droopy pants wearing, nasty and just as droopy sweatshirt wearing, big gym shoe wearing child wrong.

"What did you say, baby?"

"I asked you did you get high, ho." The boy took another gulp from the bottle, letting the excess drip from the corners of his mouth.

"Why, baby?" Terri asked through the pain of breathing.

"'Cause I want my dick sucked, ho!"

The boy's words did not falter. They were direct and struck Terri hard. Was this what he had become, someone who children could talk to like slime? Someone to be robbed at will? Someone whom no one respected was what he'd become.

"I give you a nickel rock if you take care of me, and a ten dollar one if you swallow."

Terri needed a hit. The boys down the street had taken his last twenty dollars and five dollars worth of cocaine was better than no cocaine. Terri led the child under the elevated tracks and took care of him. He was a child, with a child's organ. When he came, Terri recalled the taste of the warm milk Madear gave him on cold school mornings.

"Damn, ho, you alright. I'ma tell my boys about cha."

The beatings slowed down. The youngsters didn't want Terri's mouth messed up. Terri began to dope date, turning tricks with the young dope dealers for cocaine rocks. He took whatever they gave him and did whatever they asked. Day after day was the same; if he couldn't get a date for cash, he'd walk down Division Street until he met one of his young providers.

Weeks turned into months. He stayed in the same room and did the same thing day after day: turned tricks, dope dated, got high, went to jail for solicitation, and dreamed of Birmingham.

Men who had paid him fifty dollars in the past got his services for ten. He sold most of his clothes for cocaine rocks and rent money. He didn't bathe very often because no one wanted to fuck him. If someone did request a fuck, he would tell them, "I have the best pussy in the world—above my shoulders."

Chapter Five
Mo-red

"Damn, Mo-red! You looking good yourself, baby. When did you get out?" Terri sat in the passenger seat of Mo-red's Blazer trying not to show his fear.

"A couple of months ago," Mo-red said, pulling the Blazer into the street.

Damn, where is this crazy motherfucker taking me? was Terri's concern.

"Terri, I wasn't lying to you, baby. You looking damn good. Niggas was saying you was turned out and shit. They said that crack pipe had your ass. I knew you was too strong for that. I knew my baby wasn't fucked up."

Here we go, Terri thought. *That 'my baby' shit.* Terri knew Mo-red's moves: sweet words and vicious ass-kickings. He had to get out of the Blazer without pissing Mo-red off. Maybe a quick blowjob would do it.

"You know niggas, Mo-red. They're always talking. Half of them are probably mad because I wouldn't fuck them," Terri said with a short, edgy laugh. He looked out the window, wishing he were one of the afternoon strollers outside the Blazer.

"Damn, girl, it's good to see ya! I missed you. How come you didn't write me?"

Think, Terri demanded of himself.

"I missed you too, Mo-red. I thought you would be mad because of how I left. I didn't spend my last days with you."

Terri couldn't believe he made reference to what he didn't want Mo-red to remember. His mind was filled with fear and he was being stupid. He had to get a grip on his words and thoughts.

"I got crazy my last days, Mo-red, but once I got out, all I could think about was your sweet thang. No one out here is as good as you. You knew how to make me feel like a woman. I missed you, Mo-red. I wanted to write you so bad, but I was scared. I missed you, Mo-red. I missed you bad, baby." Terri reached over and began rubbing Mo-red's crotch while he spoke.

"You ain't send me one letter."

"I know, baby. I know, and it hurt me. You'll never know how much it hurt me. I was scared you wouldn't want me anymore, Mo-red. I missed you, Mo-red. I needed you." Terri unzipped Mo-red's pants. "I needed him, baby." He dropped his head to Mo-red's lap.

Terri sucked for dear life. He slobbered and smacked on Mo-red like a baby on a tit. Terri remembered Mo-red liked to hear sounds, and he gave them to him. He moaned praises of the size and taste of Mo-red. He told Mo-red how good it was and how much he missed it. He licked it, kissed it and talked to it.

"Where you been, sweety? Mo-red kept you away from me? I know you missed me. Mmm-mm. That's my sweet baby." He pampered it, rubbed it against his budding breasts. "You haven't seen these before, baby. Like them? They all yours, baby. Are you going to cum for me, baby? Please cum for me. Spit on me, baby. Spit that sweetness all over me. Now, baby, now, please." Mo-red complied.

Terri looked up and saw Mo-red sitting with eyes closed and mouth open. They were parked in front of a school on State Street, four blocks south of the Cedar Arms. Terri's first impulse was to run, but he couldn't allow fear to control him. He had to play Mo-red, not run from Mo-red.

"Thank you, Mo-red. Thank you for letting me feel him again."

Mo-red opened his eyes and closed his mouth. "No problem, baby. Anytime."

"You're not going to keep him away from me that long again, are you, Mo-red?"

"Naw, Terri. Shit, we just had a misunderstandin'. You's my girl. You know that. I missed all the proper talkin' and shit. You wasn't ignorant soundin' like all them others hoes. Any time you need this here, Terri, it's here fo' ya." Mo-red zipped up pants.

"Thank you, Mo-red, because you know I need him. There is nothing out here as good as yours, baby."

"You right about that, Terri," Mo-red bragged as he pulled out a thin glass cylinder cocaine pipe. "I need a hit after that. You still got skills, girl."

Mo-red snatched a large Ziploc bag full of cocaine rocks from under his seat. He loaded the pipe and took a hit.

Terri tried not to appear frantic, but he wanted a hit badly. Mo-red passed him the pipe and gave him a handful of rocks.

"Hold on to those, baby. You know Mo-red gon' take care of ya. So whatcha doin' today?"

Terri hit the pipe before he answered. The smoked that filled his lungs knocked off some of his edginess. "Not much, Mo-red. I was going downtown to take care of a little business but it could wait. What's up with you?"

Mo-red was dangerous, but Mo-red had rocks. A bag full of cocaine rocks. Fear continued to slip away as Terri hit the pipe.

"I ain't got shit planned today. I already made my dope drops. I was going to hang out, maybe go to the show or somethin'."

"What show are you going to?"

"I was going to the Plaza, but if you want to go, we got to go someplace else. I cain't be seen taking you to the show. You know how that shit is. Niggas get to talkin', saying crazy shit."

Terri was silent. Even the high couldn't soften the blow. Good enough to suck him in broad daylight and be his hag in the joint but can't go to the Plaza with him. Nigga shit. Mo-red's words hurt. Terri took another hit.

"I know that, Mo-red. You can drop me at the subway and I'll go on downtown."

"Naw, now girl, it ain't like that. I want to get with you. I just got this rank in the organization now. Everything I do niggas be watchin'. They be waitin' to report some shit. When

I got out of the joint they gave me the whole southeast side to manage.

"It's major money, baby, and you know them young boys is jealous. They waitin' for me to slip. I cain't even get high around the crib. Chiefs ain't suppose to smoke this shit. I came up north lookin' for you.

"You know I like to get high and fuck, but I cain't trust nobody. All the hoes is plugged in with the organization. They'll tell on me to get they own rank. It seems like everybody in the city knows me. I cain't go nowhere.

"So when my boy told me that shit about you, I came north lookin' for you. I want to spend some time with you. I just cain't do it in this damn city. What I suggest is we take it to the suburbs, hang out with the white folks. Whatcha think?"

"Are you serious?"

"Yeah, girl. Shit, a nigga like to get away for a bit, and besides, I want some Terri coochie and we cain't get down in the truck the way I like to."

Terri knew most of what Mo-red was saying was bullshit. Mo-red could find plenty of women to get high and have sex. What he couldn't find was a queen to kick it with. Doing it to a queen was okay in the joint but not in the streets. On the streets it was taboo, a weakness.

Mo-red wanted some queen coochie, and that was the bottom line. That was why he came looking for Terri. It wasn't about leaving him in the joint or writing a letter. Mo-red was not angry, he was horny—horny for some Terri.

He was a trade, a trick. A simple trick and nothing else. Terri smiled at the fear he'd had upon seeing Mo-red. All Mo-red wanted was to take him to the suburbs and screw him. Fine, but it would cost him more than the handful of rocks he freely gave.

The afternoon went well. Mo-red treated for lunch and the movie. They were both high and feeling good. The suburbs provided the cloak Mo-red needed to relax. Free of recognition, he played the lover openly. Small kisses and hugs throughout the afternoon added to Terri's comfort.

Parked in the motel lot, Mo-red's tongue was deep in Terri's mouth. He was stretched over the back seat of the Blazer grinding with Terri like a hot high school boy on date.

"Terri, I want you bad, but not here. Not in a motel. I want you in my bed. I know it's stupid, but let's take this party to my spot. Shit, you look enough like a woman to pass. We'll just shoot straight upstairs through the back. Okay?"

Mo-red was asking—no, begging Terri to sneak into his place. This was a different Mo-red. Maybe it was a deception of some kind; Terri didn't know. He knew he was high and Mo-red got him horny. The kisses, the hugs, the strokes, all added up to affection, and affection got Terri horny. He wanted to go.

"Are you sure, Mo-red?"

"Yeah, girl."

Terri rode with Mo-red from Palatine, Illinois to the southeast side of Chicago. All during the ride he talked about how much he missed and needed Mo-red's good loving. He caressed, licked and nibbled on Mo-red for most of the ride. Terri's cooing sped Mo-red through the city. Mo-red parked his Blazer without Club or alarm. He rushed Terri up the back stairs.

They didn't undress. Mo-red flipped Terri's leather skirt up and entered him by the back door. They dropped to the floor like dogs and humped from the kitchen to the bedroom—a dry, forceful hump. Mo-red didn't say a word, but Terri felt Mo-red's ejaculation before he collapsed across his back.

The dry, hard sex reminded Terri of prison and Mo-red's abusiveness. He no longer felt the affection Mo-red displayed in the suburbs. Mo-red was the same uncaring asshole he always was, doing him dry, not caring if Terri was in pain or not, only satisfying himself. Terri wanted out. The high was fading and reality was present. He was with Mo-red. He had to get up.

Terri squirmed free of Mo-red's heavy embrace. He stood above an exhausted Mo-red. Mo-red's sperm was dripping down his fishnet pantyhose. He needed to clear his mind and clean his body. He stumbled to the shower.

Hot. He needed a hot shower. A hot shower would cleanse his body and his foolish mind. He looked at his teary face in the mirror. He cried not from the pain of the forceful sex but from his own stupidity. How could he think Mo-red was different? A few kisses and hugs and he was fooled. He stripped and stepped into the hot shower.

Mo-red was trade, a trick, and he couldn't forget it. The fantasy was for trade, not him. The fantasy was for Mo-red, not him. Terri couldn't allow himself to be tricked. He was the creator of the fantasy. The hot water was working. His mind was clearing. Mo-red had tricked him, but now he was thinking clearly.

Mo-red entered the shower. "Let me soap you up." Before Terri could object, Mo-red grabbed the soap and began. He soaped Terri adoringly, taking care with his young breasts. He ran the towel over Terri's body as gently as he would a newborn. Mo-red's soft touch and lustful moans lulled Terri.

"You are more of a woman now than ever. You always had a damn fine body, but now with those little titties . . . Mmmm, Terri, you just too much. Every nigga in the world would want you. Damn, you fine, baby. You look just like a lil' ole girl."

Mo-red rinsed Terri's body with cool water and kisses. He carried Terri from the shower to the bed where he dried and powdered him.

"You see, this is why I wanted you here instead of a motel. Here I can show you how much I want you. Here I can show how sorry I am about the way I treated you in Statesville. I didn't know any other way. I didn't know how special you were. It wasn't until you were gone that I missed you. You're special to me, Terri, and I don't want to lose you again."

"Where is all this coming from, Mo-red? What do you want from me?" Terri tried to roll out of the bed, but Mo-red wrapped him in his arms.

"I don't want to lose you."

"Lose me? Mo-red, I don't understand."

"I want you to stay with me."

"I can't. You can't. Everyone knows me, Mo-red. Everyone knows what I am. You can't have that. Can you?"

"I don't know how. All I know is I want cha. Only you can please me. I need more than a woman. Do you understand?"

Mo-red released Terri from the restraining embrace and began stroking his thighs. Terri watched the red fingers dance on his thighs.

"Understand, Terri?"

This motherfucker is out of his mind, Terri thought, trying to pull away.

"I want us to be together, Terri, really together, better than in the joint."

Mo-red lowered his head to Terri's crotch. Terri's eyes opened wide in disbelief. Mo-red was sucking him. Mo-red, gorilla pimping Mo-red was sucking him and sucking him good. Mo-red wanted Terri to live with him on the outside. Mo-red brought Terri to his house.

Mo-red had Terri's thighs in the air, licking him good. Mo-red's tongue was between his toes, around his knees and back to his crotch. If Terri ever needed a hit on the pipe he needed one now. The man he feared for years was now lying between his thighs, licking and nibbling on him like a starved kitten. And it felt good. Damn good. Mo-red wouldn't stop. He was starving for some Terri. Terri closed his eyes and stopped thinking. He let Mo-red devour him.

"I'll be damned," Terri said quietly as he released in Mo-red's mouth. Mo-red gagged when Terri released. He jumped from the bed and ran to the toilet.

"I guess he can't swallow," Terri said, smiling.

Terri rolled out of the bed and found his own pipe and the cocaine rocks Mo-red had given him earlier. *Charlene is not going to believe this,* Terri thought. He sat on the side of the bed and lit his pipe. He was lighting the pipe again when Mo-red entered the bedroom and stood over him.

"Put that shit down and suck me off."

"One second, baby. Let me finish this hit."

Terri didn't see it coming. Mo-red slapped him hard, forcing the pipe from his mouth and snapping his head back.

"Ho, you do what I say when I say it! You don't tell me to wait a fuckin' minute! I'm Mo-red, ho! I will tear the linin' out yo' faggot ass!"

The beating was less severe than the hundreds of others Mo-red had given him. He'd broken no bones. He beat him with a wet, knotted bath towel. Terri lost one molar and his shoulder felt dislocated.

He lay on the floor of the bathroom trying not to cry. He knew better; going to Mo-red's house was plain stupid. Crying wouldn't make it better. Mo-red stood above him, pissing in the toilet and on him.

"Get the fuck off the flo', ho. I'm tryin' to take a piss. Getcha ass in the motherfuckin' bed and wait for me."

Terri crawled from the bathroom to the bed and waited.

"Shut up all that gotdamn cryin'. I still love yo' ass. You just cain't forget I'm the fuckin' boss. When I say do somethin', you got to do it. I'm still goin' to beatcha ass when you doin' wrong. Love ya or not, I'll whip yo' ass. Now, to show you I still love ya, when I finish snortin' the heroin, I'm gonna dope dick ya. You used to love that in the joint. Get full of this dope and I'll never cum. You hold on a minute."

When Mo-red finished snorting the heroin, he fell across the bed in a drug-induced nap. He rolled from the bed to the floor, waking for a brief moment. He grinned and nodded back off. Terri's first impulse was to stomp on his head, beat him with the lamp, cut his throat, slash his face, hurt him—anything to cause him pain. This man needed to feel pain; the pain that Terri felt now.

Sweet words and vicious ass-kickings were Mo-red's M.O. Mo-red had not changed. He was the same bastard who stole Terri's joy in Statesville, the same bastard who beat him to nothing—no pride, no love, nothing. Mo-red beat it all from him in prison, and if Terri let him, Mo-red would destroy the little bit of self he had now.

Mo-red was the destroyer of joy and the giver of false hope and pain. Terri stood from the bed. He slammed his shoulder into the wall, putting it back into position. One of his patrons from Statesville had shown him how to do it after Mo-red first dislocated it. He went in the bathroom and rinsed the blood from his face and quickly washed up.

Mo-red was still passed out when Terri returned to the bedroom. He found his clothes and got dressed. Terri wanted out. He couldn't return to the beatings and worthlessness Mo-red gave. Mo-red had not changed, but Terri had.

Never before did he think of causing Mo-red pain. He accepted the pain Mo-red gave him with no thought of returning it. In prison Mo-red controlled him, but they were not in prison. Escape and revenge were options on the outside.

The keys to Mo-red's Blazer were in the back door. He could take the Blazer and drive it to Birmingham. He could get away. He needed money. Mo-red's pants were on the side of the bed. Too close to Mo-red. There had to be money someplace else. Terri quietly crept through the apartment, searching.

97

In the kitchen under the sink he found a safe. He didn't think it would work, but he tried the combination Mo-red used on his footlocker in the joint. It worked.

The safe was the jackpot. It held three large bricks of cocaine and stacks of money—too much money to shove down his skirt. Next to the safe was a box of white plastic garbage bags. He pulled one from the box and stuffed it with the safe's contents. He took it all. He would leave Mo-red with nothing. Taking it would cause Mo-red pain and give Terri a good start on the future.

His head started to spin as he loaded the cash into the plastic bag. This was the motherfucking motherload. He needed his cocaine pipe; it was in the bedroom. He had to have it. No way could he pull this off without taking a hit. He left the bag in front of the back door and peeped into the bedroom. Mo-red was still out. His pipe was at the foot of the bed, two steps away.

For a small glass cylinder stuffed on one end with copper Chore Boy, it was invaluable to his life. He had other pipes, but this small glass one was his favorite. He'd had it longer than any of the metal car antennas he would use from time to time. The metal pipes served the same purpose, but they got hot and burnt his lips when he smoked with them. The telltale sign of a crackhead: burnt lips.

The little glass pipe didn't burn his lips. It was his friend. Smoking with it allowed him to watch the smoke being pulled into his lungs, and it was loaded with resin from the rocks Mo-red gave him earlier. The resin was important. It was pure cocaine. He wouldn't leave without the glass pipe or the handful of rocks on the nightstand.

He glided in and out of the room in the blink of an eye with the rocks, a lighter, Mo-red's pants and his own pipe. Mo-red's pants held thirteen hundred dollars and a straight razor. Terri put the cash and the razor in his skirt pocket. He opened two of the bags Mo-red had given him, stuffed his pipe with one and lit it. He took two large hits, filling his lungs. He put the second rock on the pipe while it was hot. He wanted the rock to melt so he could hit it later. He held the pipe with his teeth and lips as he mentally organized his escape and vengeance.

Taking the loot would hurt Mo-red, but Terri wanted more, much more. On the kitchen table Mo-red had fifths of grain alcohol. Terri grabbed three. He emptied two in the front room then poured a trail to Mo-red's bedroom. He emptied one at the foot of Mo-red's bed and around Mo-red, taking care not to splash him.

If Mo-red woke now he would kill Terri but that thought didn't stop him. The thought of revenge was stronger. He owed Mo-red for this day and for Statesville. He got two more fifths off the table and soaked the bed and the doorway. He poured a trail to the kitchen door. He turned the lock and opened the door.

"Goodbye, you red bastard."

Terri lit the grain alcohol. The blaze moved so fast that it snapped Terri out of his vengeful daze. He ran from the inferno to the Blazer, carrying the white plastic bag.

As he started the Blazer he heard Mo-red screaming. He slammed down on the gas pedal.

"Fuck you, Mo-red! Burn in hell, you bitch-ass motherfucker!" he yelled as he sped away.

Chapter Six
Old-Timer

Ten blocks later he slowed down. The Blazer's digital clock read 8:30 P.M. It was the perfect time for traveling on the road. He pulled the Blazer into an alley, shutting off the lights. He parked behind an abandoned garage and turned off the engine. He felt comfort in the darkness of the alley.

He did it. He got Mo-red's ass good. He took a couple of deep breaths to relax. Where did the courage come from? How did he think of it? Was Mo-red dead? He hoped so. He saw himself light the fire, but it didn't seem real. It was real, though. He did it. He got even. He protected himself. Mo-red hurt him, and he hurt Mo-red back.

He felt at ease, satisfied. He felt the deep satisfaction of revenge. At that moment all was right with the world. He couldn't remember feeling better. When he flicked his lighter the thought of Mo-red running all aflame entered his mind. He laughed openly while he lit his glass pipe. This was the first time he could remember getting even with someone who did him wrong. It felt good.

"Mo-red is more red now. He's a red-hot motherfucker. Scorched red. Sco-red, they gon' call his ass now. Crispy-red. Burnt-up-red. Dead-red. He fucked with the wrong girl today. Today Terri wasn't taking any shit! Caught the bitch on the wrong day."

Terri opened another bag. He put rock after rock on the pipe, not allowing it to cool. The smoke continuously filled his lungs. The interior of the Blazer was a cloud of cocaine smoke.

"Sonofabitch. 'I want us to be together, Terri . . . better than in the past.' Yeah, well it's better, motherfucker—a lot better."

Terri put the pipe in the ashtray and went through the contents of the white plastic bag. The two large bricks of cocaine were processed into crack for the streets. Terri didn't know the street value, but he knew it was more than enough to start over with style in Birmingham. He knew a little about

101

selling cocaine from the time he spent with Clyde. He knew enough to get started, and he was sure Charlene knew some people in the business. It would work out fine.

When he started counting the money his thang got hard. It was over a hundred grand. He lit the pipe again. This was some serious shit. This was bigger than Mo-red. If the fire didn't kill him, the people he worked with would. Even chiefs couldn't fuck up like this.

Between the crack and the money, a fortune was in the bag. He closed the bag and forced it under the passenger seat. Under the driver's seat he found the bag of rocks Mo-red had stashed earlier.

"Damn, I got more cocaine than Kellogs got flakes." He looked around out of reflex. The alley was empty except for him. It was time to go.

Terri started the Blazer. The gas gauge read a quarter of a tank—enough to get out of the inner city. He would fill up in the suburbs. The further away from Mo-red and his soldiers the better. He was feeling the effects of the cocaine and his situation.

He might have just killed a gang chief. He did just steal a fortune from one of the largest gangs in the city. Sitting in a dark alley in the chief's truck getting high was not smart. The cocaine had his jaws tight. He doubted his ability to order gas or anything else. The drive to the suburbs would allow him to sober up a bit and think. He needed a map, some food for the road, a couple of lighters and maybe some beer.

The logical thing to do was leave the alley. What he did was take another hit. He was sweating profusely. His eyes were bucked and he knew he had to leave. One more hit, he told himself, then he would leave.

One big hit would do it. He stuffed three rocks in the glass pipe and lit it. His hands were trembling too badly to hold the pipe and the lighter. He held the pipe with his teeth and lips and with both hands he brought the flame to the pipe.

He inhaled deeply and exhaled greatly. He spit the pipe into the ashtray. That was enough. His movements were squirrel-like, quick and jerky. His mind was racing. He had to go. He had to escape. He turned on the lights and hit the gas. He pulled from the alley.

He drove slowly; his heart was pounding in his head. He'd gotten too high. His hands were trembling and the sweat was pouring into his eyes. He was too high to drive and too high to stop. He wiped the sweat from his eyes and pulled onto 79th Street at fifteen miles an hour. He rolled down the all four of the Blazer's windows and let in the cool evening air. That helped. He caught the pace of traffic.

He needed a drink. A strong drink would calm him. He passed several liquor stores, but each had a small crowd in front of it. Anyone who saw him would know he was high. He was geeked to the max. The drink would have to wait. He got on the expressway at 79th and the Dan Ryan. He pushed down the pedal and the V8 hummed. He was moving, on his way. Fresh air rushed through the windows and partially cleared his head.

"Ahh, yeah! It's going to be alright."

As the wind rushed through the Blazer, increasing with his speed, his mind cleared more. His trembling settled. He was still high, but he wasn't geeked as much. His jaws remained tight, but the rushing wind eased the sweating. He noticed himself passing other vehicles on the expressway. He slowed the Blazer. The last thing he needed was to get stopped by the police.

He glanced into the ashtray and spotted a long cigarette butt. He pulled the Viceroy from the ashtray and lit it. It was stale but it served the purpose. He was getting calmer. His heart was no longer beating in his head.

He glanced at his eyes in the rearview mirror; they were still bucked. The Viceroy tasted horrible but he continued to smoke it. He was cruising with the traffic at seventy-five miles per hour. He thought about the radio but didn't want the noise. His own thoughts would have to do.

He tried to think of something other than pulling off the expressway and taking another hit. Birmingham entered his mind, then the best thought in years took hold of his mind. He could afford the change now. The operation was within reach. With the fortune he now possessed, he could become the lady he dreamed of. A grin broke through his cocaine-restrained jaws.

As the cocaine eased its grip on his mind, he noticed the fuel light blinking. Not sure how far he could travel with low fuel, he decided to exit the expressway. He took 94 east to 57 south and exited on Halsted. He pulled into the Shell station at 99th and Halsted. He pulled alongside the self-service pump. He sat gathering his thoughts.

It was a simple enough task. Pull three twenties from the money he had taken from Mo-red's pants then go into the station and buy the gas. Get some unwanted food, a map, and come back to the Blazer. Pump the gas and go.

The task did not require taking another hit. He closed the lid of the ashtray on the pipe and opened the door. When he stepped to the pavement his shoulder ached. He deeply inhaled the last of the Viceroy butt and snapped it to the ground.

He took a deep breath, closed the door and walked stiffly toward the station. He stopped when he remembered the keys. They were still in the ignition and the Blazer was running.

"Get it together, Terri. This shit is not hard." He opened the door, turned off the Blazer and pulled the keys from the ignition. He thought about the fortune under the seat and decided it would be safer where it was.

The sound of his own voice calmed him. "Okay, girl, let's get this over with."

The blast of a car horn from the busy street caused him to jump. He was still on edge. He took another deep breath and surveyed his surroundings. It was a busy night. Traffic on the street was heavy, and the station was crowded. He locked and closed the Blazer door and continued his stiff walk to the station.

Once inside he decided against the map and the food. There were too many people in the station to shop. He stood in line behind a couple of loud teenage boys. They were talking about a party and the fat blunts they would smoke once they arrived.

They bought a pack of Swisher Sweets cigars and three dollars worth of gas. Terri handed the young gas attendant two twenties and told her three packs of Newports and the rest in gas.

The look the attendant gave him was not to be missed. It was a look he'd seen too many times, a look he hated. It was that *who is this fag trying to fool?* look. That *I know you're a man* look. That *I am a real woman, and nigga, you ain't* look.

If Terri was sober he would have given his *ho, I can take your man* look, but he was too high to call it up. He settled for leaving.

The pump was pumping fast, but not fast enough for Terri. He stopped it at twenty-eight dollars knowing he had a couple more dollars to go but he was compelled to leave. He shoved the nozzle back in the brace and leaped into the Blazer. Fear was upon him. He didn't know why but he felt danger. As he started the engine he saw a red mass splatter on the windshield.

It was followed by what Terri guessed was a cheeseburger and fries. Two paper cups of pop added to the mess on the windshield. Through the smear of the windshield wipers Terri saw the two teenagers from the station laughing at their assault. He couldn't hear what they were screaming at him, but he knew what they were saying: "Faggot, get the fuck away from here." He agreed completely. He gassed the Blazer, exiting the station onto Halsted Street.

He put the boys and the clerk out of his mind. Growing up on the south side of the city, this behavior was not new to him. Drag queens were hated during the early hours, but those same boys, alone in the wee hours of the morning, would pay him to suck their horny thangs. Together in the evening they played the role of fag haters.

He needed a drink, and felt sober enough to stop again. Four blocks from the gas station he spotted two liquor stores across the street from one another. The larger one was a Prestige liquor store. It had a crowd in front. The smaller one looked like it was closed or about to close. Only one old man stood in front. It appeared the safer of the two. Terri parked by the smaller store. He pulled another twenty from his pocket. This time he cut off the Blazer and took the keys out of the ignition before he prepared to exit.

He was stepping out of the Blazer but suddenly decided against it. He was still uneasy; something wasn't quite right. Something more than the teenagers was endangering him. He closed the door and locked it. He couldn't see who was inside the store. The advertisement poster covered the windows, blocking his view. He rolled the passenger window down and beckoned the old man who was standing in front of the store.

"Hey, baby, come here for a second."

The old man didn't hesitate. Terri guessed his intentions were to beg whoever was in the truck anyway. Being called over was a plus.

"Hiya doin' dis evenin'? What can I do fo' ya?"

"I want you to go in the store for me buy me a fifth of Richards red and a pint of hundred proof Grand Dad. Here is twenty dollars. You can keep the change."

"Fine, sugar. Be right back."

The old man grabbed the twenty and darted straight in the store. The door hadn't swung shut before he was back out with the liquor.

"Here ya go, sugar." He put the bag through the window. "Dis here a nice truck. I see ya got dat LoJack thing on it."

"LoJack?"

106

"Yeah, that fancy alarm that helps the police track it if somebody steals it."

As the wino spoke, Terri noticed two squad cars slowing at the end of the block.

"Shit!"

That was the danger he felt. He reached under the seat, grabbed the white plastic bag and the Ziploc bag of rocks. He snatched his pipe from the ashtray and slid it into his pocket. He handed the liquor back to the old man through the window then exited on the passenger side. The patrol cars hadn't moved.

"Hey, baby, I need to get away from this truck real fast and easy. If you help me, I'll give you a hundred dollars."

"Follow me, sugar."

The wino disappeared in the dark gangway on the side of the store. Terri was right behind him. He heard the squad's sirens. The old man reached back, grabbed Terri's hand and led him through the darkness. They made a sharp left down four stairs to a landing, then four more steps. The old man leaned into the blackness and pushed opened a door.

"Come on in here, sugar. Dis my place. Ain't nobody gon' getcha down here. Watch ya step. It's some holes in da flo'. Wait a minute and let me get da light."

When the old man pulled the string he brought light to the darkness. Terri saw there was no floor. There were holes, but there was no floor. It was dirt, rocks and sand. They were in a cellar.

"You live here?" Terri asked, trying to hide the disgust. True, the Cedar was a dump, but it wasn't a hole.

"Yep, damn near rent-free. I do a little work fo' da lady dat owns the store. She let me sleep here. It ain't much, but I don't do much fo' her. I was married to her once."

The cellar was furnished with plastic chairs and wooden milk crates. The table was a cable wire spool. The walls were gray concrete cinderblocks with pictures of Lena Horn, Red

Foxx, Vanessa Williams, Ali, Joe Frazier, Duke Ellington and other faces Terri didn't recognize. They were taped to the concrete blocks with duct and masking tape.

The only light in the room hung from open wires stretched across the ceiling rafters. Terri's eyes followed another wire down to an electric hot plate and a small table of spices and cooking utensils. Hanging from the rafters against the far wall, Terri noticed two hammocks. One was filled with quilts and pillows; the other held clothes.

"Dat's my bed. Da other one is fo' company. I know da place ain't much, but I gets visitors. Mostly folks like yaself, lookin' for a place ta hide, and ain't no better place dan Willie's hole.

"I got da idea fo' hammocks after I got tired of da rats and bugs bitin' me. Sometimes one or two will find dey way into em', but it's nothin' like it was. Shit, I was gettin' bit by somethin' every time I went ta sleep. Dat's all I do down here mostly is sleep and drank. What's yo name, sugar?"

"Terri. And you said yours is Willie?" Terri asked, still standing. He was looking around for crawling insects.

He hated crawling insects, roaches and spiders in particular. In each corner of his room at the Cedar was a roach motel; boric acid outlined all the wall moldings. The sight of a roach or spider made his skin crawl. If one touched him he went into a tizzy. He would not and could not share a room with either roach or spider.

Although the hole was not nasty—no garbage, no empty bottles or food wrappers—it was still a perfect haven for crawling insects. Before he sat, he was going to be certain he saw none. If he had to, he would take his chances on the streets.

"Dat's me. Willie. Willie Jones. Not William, but Willie. Willie's my name, and it ain't short fo' William. Go on and grab yaself one of dem stools. Dem police gon' be circlin' fo' a while. Ya got a drank, I got a drank. Let's sit and talk a while."

"Sounds good to me, Willie. I could use a rest."

Satisfied that none of the insect or rodent population was present, Terri pulled a blue plastic crate to the spool table. He placed the plastic bag between his feet and sat down. He pulled the Grand Dad from the paper bag, broke the orange seal and took a gulp.

"Dere ya go, sugar. Drank like ya at home." Willie pulled up a wooden crate with a back nailed to it, and sat across from Terri. "Ya didn't know dat truck had LoJack, didja?"

"No, Willie, I sure didn't. I'm grateful to you for pointing it out to me."

"Ain't no problem, sugar. Da only reason I said somethin' was because I saw you was nervous, and I saw dem police circlin' da block. I didn't thank dat big truck was your'n, but you ain't look like no car thief."

"I'm not. I took it from my boyfriend." Willie obviously thought he was a woman and Terri saw no need to have him think differently. He might not have been as helpful to a queen.

"He made ya mad, huh?"

"Yes, Willie, he pissed me off." *An understatement,* Terri thought.

"Must not be much of a man, calling da police and everything." Willie cracked his pint of Calverts blended whiskey and turned it up.

"Yes, you're right about that; he's not much of a man. Those police probably work for him. I can't see him calling the regular police. He's a criminal."

"Y'all got in a fight?"

"Sorta, Willie. He beat me and I got even." The thought of the beating pulled the bottle to Terri's mouth.

"Good for ya, sugar. Dis da nineties. Ain't no woman suppose ta take no beatin'. Shit, most of y'all making just as much money as mens nowadays anyhow. Y'all ain't got to take no shit off no nigga."

"Amen to that, Willie." Terri took another gulp of the Grand Dad. "How long you been living down here, Willie?" The Grand Dad was making Terri's chest warm.

"About fifteen years."

"Fifteen years!"

"Yep."

"Why?"

"Why what?"

"Why you been living down here so long?"

"'Cause I still love da woman upstairs. She da reason I'm down here."

"What?"

"My ex-wife lives upstairs. I wants ta be close ta her."

"She owns the store?"

"Yeah, I gave it to her."

"What happened?"

"Naw dat's real personal, sugar. Maybe after I oil up a bit, I talk about it. I usually do."

"You love her?"

"Love dat woman's dirty drawers."

"What do you mean she is the reason you're down here?"

"It wasn't her directly, but my love fo' her is why I'm down here."

"That's a lot of love to make a man live like this."

"Aw now, sugar, it ain't dat bad down here, but I do love her a lot—a hell of a lot—and I owe her. I owe her a lot." He took another gulp of his Calverts.

Terri sipped his Grand Dad and wondered what kind of love would make a man live in a hole. What could a man owe another person that would justify living like a worm?

A sobering thought entered Terri's mind: Mo-red was alive and looking for him. He wanted to take a hit on his pipe but he suspected Willie would disapprove. Most old men didn't like crack or the people who smoked it. Terri tried to put his desire for a hit and Mo-red out of his mind.

110

"You cook on that hot plate?"

"Oh yeah, sugar. I jams on dat lil' old thing. I got a burner in da back. Sometime I use dat, but most of my meals I cook wid dat hot plate dere. I can burn a lil' taste too. Folks like my cookin'. Maybe one day I a fix ya somethin'.'"

"That would be nice, Willie. It's been awhile since I had a good meal. My place isn't much better than this. I know it's smaller, and there's no place to cook."

"Ya live wit'cha boyfriend?"

"No. I rent a room at a hotel." The Grand Dad was beyond warming; it was burning his chest, but he continued to down it.

"When me and my Delphine started out, we lived in hotel rooms and boardin' houses. Nothin' but holes in da walls, but we was together and in love. I promised her da world then gave her hell." The Calverts bottle went up again. "A man—a real man—always wants da best he can for his woman. He wants her ta wear fine clothes and live in fine places. I promised her dem things, but I never gave 'em ta her. I gave her eight kids, a bad back, sore feet, and a hard heart. I owe her."

"Eight kids?"

"Yeah, eight. One right after da otha. I stayed inside dat woman. Lovin' her made life sweet. She was all I had in dem days. A woman had to be everythin' t'a man. It was hard on a nigga back den. Da white man worked you from sun up to sun down. Kept his foot up yo' ass. If ya wanted somethin', just a little somethin', you had ta work for it and work hard. Shit, I worked in da slaughterhouse in da day and da hotel at night. Da only sweetness I had in life was my Delphine.

"I was a hard man den. I ain't know how ta treat her soft. When I came home I dug into her. I came in da house fuckin'. No talk, no listen. Just fuckin' and drankin'. It was all I knew. Dat's how my daddy lived, dat's how I was gon' live. It was Delphine's job ta please me, ta ease the pain of da life I had.

"She was supposed to make me feel like a man, even though Whitey was callin' me boy eighteen hours out of da day. 'Boy, slop dem guts. Boy, tote dat pail. Boy, wash dem sheets. Nigga, come here.'

"Yeah, she had a hard job. I carried a lot of pain in dem days, a lot of anger. I was mad because I was black, and I was mad because I was po'. She use ta tell me it would get betta, but it didn't. Babies was comin' every year, and da money was always gone. No matter how much I got, it was always gone. Dem was some hard days, and I was a hard man." He took another drink, finishing his bottle. Terri passed him his.

"Thanks, sugar. It was a soft man dat took my Delphine from me. A soft, pretty, yellow nigga wid gray eyes. Worked at the hotel wid me. I brought him home from time ta time ta eat wid me and my family, since he ain't have one of his own.

"Nigga got to be so friendly wid us, he was dere when I wasn't. I ain't thank nothing of it. Shit, my Delphine was mine, and he was a good friend. While I was cleaning up pig and cow guts, dat nigga was soft fuckin' my Delphine. I thought he was a sissy boy. Shit, bastard proved ta be more man dan me.

"After eleven years of marriage and eight kids, I know'd Delphine was mine, and I ain't thank nobody else wanted her but me. Shit, she wasn't never no pretty woman—big lips, flat nose, no titties, but a nice ass.

"She still got a nice ass. Eighty-three years old and the ass still sits up. I don't know why she gave dat nigga my pussy. I figured it was since he was so different dan me. Soft and all. He brought flowers and shit ta da house. She didn't hide dem. Put dem on the table fo' me ta see. I didn't thank nothin' 'bout it.

"He brought dem damn flowers fo' my Delphine. I ain't never brought her no flowers—still ain't. Now I cain't. Every time I see a flower I thanks about dat soft nigga.

"Turns out dat nigga's daddy was one of da owners of da hotel we worked at. Dat nigga's family was rich. He took my Delphine and my kids. Dey sent me a letter from a lawyer saying we was divorced. It was a lie, but I didn't know no better den. Da way I looked at it, da motherfucker took da only sweetness I had in life. He took it right from under my nose. Moved my whole family ta Hyde Park, bought a nice house and everything.

"I never beat Delphine or nothing. Sure, I drank, but I worked hard, and loved her; but I wasn't soft wid her, and I never brought her flowers, and I cain't now. Dat pretty, soft nigga took my only sweetness. He took my family and gave dem more dan I could. I drank for three weeks; ain't go ta work, just drank. I drank myself crazy mad.

"I loaded up my shotgun, caught da street car to Hyde Park and killed dat soft nigga. Shot him dead on his new porch, in front of my family. I spent forty years in prison because a soft nigga took my family. Kids grown up, and my sweet Delphine is old, just like me.

"Wid me in jail and her new husband dead, Delphine had it hard. I made it hard for her. I killed her chance. I killed dat soft nigga dead. I killed her sweetness. When I got out of prison, I robbed the first National Bank of Wisconsin. Me and three old boys I met in da joint. My first and only robbery.

"I bought her dis store. She didn't want it at first; told me ta get away from her, but she took it after my oldest daughter talked her into it. Now, for fifteen years I been tryin' ta get close to her. Last Christmas she kissed me. I'm making progress. I owe dat woman."

"Seems like you both owe each other."

"How ya figure dat, sugar?"

"Willie, you been locked up for fifty-five years—forty years in the joint and fifteen down here. That's a lot of time to say I'm sorry. I know it's not my business, but she did leave you. It seems to me that she owes you too. She was supposed to stand by you in good and bad times, not leave when she got a better offer. You all had a life, a family, and she let a pretty man break it up."

"I use ta thank like dat. I was mad at her fo' years. Hated her. But hate eats at cha. Ya cain't hold it inside. Once I let it go, love filled da space. I fell in love wid her again locked up behind dem walls. Dat woman birthed eight of my children. Eight parts of me are on dis earth because she gave dem life. She deserved some softness in her life, some flowers and tenderness.

"If I had known what I know now, I would've gave it ta her, but I ain't know how ta back den. Believe it or not, prison taught me how ta be soft; how ta slow down and appreciate shit; how ta enjoy the taste of biscuit and the smell of rain; how ta wait, really wait, and be patient. Dese fifteen years have passed like fifteen days, and ya don't understand dat, 'cause ya too young. Days and years is da same. It's all time.

"It don't matter 'cause I know we gon' get back together. I see the old love in her eyes when she looks at me—da love I didn't understand when I was younger. I ain't know its value. Love goes beyond time and dis life. If I die in dis hole, I know dat woman upstairs loves me, and I a meet her where souls dat love each other meet. Naw, sugar, she don't owe me. I took from her."

Willie was tired, and Terri was trying to understand what he just heard. As a result, the hole was silent until Terri figured out it wasn't for him to understand. He asked another question.

"You ever love any other woman?"

"One. I sho' did. She ran a ho' house on Fifty-first in Princeton. The fanciest black woman I ever seen in my life. She'd love me good, take my money and tell me to go home to my good wife. She never took more dan what she charged, and wouldn't let me get too drunk. She wanted to make sure I made it home before da sun came up.

"She told me as long as I had a home ta go home ta, we would be fine. She wasn't a home, just a feel-good place, but I loved her. She was right. When I lost my home, I had no interest in her or anything else. She was a fine woman—talked all proper, and knew how to cook all kinds of shit. She da one got me started cookin'. I would sit in her big kitchen fo' hours watchin' her prepare for her big Fridays.

"All da big shot niggas came ta her place on the weekends: musicians, politicians, gangsters and doctors. I snuck over through da week, but I coulda went on da weekends. She always invited me. She knew how ta make me feel special, even though I didn't have the money dem big-timey niggas had. She treated me just as good, if not better dan she treated dem.

"I doubt if any of dem big-time niggas ever sat in her ketchin fo' hours, and I know she didn't bake dem pies like she baked fo' me. Whenever I told her I loved her she would just smile and give me a lil' ole kiss. Tell me it was good I loved her, but I had a family ta love and take care of, so she couldn't let herself love me.

"One year on my birthday she didn't charge me fo' da lovin'. I remember every second of dat time. She came ta see me twenty-two times when I was locked up. Brought me pictures of herself naked. She loved me, but she would never tell me. She knew if I heard dem words out her mouth, I might've left my family. I heard she met some nigga got her strung out on dat shit. I guess dat's why she stop vistin'.

"I know what temptation feels like, I know what my Delphine had ta fight against. Dat soft nigga was selfish. He didn't care about breaking up a family, but Florence cared, so she never told me she loved me, but she let me in her ketchin, and she baked pies fo' me.

"She was the only other woman I loved; Florence, Florence Parish. Da most attractive, classiest, and damn near sweetest woman I know'd, beside my Delphine of course. I went ta her funeral a couple o' year or so back, and fo' da first time in my life I really felt close ta death. Almost everybody I know'd is dead. Seein' Florence in dat box made me cry.

115

"Life is too short. I came back around here, and started paintin', and nailin', and fixin' on shit I'd been puttin' off. I wanted ta kiss her face, when I saw her in dat box. A friend I loved was gone. Delphine thought I was losing what was left of my mind, da way I was fixin' and cleanin', but I wanted ta keep busy fo' some reason. I didn't want ta slow down. I didn't want ta stop, and I been busy ever since."

Terri hadn't cried at Madear's funeral, he didn't cry when he thought of her at night alone, but he cried now. Hearing the way Willie remembered her made him cry. The tears poured from his eyes. He didn't try to stop them. Maybe it was the liquor, maybe the stress of the night. He didn't care. He let the tears run. They were for Madear.

"Sugar, ya okay?"

"Yes, Willie, I'm fine."

"What's wrong wid cha, sugar?"

"Nothing, Willie. I'm okay."

Willie didn't need to know who he was. He didn't need to know Madear was his mama. He didn't need to know that she was everything that was real in his life. It wasn't his business. Willie had his memory of Florence Parish and Terri had his.

It wasn't a knock; it was a bang, a summons, a demand to answer the door. Willie pointed to a pile of blankets and clothes on the ground in the far corner. Terri nodded and hid within the pile, taking the plastic bag with him.

It was three of them—two police officers and Mo-red. Terri heard the questions. One officer asked and Mo-red repeated them. Did Willie see anyone driving the truck? Did he see anyone offer to help the woman driving the truck? Was he sure? Why were there two bottles of whiskey on the table? Was Willie lying?

Willie assured them he was not a liar. He told them he had not seen the truck they were asking about and that he often drank more than two bottles of whiskey a night, and he didn't appreciate the police breaking into his place. He knew the alderman, and they should rest assured knowing that he would report this intrusion on his evening.

Mo-red was alive and in the room. Breathing normally was out. Terri breathed through his mouth. After he heard the three leave he was still unable to move. Mo-red was alive and on his ass. Willie dug him out of the pile and forced him to stand.

"It's okay, sugar. Dey gone. Come on, baby, get it together."

Get it together? No, he couldn't get it together. He had to get away.

"I guess dat was yo' boyfriend wid dem. He seems a mean bastard. His hands were blistered bad, but he ignored da pain. I know dey was hurtin'. Dem blisters was fresh. A man ignorin' pain like dat is either pissed off or crazy. He looked like he was both.

"Spit was flyin' out his mouth while he was askin' questions. He walked around dis table like a fenced-in red Doberman. Dat man is pissed. Ya better stay here a little while longer. Take yaself another drank. Come on now, sugar. Sit on down." Willie pushed a crate to Terri.

Terri sat on the crate and took another gulp from the bottle of Grand Dad. Mo-red was alive. Mo-red was close. Mo-red had help. Terri pulled his pipe from his pocket.

"Willie, I need to take a little hit. Would it be okay with you?"

"Baby, if dat mean bastard was lookin' fo' me, I'd smoke some of dat shit too. Go on, girl. Smoke dat shit. Did ya burn him like dat?"

"Yeah, I tried to kill him. I set his bed on fire."

Terri lit his glass pipe, knowing there was enough cocaine left from earlier on the copper Chore Boy. He filled his lungs.

"I couldn't tell if mo' dan his hands was burned, but cha fucked his hands up. If ya gon' smoke dat shit, I'm gon' drank da rest of da Grand Dad. Okay?" Willie asked, reaching for the bottle.

"Knock yourself out, Willie. He was really pissed?"

"He was madder dan a wet hornet. He want cha bad, sugar."

Terri put the pipe on the table. It wasn't calming him and he didn't want it to add to his edginess. He had to think. He couldn't afford to get stuck on stupid now.

"Where am I exactly, Willie? What street?"

"Ya on a Hundred-nineteenth and Halsted."

"Do cabs come out here?"

"Not many of da regular ones, but I can get cha a bootleg cab. Andrew live next do'. He hacks, and I seen him parked out back. Looked like he was in fo' awhile. He don't do much business at night, but I'll tell him ya my niece."

Terri reached into the plastic bag and pulled out a stack of twenties. He placed the stack on the table. "That's yours, Willie. Thanks for everything, but it's time for me to get going. Will you go and check on the cab for me?"

Willie picked up the stack. "Ya sure ya ready now? Ya can stay da night if ya need ta."

"Thank you, Willie, but I got to get moving. Sitting still will drive me crazy. Tell your friend I want to go to Midway airport. I'll pay him a hundred dollars."

"Shit, sugar, I ain't gon' tell dat nigga dat. He might die from da shock. You can pay 'im what cha want, but I cain't tell him ya gon' give him a hundred dollars. Dat might scare him. I know he seen dem police. I'll give him a twenty out of dis here. Dat will get you dere. Now hold on while I go an' hook it up fo' ya. Don't move. Stay here. I'll be right back." He stood to leave. "Ya know, sugar, I ain't had dis much money in a long time. I'm gon' give it ta my Delphine ta fix up around da store. Thank you, sugar. Now sit and trust ole Willie. I be right back."

The issue of trusting Willie hadn't entered Terri's mind. Charlene warned him that he trusted too easily. He saw no reason not to trust people until they proved untrustworthy. That practice left him often with a broken heart.

He had no choice but to trust Willie. Fear wouldn't allow him to leave the hole. Mo-red and the police could be waiting outside. Why did Willie tell him to trust him? Was he planning to betray him? Did he see the money in the bag? Was there a reward for him? Did Mo-red make him a deal? Why did he tell him not to move?

"Forget it. I'm here. Whatever happens, happens."

He lit the pipe again. He envisioned Mo-red pacing the hole with blistered hands, foaming at the mouth with anger. He didn't know why, but it tickled him. He laughed out loud.

Willie said the blisters had to hurt; that made Terri laugh more. Mo-red was in pain and frantic. Willie was okay. He wouldn't betray him. Terri felt sure of it. His mind drifted to past betrayals. The one that stood out in his mind was his agent, Don Wilkens.

He met Don when he was out one night with the swim coach. They were celebrating Terri's graduation from high school. The coach took him to the Baton Show Lounge. Terri was under age, but the coach was able to get him in. It was only his second time out in drag. The club was walled in mirrors, and he was pleased with his reflection. The coach told Terri he looked marvelous, and judging by the response of the men there, the coach must have been right. They were all buying him drinks, offering to take him to breakfast and giving him their phone numbers. Don approached him by mistaking him for one of the performers.

"Hey, girl, you'd better get backstage. The show is starting in twenty minutes and you girls know you need your time."

"I'm not in the show," Terri said, showing all thirty-two pearly whites.

"Well, you should be. Child, do you have an agent?"

"No."

119

"Well, girl, you do now. Here's my card. Call me in the morning, but not too early. I take my beauty sleep serious."

Don Wilkens' agency was located in his house, a two-story building on Roscoe Street on the north side. Don wasted no time hiring trainers and drawing up contracts for Terri to sign. Terri pushed his age up a year and signed the contracts.

Terri became an employee of the Wilkens agency. The contract was good for three years. The coach and some of his friends warned Terri that Wilkens was a crook. Terri interpreted their warnings as jealousy and stopped seeing the coach. Wilkens was paying him three hundred dollars a week. No one else was offering that much steady cash.

Wilkens, who referred to himself as a flaming drama queen, stood five feet two inches and weighed ninety-eight pounds. Terri could see no dishonesty in Don's clear blue eyes, and he adored his blond ponytail. He hung on Wilkens' every word and followed his directives to the letter.

If Don's people said wear false breasts, he wore false breasts. If Don's people said use foundation, he used foundation. If he was told he should sleep with a club owner, he slept with a club owner. Within a month he was doing two nights at the Baton, and one night at Victor Victoria. He was under the magic lights. Don's people suggested Stephanie Mills and Tina Turner as his act. He did them.

When Madear came to see her first show she cried tears of pride. "T.T., you looked so good up there, and you smiled so pretty. You made me proud. Keep going, baby. Get all you can while you can. But baby, your manager is a snake. He's a pimp, baby. If you have trouble with that little white snake you come tell me, baby. You promise?"

"Madear, he's a nice man. He just comes off cold sometimes."

"Baby, that man tried to stop me at the door and he knew who I was. I didn't mind you moving out, but keep in touch with me, baby. Everyone needs their family, and only snakes

120

try to keep you away from them. Now that's all I got to say about that. This is a happy time. Give me a kiss, you little star, and order me one of those drinks with the umbrella. I'm dressed fancy; I might as well have a fancy drink at my table."

Madear's warnings didn't fall on deaf ears. Living with Don gave Terri some concerns over time. Don dated a young, black man named Jessie and when he visited, Terri would hear the strangest sounds coming from Don's bedroom. If it was lovemaking, it was rougher than any he'd experienced in his young life. It sounded to Terri like Jessie was whipping Don's butt.

Jessie openly flirted with Terri in front of Don. Don tried to laugh off Jessie's advances toward Terri, but Jessie never laughed. He let it be known that he was serious.

Jessie kept insisting that he and Terri knew each other, and once Terri remembered from where, they would be together because it was a special memory.

Terri found Jessie dangerous, and even though his skin was darker than a burnt match, he found him attractive. Out of respect for Don he ignored Jessie's advances.

Don and Jessie's relationship was based on money. Don, who was on the other side of forty, had no problem paying for sex. "When I had the sizzle, others bought it from me. I ain't got it now, so I buy it," he told Terri with a wink.

Terri didn't understand Don's reasoning. He thought Don was a good-looking man. He tried to sleep with Don once, but Don rejected him cold. "Girl, you way too fishy for me. I would love to feel that log of yours inside me if it was attached to some muscles and a hairy chest. But that plump booty of yours along with those pretty eyes . . . no, no, child. I would get sick. We are two of a kind. I like them hard and mean; you soft and sweet."

Jessie, Terri guessed, was hard and mean.

One night when Don was in Detroit visiting his parents, Jessie suggested he and Terri go to the Jeffery Pub, a gay club on the south side of the city. At first Terri refused, until Jessie told him about the contest and the three hundred-dollar prize money. Terri was gaining star status on the north side of the city, but Don kept him off the south side. In Don's opinion there was no money on the south side and the competition was too tough.

"How long are you going to let that white man tell you where to play ball? Superstars play where they want to play, and they always try to play against the best. You'll never know how good you are competing against only white people."

Jessie was sitting at Don's kitchen table and drinking Don's tea and talking against Don. Terri saw him as an ungrateful hustler.

"I compete against Blacks on tour all the time."

Terri sat at the table nibbling on an egg sandwich. The poise trainer Don had hired, a woman Terri guessed was at least a hundred and six years old, had him on a high protein diet.

"Oh yeah? How many times have you won?"

Terri had never defeated a black queen, but he didn't feel a need to share that with Jessie.

"Don will keep you where he got you because he's getting rich off you. You got to grow on your own. It's just a little show. I tell you what—you don't have to compete. Just go and see the competition. I'm sure once you get there and see the talent you won't want to compete."

Terri heard the challenge in Jessie's voice and wanted to accept it. "Just you and I?" Terri asked guarded.

"That's all, girl. We don't have to let the world know our business."

Jessie winked one of his hazel-colored eyes at Terri. Terri never would have thought hazel-colored contacts on a man as dark as Jessie would be attractive, but they were.

"And all we are doing is going to the pub? You are not gonna try nothing?" Terri asked, swallowing the last of his egg sandwich and ignoring the wink.

"Now, I didn't say that. I want you too bad to lie to you. If I think you in the mood, I'm going for it," Jessie said, pushing his chair back from the table.

"Well, I won't be in the mood," Terri said while flicking the remains of the egg sandwich from under his manicured nails.

When Terri stepped out on the porch and saw Jessie standing next to his granite-gray 330i BMW dressed in a coal black Armani double-breasted suit with no shirt and purple snakeskin sandals, he knew he'd lied. He was in the mood. The streetlight shone on Jessie and his BMW; they were both in the spotlight. Terri didn't know what it was about a finely dressed man and a fine car that got him going, but going he was.

Jessie wore his black, wavy hair to the back, and his shoulders were broad even without the aid of the Armani padding. He was tall enough to play professional basketball and big enough to play football. He had a barrel chest with a smooth patch of hair in the middle.

Terri didn't trust himself. Upon seeing Jessie he turned a half-circle and was headed back in the house, but Jessie ran up on the porch and took his hand.

"Oh, no you don't. You already said you would go. You're dressed up now. It would be a shame not to let folks see you in that fine dress. What color is it?" Jessie asked, standing close enough for Terri to feel the heat of his body.

"Turquoise," Terri said, stepping back against the closed door.

"Silk?" Jessie asked, moving a half step closer.

"Rayon. And back up. This is a big porch."

Terri put his hand against Jessie's chest with the intention of pushing him back, but when he felt the heat that escaped through Jessie's skin he quickly removed his hand.

"It fits you nice," Jessie said, not stepping back.

"Thank you." Terri stepped around him and went down the stairs.

"You got Indian in your family, don't you?" Jessie asked, walking beside him on the walkway.

"I don't know. Why?" Terri answered with irritation, not at the question but with himself for what he was feeling. Jessie was Don's, and Don was his friend and boss. His mind shouldn't have been where it was.

"Because your hair is so thick and looks so soft. I ain't seen a queen in this city with skin as clear and pretty as yours. Don't let them ruin your skin with all that foundation and shit. You don't need it." Jessie opened the passenger door of the BMW.

"Look, I'm going, okay? You can stop the bull. I'm not paying you."

Terri wanted the complimentary words to stop; any more might have caused him to forget Don was his friend. Flattery was one of his weaknesses, especially when it was directed toward his feminine attributes.

"That's why you know it's not bull: because you're not paying me." Jessie kissed him on the cheek.

"Tssst." Terri sucked his teeth. That was the first time in months Terri made that sound. The training coach had made Terri conscious of the sound, saying it was an ignorant audible and should be extinguished from his vocabulary. However, being around Jessie brought back a lot of Terri's old behaviors.

The interior of the BMW smelled of Gray Flannel cologne. "I thought Don told you that was a winter fragrance. Why are you wearing it now?"

Terri had to bring up Don in the conversation for himself and for Jessie.

"You don't like it?" Jessie started the car.

"It smells okay." It smelled damn good to Terri.

"That's the problem with white folks; they think they can tell you everything. This is the only fragrance I wear. I was

124

wearing it when I met Don and it was July. He liked it then," Jessie snarled.

"Don knows what he's talking about." Terri let the passenger window down.

"True, he knows 'bout some things, but not everything." Jessie reached for Terri's hand.

"He told you to wear a shirt with your suits. You're going to stain the lining when you sweat." Terri pulled his hand out of Jessie's reach.

"Don't nobody see the lining but the cleaners, but plenty of people going to see my chest tonight. I'm showing off."

Jessie took the corner without braking, causing Terri to lean toward him.

"Why are you showing off?" Terri asked, sitting erect.

"'Cause I got the freshest star in the city with me." Jessie tried for another kiss.

Terri moved against the passenger door. "Tssst. That's a red traffic light, nigga. Most people stop for them."

Jessie was turning him on; he had to keep his distance. Don was his friend and boss. He told himself he was only going to check out the competition, not to check out Jessie. He told himself that if he thought it enough, he would believe it.

The pub was packed. Thursday night was show night, and immediately Terri knew what Don meant by tough competition. Terri could barely distinguish the queens from the real fish. What he began to notice was that the queens were dressed better, smelled better and profiled better. The show was among the crowd on the dance floor, not on the stage.

Jessie was pulled to the dance area by three queens. Terri found a space against the mirrored wall and watched. The queens had Jessie in a circle and they were freely putting their hands wherever they wanted on his body while they danced to the pounding house music.

Terri didn't like house music. It was all beat. He liked love ballads, and rhythm and blues. Anita Baker and Luther

Vandross were his favorites. Terri tried not to watch Jessie dancing, but his gaze remained fixed. When he noticed Jessie smiling at him he looked away.

A waitress brought him a drink and pointed to a red-eyed, silver-toothed older man sitting at the bar. Terri refused the drink but smiled and mouthed thank-you to red-eyed man. Jessie broke away from his three admirers and escorted Terri to a table in front of the stage.

"This is my table. They hold it for me every Thursday." He pulled the chair out for Terri.

"That doesn't surprise me. I can see you're popular here."

Terri sat with his newly learned poise, crossing his legs at the knee. He was sitting to the side of the table, displaying the legs that were second only to Tina Turner's.

"I'm popular everywhere. Are you jealous?" Jessie asked, seating himself.

"Tsst. You're not mine," Terri said, looking away.

"I could be." Jessie held one of Terri's manicured hands between both of his football catching, or basketball palming hands.

"No, baby. You cost white man's money and besides, I'm not buying." Terri pulled his tiny, slender hand back and placed it ever so lightly on his own knee.

"You're making white man's money. You just don't know it. And I'm not always for sale. I got a heart."

Terri's eyes were filled with Jessie's.

"Buy me a drink." Terri looked away and wondered if Jessie really had a heart.

"Are you old enough?" Jessie asked, smiling.

"Fuck you," Terri snapped, rolling his eyes.

"When?" Jessie asked, beckoning the barmaid.

The show left Terri speechless. The performers were better than any he'd seen on the north side or on tour, and this was amateur night. There was no lip-syncing. These queens sang, and sang well. The Aretha Franklin brought tears to Terri's

CHASIN' IT

eyes. He was still crying on the ride home.

"Why ain't they pros?"

"Because they black."

"I'm black."

"But you're not as good as them. Not yet anyway. You just a little better than the white queens. When you get a lot better, then the shit starts. When you start drawing headliner crowds you'll feel the heat. When that three hundred dollars a week Don is paying becomes nothing and you want more, then you will see the real deal.

"You're going to know you're worth more, but the white man will never give you what you're really worth. He will let you be a pretty weed, but when you bloom into that rose, he's going to try to clip you."

"Not Don."

"Carmel used to work with Don."

"Which one was Carmel?"

"Aretha Franklin."

"No."

"Yeah, she did."

"What happened?"

"He cut her off. She wanted more, he said no. She tried to go independent, he put the word out on her and nobody would give her a gig. She made her move too soon. She wasn't a headliner. She was good, but she didn't have a following. Fans—that's the secret."

"I don't want to talk about this anymore. Take me home."

"Stick your head in the sand if you want to, but remember when your ass is out, you don't know who's fucking you."

"Tssst. Shut up!"

* * * * *

Terri's anxiety returned when he saw the tattered wooden door of Willie's hole being slowly pushed open. He pulled Mo-red's straight razor from his pocket. Although the door was moving slowly, it was moving too fast for him to jump up and pull the light string without the sudden darkness being noticed. He opened the razor and waited.

The face he saw relaxed him. It was a round face, a brown face, an aged face. A face that made him think of Madear's warm hugs and her pies. The face wasn't smiling, but the big eyes were warm.

The tiny old lady was dressed in a man's blue terrycloth robe tied together by a pink, flowered satin belt from a lady's robe. Her gray cotton sleeping shirt hung past the robe to her ankles, just above a pair of once-white canvas deck shoes. The backs of the shoes, along with the baby and big toe areas, were cut out. Her hair was covered by what Terri guessed was the corner of an old pillowcase tied with a stocking. She was carrying a plate of food covered with a dishtowel. Terri smelled the greens and he caught a hint of sweet potatoes. Terri knew this was Delphine, Willie's wife.

"Oh, excuse me. I didn't know Willie had company. I was just bringing him a little late dinner." She paused in the doorway and peeped around the hole. "Is Willie here?" She walked to the table, leaving the door open.

Terri dropped the razor to his lap and slid the glass pipe in his pocket. He hoped she didn't notice either. "I'm not really company. Willie went to get me a cab. You must be Delphine," Terri said, smiling and with his most cordial voice. The last thing he wanted was for Delphine to mistake the situation, get upset and throw him out.

"Yes, I am. Do I know you?" Delphine asked, looking Terri straight in the face. She looked as if she might know him, but her eyes said no to Terri.

"No. Willie was talking about you, so once I saw you I knew it had to be you." Terri managed to slide the razor into his pocket.

"Yeah, people tell me he talks a lot about us, especially when he's drinking." Terri saw her face was smiling, but her eyes said she was cautious.

"He's got nothing bad to say about you." Terri decided against standing. Sitting was less of a threat.

"Now I know he was drinking. I'ma leave this plate here. Tell him I left it and I'll see him in the morning." Terri followed Delphine's eyes to the two whiskey bottles on the table.

"Why don't you wait? He'll be right back." Terri opened his hand and gestured toward the other crate at the table.

"No, no, that's okay. I was just a little worried. I saw the police leave." Her eyes were questioning Terri.

"I know he'll be sorry he missed you." Terri ignored the unasked question.

"He knows where I am. Seeing me down here might shock him. He might go to thinking crazy." Delphine's face continued to smile but the eyes were serious.

"Crazy?"

Terri wanted her to talk; talking relaxed most people, and he wanted those eyes to relax.

"Yeah, the old fool still thinks I love him. If he see me down here it might add coal to a dying fire." The smile was gone; the face matched the seriousness of the eyes.

"Would that be so bad?" Asking the question was taking a chance, but Terri wanted to keep her talking.

"Just tell him I was here, darling, okay?" Her eyes told Terri the conversation was over.

"He does love you."

A street bitch has to have balls. Terri pushed the conversation past what he thought was safe. The Grand Dad had kicked in, and he was throwing caution to the wind. Willie wasn't the only one who talked when he got oiled up.

"So he says. What did the police want?"

"They were looking for the driver of some truck."

129

"The one in front of the store?"

"I think so."

"You were driving that truck."

"Yes, ma'am, I was."

"So the police is looking for you?"

"My boyfriend is looking for me. Those police work for him."

"Willie don't need no trouble."

"I'm not bringing him any. Like I said, he went to get me a cab, then I'm gone."

"You met Willie tonight?"

"Yes, ma'am. In front of the store."

"And that fool just brought you in his home?"

"He saw I was in trouble. He saved my life."

"And risked his own. Sweetheart, please leave soon. We don't need no trouble." She turned to leave.

"Willie told me you kissed him on Christmas. That was months ago and he talks about it like it was yesterday. You said the fire was dying, not dead. I know you know him, but I don't know if you know how bad he needs you. He told me tonight that all his friends were dead. All he's got left is his children and you. Why don't you stay until he gets here? He needs to see you here, and I could use the company."

She turned around.

"Honey, me and that old man's business ain't none of yours. Those police is your business. Don't involve Willie."

"I have no intentions of involving Willie in this mess, and you're right, I was overstepping my place telling you he needs to see you here. It's just he talks so much about you and the love he has for you. You should've heard him talking about that kiss."

A slightly embarrassed smile crept across Delphine's round, wrinkled face. "What did he say about that peck I gave him?"

"Peck? Delphine, he talks about it like y'all had lips locked for ten minutes."

"Old fool." She returned to the table and sat. "I got a house full of furniture upstairs and he won't take none of it. The man works around here like a dog and won't take a dime from me; won't even take free whiskey from me. He'll beg folks on the street but won't ask for my help. We both old and stuck in some old mess. I wanted that man to come upstairs ten years ago, but we can never seem to find the words for each other. I don't want him to die in this hole, and I don't want to die in a empty bed. He ain't the only one without friends."

"So you love him?"

"Yeah, I do, but I cain't tell him. The words are down too deep, stuck in the mess. Christmas, when all the kids and grandkids are here, is the closest we get all year. When they leave, he leaves. I need him too."

"You two ever take some time away, just the two of you?"

"No. It ain't never been just him and me, not since the kids anyway. Kids changed that man. He was a fun-loving soul, always a smile on his face and a laugh in his heart. Nothing could get him mad. He worked hard, damn hard all day, and come home smiling and telling me jokes he heard at the stockyard or on the streetcar. He'd tell folks his jokes, and they would tell him theirs. One night we went to the Golden Lily—I know you don't know nothing about the place.

"It was a Colored nightclub on Fifty-sixth and State Street. It was way before your time, probably before your mama's time. Anyway, we would go there when Willie got paid off. We'd dance and drink all night, and listen to the singers. We heard Bessie Smith there, and Ethel Waters. Child, that was music.

"Anyhow, the owner of the club knew Willie, and he knew Willie could tell a joke that could bust your side. One of the singers was sick on that no-good moonshine, so he asked

Willie to get up on stage and tell some jokes. Child, that man of mine didn't hesitate a second.

"Sugar, he got up there and had them folks crying they was laughing so hard. The owner gave Willie some money, and we drank free all night. Child, those was good times when it was just me and him. Us going away together, sugar, that would be nice."

"How did the children change him?"

"Some folks take things too serious. Willie took kids serious. Our first boy wasn't even born and Willie took on another job. We didn't know how much a kid would cost. Willie just figured we didn't have enough.

"As soon as he found out I was pregnant, he went to working nights, and child, it was all downhill after that. Two jobs is too much for one man. He started drinking hard and got mad at the world. He turned into his daddy: a mean, hateful bastard who beat Willie's mama worse than he beat his mule.

"Willie have never beat me—with his hands, anyway. He did worse. He took his self away from me. All I got was what was left over from two jobs and the whiskey. I tried not to have no more kids, but they kept coming. Every year another one came.

"I had to love them because they was mine, but I knew they was pushing my Willie further away. After a while all the love I wanted to give to Willie went to the kids. I remember thinking he didn't miss it anyhow.

"His friend Clarence told me he was sleeping with a whore. I didn't believe him. Then Clarence took me to the whore's house and I seen my Willie kissing that fancy whore goodnight. He was kissing her soft and gentle, like he used to kiss me. I gave myself to his friend Clarence that night. I only slept with two men worth remembering—one is dead, and the other is cold on me."

"He's not cold on you. That man loves you."

"So his mouth says. It's more to love than words, and it's more to the story than you know."

"I don't need to know the whole story to see the love Willie has for you."

"You can turn bad to good, T.T., if you want to. Nothing or nobody is all bad or all good. If you in a bad situation, do something good and watch it turn around. There are no perfect people in the world, T.T." Terri recalled Madear's words.

"Delphine, Willie doesn't know this, but he was good friends with someone I loved very much."

"In prison?"

"No, she was never in jail, but she sent me to him tonight. I realize that now. I want to do something that she wants me to do."

"Who was she?"

"Florence Parish."

"I remember that name. She used to visit him in prison. I figured she was his fancy whore. She died maybe one or two years ago. I drove him to her funeral. First thing he asked me to do for him in years."

"She was my grandmother."

"I'm sorry for your loss."

"Yes, it was a loss. Delphine, you two need some time alone, and Florence Parish would like to make it possible. She owed Willie some money and she left it in her will. I came to see if he was in his right mind to accept it. If he was not, I was going to keep it. I have my doubts. As you said, he is an old fool, but you are solid as a rock.

"The money, in your hands, would benefit you both, and maybe allow for that much-needed trip. The only thing I ask is that you do not tell him who I am or what my purpose was until I'm gone."

Terri pulled five thousand dollars out of the plastic bag and handed it to Delphine.

She refused it. "Willie ain't never had that much money to loan nobody."

"I didn't say he loaned it to her, I said she owed him. What the arrangement was I don't know. All I know is that this is his money, and if you don't take it, I'll keep it. With the money you two could take a real nice trip, and the words will come, believe me. I haven't known two people yet to go on a nice trip and don't talk. If you don't do it for yourself, do it for Willie. He shouldn't die in this hole."

Terri put the money on the table.

"Who are you?" Delphine asked.

"The grandchild of Florence Parish."

"And you want me to take this money based on that made up mess you pushed out your mouth?"

"No, ma'am, I want you to take the money because it would make Madear happy."

"She was his whore. It was her that started all the mess."

"I thought you said it was the two jobs that started the mess."

"I don't need no whore's money."

"It's Willie's money."

"We don't need it."

Terri took the money from the table and put it back in the bag. "Fine. I need it."

Delphine stood from the table.

"It was nice talking with you. I really mean it. And I am sorry about your grandmother. We really don't need her money. I'm going to sell the store to them Arabs across the street. They been trying to buy me out for five years.

"It's time to sell. I stayed open so me and Willie would have something to do together. I never thought about traveling with him. You put something on my mind. Would you do me one favor?" Delphine sat again.

"It depends," Terri answered.

"Put it on his mind. You're good at talking. My oldest is a sissy and he's good at talking too. Talked me into taking the money from Willie to open this store."

"Willie said it was his oldest daughter that talked you into it."

"That's what he calls him, his daughter?"

"Damn."

"What?"

"Willie knows I am a queen?"

"Sweety, you'd have to get up damn earlier to pull the wool over either one of our eyes."

The door creaked open. Willie and a young, short man with eyeglasses thick as glass blocks entered the cellar.

"Delphine? Girl, whatcha doin' down here? Ya gon' catch ya death of cold down here." Willie hurried to her.

"Just talking with your company. I brought you some food, old man. When you finish eating it bring the plate upstairs. I'll leave the door open for you. Bring it up tonight. I don't want none of them rodents crawling on my dishes."

"Ya wants me ta bring da plate up tonight?" Willie whispered the words in Delphine's ear.

"That's what I said, ain't it?" Her eyes rested softly on Willie's.

"And ya gonna leaves da do' open fo' me?"

"I didn't know you was losing your hearing, old man. Good night, all, and you, the grandchild of Florence Parish, you take care of yourself."

Delphine left the three at the table.

"You is Florence's grandchild?" Willie asked with his head cocked like a puppy looking at a butterfly for the first time. "Well I be damned."

"No, you be blessed." Terri gathered his belongings and stood to leave.

"If I was you, I'd take that plate on upstairs right now." Terri turned to the thickly eyeglassed cab driver. "You're Andrew?"

"That's me. You wanna go to Midway, right?"

"As fast as you can get me there." Terri was walking to the doorway. "Get on upstairs, Willie. Study long, study wrong. Madear, Florence Parish to you, taught me that. I haven't met a finer man, Willie. Goodbye." Terri kissed him on the cheek and walked into the darkness.

Outside Terri removed the straight razor from his pocket, unfolded it and followed Andrew to his cab. Andrew's cab, a white '80 Toyota Corona was parked in the alley behind the store. The interior of the car was spotless. Terri could smell the Comet cleanser Andrew used to scrub the vinyl. Another smell was present, a familiar scent: grain alcohol.

It should have been a bang, but it wasn't. It was muffled; the sound of a child popping a blown-up paper bag. Two muffled pops and Andrew only had pieces of a head.

The arm went quickly under Terri's chin to his neck. The hot muzzle was against his temple.

"Bitch, I should kill you now, but I ain't. I'ma cut your thang off and burn it in front of you. Open the fuckin' door."

It was a reflex more than anything else. Terri sliced the arm around his neck. Fire leaped from the pistol, shattering the front windshield. Terri rolled from the car with the plastic bag and razor in his hands. The corner of the door scratched his shoulder as he squirmed under it to the pavement.

Once his knees hit the ground, he crawled for dear life. He saw sparks flying from the pavement. Bits of concrete tore into his forehead. He continued to crawl. The alley became flooded with light. He got a foot under himself and stood to run. There was a loud bang from a distance. A short fence was a step away.

He was over the fence and heard another bang. He ran through the yard. The plastic bag slipped from his fingers. He turned back to pick it up and saw four bright lights on top of the liquor store lighting up the alley. He heard another bang and Delphine's voice on a loudspeaker announcing she was calling the police, warning the intruders to get off her property. The next shot, she promised, would not be in the air. No one was following him. He flew into the night, pumps clacking on the sidewalk.

He ran down three residential blocks, watching the lights and hearing the traffic on Halsted Street. The only sounds on the residential blocks were his clacking heels and his heavy breathing. He expected the Blazer or a squad car to turn the corner at any second. He forced himself to stop, catch his wind and think.

He couldn't stay on the dark, quiet blocks. Halsted, with its lights and traffic was more inviting, but also more dangerous. He increased his chance of being seen on the busy street. Uncertain of what to do, he stood on 115th and watched the traffic one block east on Halsted.

A gray cat skulking out of the back window of a car caught his eye. He took three careful steps in the direction of the car. It was parked in a good spot, in the shadows, out of the gleam of the streetlight.

The two back tires were flat—a good sign. He took another step closer. On the windshield, he saw handful of parking tickets—another good sign. The hood of the car was missing; there was no engine. He peeped through the window—no more cats, no kittens. The cat would not return once it smelled Terri's scent.

The window was cracked only enough to allow a nimble feline body. He tried the back door; it was locked. The front door next to the sidewalk was also locked. Terri didn't want to risk standing in the street to try the other doors.

It was tight, but his arm did fit through the space of the back window. He was in up to his shoulder before he could get a grip on the release lever. He pulled up and the door creaked open.

"Thank you, Jesus."

He was inside with the door closed in less than a second. The window was stiff, but he managed to roll it up. The car was in a good spot. He could see behind him and in front of him, and no one could see him. He leaned back in the damp seat and exhaled.

The scratch on his shoulder began to sting. He opened the plastic bag, and got the Richards Wild Irish Rose. He uncapped the liter and poured a little on the wound. He poured some in his palm then dabbed his forehead. He took a couple of gulps and capped the bottle. Getting to the airport was out. He was not moving from the car.

The next day was Saturday and if memory served him right, there was only one flight out to Birmingham at eight-thirty at night. Outbound flight times to Birmingham on three airlines were permanently etched in his memory. The next day's outbound flight was on United, the highest priced of the three. No matter. He was rich.

He thought about Delphine. That was brave. She saved his life. Mo-red killed that poor cab driver, Andrew. Terri would try to find out if he had family. If he did, Terri would send some money.

Mo-fuckin'-red. Why was he still alive? He deserved to die. Did Andrew? Did Madear? He slumped down in the seat when he saw the headlights of a car turn off of Halsted onto 115th Street. The car speed past him. He was unseen.

Death could come so fast. In a second, a head could be in pieces. In a second, a hot gun could be put against your head. He folded the bloody straight razor and dropped it in the plastic bag.

What was it going to take for Mo-red to stop fucking with him? What was it going to take for Mo-red to die? Maybe Terri could pay somebody to do it. Who was it he knew that killed for money? Oh yeah, Jessie.

What a strange man Jessie was. He wouldn't be sitting in the back seat of an abandoned car, hiding and scared. He would be out looking for Mo-red, gunning for Mo-red. What was it Jessie told him? Fear ain't nothing but a temporary state of mind. You got to think past it.

Chapter Seven
Jessie

"I'm telling you, Terri, that white man means you no good."

Terri was running the water in the shower hard, trying to drown out Jessie's words. He didn't think to lock the bathroom door and Jessie walked in, continuing the conversation from the car and pub. He sat on the toilet while Terri showered, giving him unwanted information.

"I bet you didn't know I got you a spot on the *Oprah* show, did you?"

Terri didn't know, but he said nothing.

"Yep, it tapes in a week. Don told me not to tell you. He said you weren't ready. I told him you were. He told me to mind my own business; said managing talent was beyond the scope of what I was good at. Arrogant bastard. He has no idea what I'm good at."

"He's got some idea," Terri yelled over the noise of the shower.

"No he don't. He knows what I let him know."

Terri shut the water off. "He knows what he buys."

"He hasn't purchased. He rents me," Jessie said.

"Tssst. Rents, buys, what's the difference? You're his."

Terri didn't want to step out of the shower nude in front of Jessie. He didn't want Jessie's eyes on his body. He didn't want to see Jessie's desire.

"Jessie, could you leave while I dry off?"

"No."

"Jessie."

"You don't have anything I haven't seen before."

"Maybe not, but you haven't seen mine," Terri said from behind the shower curtain.

Jessie stood from the toilet and yanked the curtain back. "Now I seen yours." He paused. His eyes told Terri he was impressed. "Damn, you really are built like a woman. All you need is titties. Look at that ass!"

He reached and Terri didn't move.

"Such a thin waist and curvy hips. And solid thighs." He stroked each part as he mentioned them. "Girl, it's time we get together."

Terri stepped from the tub past him. "Tssst. We are not getting together." Terri pulled a towel from the wall rack and began drying himself. Jessie snatched it from him and did the drying.

"You want to hear about Oprah?"

"Oprah Winfrey?"

"No, Oprah Donahue. Of course Oprah Winfrey."

Terri kept his back to Jessie. He didn't want Jessie to see his rise. Despite trying to think the right thing, Jessie drying him off was stimulating.

"Tell me," Terri said.

"She's doing a show on female impersonators. I called and left a message about you. They called me back and asked for photos. I sent in your package. They called me the next day and said you had a spot."

"What was in the package?"

"You don't know what's in your media kit?"

"No."

Jessie was gliding the towel across the small of Terri's back and the backs of his thighs. He hadn't dried his butt.

"Head shots, dance shots, a bikini shot and a video tape."

"Which tape?" At that moment Terri didn't care which tape. He wanted to feel the pampering towel on his butt.

"From your second show at the Baton."

"Oh. Dry my butt, would you?"

Terri woke late that morning in Don's bed, on Jessie's chest.

"I shouldn't have did it."

"Why?" Jessie asked.

"Tssst. 'Cause you're Don's."

"I ain't nobody's. I could be yours."

"I can't pay your bills."

"Get dressed, Terri. It's time to show you something."

"Where?"

"All over the city. Don won't be back until Sunday."

"I can't. I have to get my hair washed today."

"I'll take you."

Giddy. That's how Terri felt riding with Jessie in his fine BMW. He was dressed in his schoolgirl outfit—a blue plaid skirt, a powder blue string-tied halter which came with C-cup padding, bobby socks, and black-and-white two-tone loafers.

Jessie's attention seemed endless. He held Terri's hand, kissed him on the cheek, stroked his thigh, caressed the hair at the nape of his neck and told him he was beautiful. They stopped on Taylor Street in front of a small store. It was more of a shack than a building.

"You ever have Italian ice?" Jessie asked.

"No. What is it?"

"You'll love it. He's about to close for the season. Next week you won't be able to get any until next year. Like most good things in life, you got to get it while you can."

He got out of the car, walked around and opened the door for Terri. "Come on, baby. You'll love this."

Terri got the watermelon flavor, and he did love it. It was sweet, cold, and full of flavor. It was much better than a Slushy or Icee. Little bits of watermelon were mixed in with the crushed, flavored ice. He got a large, so he was able to put spoon after spoon of the delightful treat into his small mouth.

"Slow down," Jessie said while starting the car. "You're going to get one of those cold headaches."

"Cold headache?"

"Yeah, you know, the headache you get from eating cold stuff too fast. I let mine melt down, then I sip it through the straw."

"Well if you don't mind, I'm going to take my chances against the cold headache and keep eating mine." Terri shoveled two quick spoonfuls into his mouth. "Mmmmph! This is good. You should eat yours."

"Suit yourself, baby." Jessie smiled. "Did Don ever tell you how he and I met?"

"Unh-uh," Terri answered without taking his eyes from his frozen treat. He was searching for another bit of frozen watermelon.

"His old partner, Juan, paid me two hundred dollars to beat his ass."

Terri noticed Jessie pause for his response. He gave none. He was spooning the Italian ice.

"He and Juan had a business together—lawn care. They were partners. Somehow Don got Juan to sign some papers that turned half the business over to him. Juan—who did all the work, cut the grass, trimmed the hedges and hired the labor—got pissed. All he asked Don to do was loan him the money to buy a used truck. Don made him the loan for a fifty-percent partnership in the business. Don turned Juan's hustle into a business.

"Customers were signing contracts, employees were being paid by check, and he even put Juan on payroll. Paid him five dollars an hour, even though the business was bringing in twenty grand a month. When Juan complained, Don called Immigration.

"By the time Juan got Immigration straight, Don had sold the business. He made close to a million dollars, offered Juan a thousand. Juan took the thousand and hired me for two hundred."

Terri felt the pressure spreading behind his eyes. It moved to the top of his head then down to his neck. It hurt. He didn't know if it was it a cold headache or hearing Don's name so often. He rested the spoon in the large cup.

"Where is Juan now?"

"He drove back to Mexico happy after he saw Don beaten black and blue."

"You beat Don?" *Yeah right*, was Terri's thought.

"I whipped his ass on the fourth of July. It was in the bathroom of Little Jim's. It was my first time in a gay club. Juan drove me there in the piece-of-shit truck Don bought for him. He told me Don was inside. He described him to a T. I sat at the bar and waited for him to go to the can. When I saw how small he was, I knew the beating wasn't going to take long.

"I followed him into the bathroom. He was standing at the urinal with his back to the door. He didn't even turn around when I entered. I grabbed his ponytail and banged his head into the ceramic wall. He squealed like a little girl. I liked the sound, so I did it again. He squealed again. I didn't want to laugh, but I couldn't help it. I spun him around and slapped him a couple of times in the face. Every time I slapped him he squealed. 'Oh! Awgh! Ohwee! Oh! Awgh! Ohwee!'

"He weighed nothing. It was like slinging around a bag of kitchen garbage. When I looked him in the face, the son of a bitch was smiling. The bastard looked me straight in the face and asked, 'Could you open your hand and slap me with an open palm?' Sure, I said, and slapped the shit out of him.

"He pulled down his pants asked me to spank him with my big, black hand. I told him that would cost him. He reached in his pocket and pulled out a roll of hundreds. I took it and spanked his ass good. My hands were callused at that time. I was laying bricks and working at UPS loading trucks. Then he asked if I liked beating a white man. I told him hell yeah. He said he understood because the white man had done so much wrong to people of color.

"I want you to get the picture, Terri. This man is bent over the sink in a bathroom getting his ass royally spanked and telling me this shit. My hands got sore—both of them—because I'm trying to take the pleasure out of it for him. I take off my work belt and tear into his ass. The bastard could have

145

moved, but he didn't. He laid there and took each heavy-ass stroke. His ass was covered with welts.

"I beat him like they beat Kunta Kente. Then he tells me he deserves it. He deserves to beaten by a black man, he says. I start to really get into then. He wanted it, so I gave it to him. I ripped his shirt off and beat welts the size of my arm all over his back. He pulled off this Rolex I'm wearing now and begged me to fuck him.

"The idea of fucking a white man in the ass turned me on. I dry-fucked that motherfucker so hard it hurt my johnson. The bastard starting crying, and that turned me on more. I tried to split his ass open, but mine wasn't the first big, black johnson that asshole experienced. Wasn't no splitting it.

"After I nutted in his ass he asked me if I liked it. I told him it was alright. Then he took the gold chain from around his neck, the pinky diamond ring off his finger and handed them to me along with his business card. He told me he would give me a thousand dollars every time I beat his ass and fucked him." Jessie took a sip from his Italian ice. "Now that's Don."

"Do you still beat him like that?" There was no doubt in Terri's voice. Jessie told the story with too much sincerity to doubt.

"No, his skin can't take it anymore. His back is all scar tissue. I just slap him around, fuck him and shove huge dildos up his ass. He still pays a thousand a pop."

"Damn."

"I told you. He's not what you think."

Jessie had parked the BMW in front of a stylish hair salon on Oak Street.

"I ain't paying their prices!" Terri protested.

"It's on me." Jessie smiled.

"I don't want to hear no stuff about they don't do Black hair." Terri sat back in the Recaro leather seat of the BMW and pouted.

"It's a Black shop." Jessie kissed him on the check.

146

"Tssst. I don't want hear no shit about they don't do *queen* hair."

Terri sipped Jessie's Italian ice. He had peach.

"They won't know. Come on."

He reached over Terri and pushed the passenger door open.

"Baby, nobody on the street can tell you're a queen. Trust me. I wouldn't bring you here if it showed."

The salon was high profile. Unlike most Black salons, it was spacious. Each stylist had her own large working area. Terri counted six chairs on the main level and four above; all but one was occupied. The second level was a balcony curved in a U-shape. The ceiling was a blue-tinted glass dome. The decor was powder blue, white and chrome. Huge photos of black movie stars hung from the chrome railings on the balcony. Terri stopped in mid-stride when he saw his picture hanging from the railing.

He said slightly above a whisper to Jessie, "I thought you said they wouldn't know." He pointed to the picture.

"They don't," Jessie answered. A woman who Terri was sure was a midget approached them grinning. Jessie walked ahead to greet her.

"I knew you'd be here today. Them receipts was stacking up. Bend on down here and give me my kiss, you rich nigga."

Jessie bent almost in half to kiss the young woman whose head barely reached his belt.

"You made me rich, Pumpkin."

"I know that, nigga. I ain't stupid. A little body don't mean a little brain. You staying for a minute or you just going to take the receipts and leave?"

"I'll be here a minute, Pumpkin. I have to pay some bills. Did the exhaust man come?"

"You don't smell any chemicals, do you?"

"I didn't smell it when you said the system was broke. All I smell is that damn Jasmine you pumping through here."

"Yeah well, whatever. The customers must like it. I did switch wine suppliers."

"Why?"

"The bastard gave every business on this block four bottles of Dom. He didn't offer us shit. I tore up the check you left for him and told him to kiss my rusty black ass."

"Pumpkin, this is Terri. She wants something done to her hair. Could you fit her in?" Jessie turned to Terri.

"Boy, I know who she is. She's the one you been raving about. Shoot, I have been looking at her five-by-four-foot face for three months. He took my Denzel down for you. He sure did, and believe me, that was a battle. I told him only movie stars were to hang from the railing, not the stars of his heart."

"I'm going in the back." Much to Terri's dismay, Jessie left as nervous as a teenager whose mother was telling his secrets.

"Look at him running," Pumpkin yelled behind him. "And don't forget to write a check for Hinckley and Schmidt. Our water ain't free. You ain't wrote them a check in two months."

"Okay." Jessie waved back at her with one swing of his arm.

"You would have some competition from me if that man was shorter, but I don't like 'em that tall. But he sho' got a nice booty, don't he? Come on, baby."

Pumpkin led Terri by the hand to her station. "Sit on down. I can look at your hair and tell you don't need a perm. And if you going out with Jessie I know you ain't getting that pretty hair cut. So what can I do for you?"

Pumpkin stepped up on the raised platform behind the chair. Terri sat down.

Don, Jessie and the coaches Don had hired told him his voice was fine. It was as light as a woman's, they told him; relax about it, Terri, they advised. Terri, however, felt that his voice was the only way a person would know he was a man. He had no Adam's apple to speak of. His hands and feet were small and he'd never shaved a day in his life, but his voice, at

148

times, especially in the mornings or when he was excited, had more bass than he desired.

Forget it. Terri relaxed his worries about his maleness being discovered. If the short woman found out it would be Jessie's fault for not telling her. He never thought of Jessie as being in the closet; he never thought of Jessie as a lover. The fact was he never thought much of Jessie until last night.

What was Jessie, Don's Jessie, doing with a hair salon? Why did Pumpkin think he was Jessie's girlfriend? Why did Jessie have that huge picture hanging from the railing? It was a good picture. Terri wondered if it was from his media kit.

Jessie took down Denzel to hang his picture? Jessie argued with his short friend about hanging his picture? Oprah Winfrey hung from the railing. Anita Baker hung from the railing. Phyllis Hyman hung from the railing. Prince hung from the railing. Why not Terri Parish?

He grinned and answered Pumpkin's question about what was to be done to his hair. "Nothing much, Pumpkin. Just a good washing. I was going to my regular shop, but Jessie insisted I meet you. I told him you didn't have to do my hair for me to meet you."

"Girl, you cain't tell that man much of nothing. Once he gets his mind set, that's it. I been trying to get him to bring you down here since he hung your picture from the railing, but he's such a private man. I told him people were going to ask who you were and he said they wouldn't because they wouldn't want to look stupid. He said if they saw your picture up there with all the other stars they would assume you were a star. Girl, you been called Stephanie Mills, Chaka Khan and even that girl from Ashford and Simpson."

"You're lying." Terri laughed.

"Not at all, girl. He was right. People made you a star. Lean back a little, Terri. I'm going to scratch your scalp before I wash it. You ain't got a perm, so it ain't gonna hurt nothing. It keeps your scalp healthy and let some air to your roots. Jessie

149

told me about them stage lights. Girl, I admire you. I could never do what you do. Not that anyone would pay to see my short body, but it would be nice to be naked in a room with all them men.

"Exotic dancer—that sounds much better than stripper. Jessie told me you was a stripper. I corrected him. I told him the correct term was exotic dancer. Has he been saying it around you? I told him you would get pissed if he called you a stripper.

"But anyway, what does it feel like to have all them men's eyes on you, knowing they wantcha bad? Seeing them beg with their eyes? Do you let them stick money in your bosom? A whole room full of mens looking at you naked, desiring you...I know it feels good.

"Jessie told me he acted a fool when he saw your show. Sent you all them roses with no card. I told him he better tell you they was from him. I saw the bill: a dozen roses every night for two weeks. Did you give him some when he told you they was from him? I know you did. I woulda. Any man that shows that much interest gonna get him some Pumpkin nookie."

Terri broke out in laughter.

"I ain't lying. Girl, I'll spread-eagle these little nub legs. Shoot, my no-good-ass old man got the nookie with a handful of grocery store daises. Roses every night for two weeks, I woulda screwed him silly!"

Terri thought the flowers were from Don. Jessie was a strange man. Terri closed his eyes and relaxed as Pumpkin parted his hair with the comb. She pressed down firmly when making the parts and scratched with the same gentle pressure. Not since childhood sitting between Madear's legs on the porch had anyone scratched his scalp. It felt good. He didn't bother to answer Pumpkin's questions because Pumpkin answered them herself.

"Girl, you got some pretty hair. Must have Indian in your family. This ain't no white man mix. This Black and Indian hair. I bet it will grow to your butt if you let it. I'ma tell you something about your boyfriend. He loves hair. Nigga cain't comb a poodle but he loves hair. He tried to get his license. He's the only person I know that flunk out of beauty school after he paid the tuition.

"They refused to give him a certificate. It didn't make much sense anyway, big old nigga doing hair. I could see if he was gay, but that man loves pussy, and I know I ain't got to tell you that. A lotta women think since he don't flirt with them and owns a beauty shop he's funny. That nigger ain't funny, just picky. Knows what he wants."

"Tell me about him, Pumpkin," Terri asked with eyes closed.

"Ain't much to tell, sugar. He's kind as the day is long. Wouldn't hurt a fly. I met him at beauty school. I was trying to help him understand his work. He loves hair, but he has no understanding of how to style it or treat it. When I finished school I couldn't get hired at this shop. A make-believe Frenchman owned it then. He told me he didn't have any Negro customers so he didn't need a Negro stylist.

"I never heard the word *Negro* sound so much like nigger in my life. Jessie drove me down here in his fine car for the interview. After the interview, I told him exactly what the man said. Jessie walked into the shop, looked the phony Frenchman straight in the eye and told him he was going to buy this shop and it would have black customers and black stylists. That was two years ago. As you can see, he made it happen. We been in this shop for eighteen months.

"Girl, I don't know much about that man. I know he gets what he wants, and I think he's a little prejudice. White people aggravate him. He leaves all his dealings with them to me.

"I asked him one time where he got the money to buy this place. He told me I didn't want to know, and the look in his eye told me he wasn't lying.

"I think he grew up on the south side. Real poor, I believe, 'cause the brother don't waste nothing. He eats every piece of meat and gristle on chicken bone and sucks the marrow. Now don't get me wrong. He ain't cheap, but you can tell he ain't always had.

"He blinks a little bit when I tell him his Armani suits cost fifteen hundred dollars and the Italian handmade loafers cost eight hundred. Do you like the way he dresses? I know you do. I shop for him. That nigga would be still be wearing work pants, studded belts and dago T's."

Terri snickered.

"Girl, I ain't lying. The brother ain't got no fashion sense. The other students didn't believe that was his BMW. They said he dressed too bad to have that much taste." Pumpkin had to stop to laugh. "Good-lookin' dark brother he was, but the boy couldn't dress a lick. He just didn't care about clothes. If he bought some new clothes, they looked like the old clothes.

"I swear to God, I didn't think stores still sold them work pants. I told him to go buy some clothes 'cause folks was talking about him. That man came to school the next day with some brand new work pants and a brand new dago T. I liked to died because he was my friend and I didn't want them no-count niggas talking about him."

"Pumpkin, what did the pants look like?" Terri was beyond snickering. He was so tickled that tears dripped from the corners of his eyes. He couldn't imagine suave, smooth Jessie dressed badly, but with Pumpkin's help he was getting a picture.

"Girl, they were them farmer pants. They didn't have just a bib; had the place for the hammer and everything. But my poor baby didn't know no better. He thought he was clean. He came in class with his chest sticking out and his head held high, like he was clean as the Board of Health. I told him they was still laughing at him and the man asked me why. And he was serious!

"My baby didn't have a clue. I told him it was the style of clothing he was buying. He told me he wore workingman's clothes because he was a working man, and they could all kiss his ass.

"Now, being short all my life, I was used to being teased. I didn't like it, but I was used to it. To this day I cain't stand to see nobody else get teased. Teasing hurts. Being grown didn't have shit to do with it. It still hurts. It hurt him; I saw it in his eyes. He tried to hide it with tough words, but I saw the pain. That man can make his mouth lie, but his eyes won't lie. Remember that, sister girl.

"I guessed at his size, so the next day I met my friend in front of the school and walked to the McDonald's down the block. I handed him a bag with six pairs of pants, six new shirts and two pairs of shoes. Oh, girl, I didn't tell you he wore combat boots—the originals, child, the kind that came up way past your ankles. He tucked them work pants in the top of them boots. Girl, he was a mess.

"I bought him two pair of Levis and four pair of Dockers. The shirts were those button-down oxfords in various colors. I got him a pair of leather Nikes to wear with the jeans and a pair of Dexter penny loafers to wear with the Dockers. When my baby came out that McDonald's bathroom he was a new man. He looked like a DePaul University professor. I was so proud of myself. And that's how we got tight. I didn't want nobody laughing at him.

"I do his hair too. You like them waves? I know you do. They soft too. Ain't no gel in his hair. I grew them waves in his hair. If he wasn't so tall and if I didn't have a no-good man with five kids, I mighta gave him some. Girl, he asked me a couple times after I bought them clothes. He sure did. Don't tell him I told you. I damn near said yes one time.

"I was mad at drunk-ass Ralph. Instead of going to school that morning we sat in front of McDonald's and talked. Well, I talked and Jessie listened. Then he asked me for some coochie. Wasn't that sweet? I told him no and we went to school. He didn't know all he had to do was take me by the hand and lead me."

"He knows how to do that now," Terri said with eyes closed again. Pumpkin's scratching and her reminiscence of Jessie lulled him into feeling comfortable.

"Oh girl, I knew it! He don't ask for nothing, do he? I know he don't. He's gentle and forceful, ain't he? I know he is. I told him he cain't always wait for a woman to make up her mind. Pull her a little, I told him. Did he pull you, girl? I know he did.

"I wish I knew more about him to tell you. He's a very private man. I accept that about him. At Christmas I bought all his presents and wasn't none for nobody I didn't know. Them flowers were the only mystery, and now I met you. It's just him—oh yeah, and the kids. He buys a bunch of shit for them kids at the Audy Home. Bad little bastards."

"Kids?"

"Them bad little fuckers. He buys them clothes and rents them busses to go places—Bulls games, Great America, that type of thing. He spoils my brats too. I have to keep them away from him because they will beg him broke. Girl, I'm telling you too much about my baby and I know it. It's just that I want him to have somebody; somebody he wants. He deserves it. I'ma let this chair back to the sink. Just relax."

The seat rose as Terri's head dipped into the sink. Terri spread his legs to stop himself from sliding too far. He hooked his feet beneath the footrest. When he opened his eyes he saw under Pumpkin's chin. She had whiskers. Was she—? No. He put the thought out of his mind as quickly as it came.

In the station across from Terri a little boy was sitting at the foot of his mother's salon chair sucking on a red Popsicle. The little boy was restrained by child straps. His mother had the other end secure in her hand under the beautician's cape. Terri caught the little boy peeping under his skirt.

The little boy obviously had a good view, because his mouth was hanging open. Since he was wearing a skirt Terri hadn't bothered to put on a gaff. He had simply slung it to the side of his bikini panties, allowing it to hang against his thigh. Terri risked sliding into the bowl and crossed his legs.

"Ma!" The little boy tugged on his leash. "Ma! Ma, that lady got a Jimmy dog."

"Boy, shut up!"

"She do, Ma. I seen it! That lady got a Jimmy dog!"

"Boy, I'ma smack you silly if you don't shut your mouth," the irritated mother said from under the running water. She snatched his leash to emphasize she was serious.

"She got a Jimmy dog," the little boy said quietly. "A big one too." He bit into his Popsicle and looked away from Terri for something else to discover in the shop. Terri laughed to himself and closed his eyes.

"Terri, I'm going to use this oil-based shampoo on your hair since you be under them bright lights. Your hair is dry. I'ma give you a bottle to take with you. If you like it, come get some more. It's twenty dollars a bottle, but it's worth it. Now close your eyes again. I flaked up a lot of dry skin and growing dandruff. It's going to take a couple of good washes and rinses, so relax. It's a coconut oil base, so it smells kinda sweet. I like it.

"I can tell you this, sugar: If you think you want to keep him, give him a child. Hold it, baby. Sit still. Don't open your eyes. If the shampoo got in it will only sting for a second. Relax."

Give him a child? A picture of him and Jessie and a small child walking between them entered his mind. It was a nice picture, but it would take more than Pumpkin's bragging to make it reality.

Terri found himself dozing. He had short dreams. One was of him and Jessie playing on a beach in Jamaica. Another was he and Jessie standing under a coconut tree, kissing. Pumpkin's massaging fingers on his scalp, the rushing water through his hair, the coconut shampoo all added to the short dreams.

Through the tropical scent of coconut he caught a whiff of Grey Flannel. His last quick dream was of Don chasing him and Jessie, yelling that Jessie was wearing the wrong fragrance for the islands. Terri forced his eyes open. Jessie was standing over him. The skin beneath Jessie's chin was smooth, no razor bumps or whiskers. Terri closed his eyes again.

"You almost finished, Pumpkin?" Jessie placed a bundle of envelopes on her shelf. "Mail these today if you can. There wasn't any postage in the machine. Terri 'sleep?"

"No, she ain't 'sleep; and Jessie, I'm not gonna have time to mail those. This is Friday, a very busy day for a stylist. Maybe not for a shop owner, but for hardworking stylist managers this is a humping day. So, sweetness, take the letters with you. Terri, ride with him with the windows down. Your grade of hair dries much better in the air than under a dryer. Demand the windows down. He's a good boy. He'll do what he's told.

"Braid and oil your hair nightly. Terri, don't press it or apply any heat for at least a month. I'm going to towel it dry for now. Your hair is damaged. You can't be under hot lights and then expect to press your hair. If you follow my advice, come back here in a month and I'll grow your hair down to your butt."

She dried Terri's hair and wrapped it in a thin towel.

"Will I see you in a month?" she asked.

"Yes."

"Good. Take care, and don't let Jessie forget to mail these letters." Pumpkin handed the bundle of letters back to Jessie.

"You ain't got to bend down to kiss me goodbye now. I bet you're glad I bought this stand, ain't cha?" she said to Jessie, who stood quiet watching her work on Terri's hair.

"I'm glad you're here, and I'm glad you're my friend. That's what I'm glad about." He kissed her on the cheek.

Terri stood and kissed Pumpkin on the cheek as well. "I'll see you before a month ends. We have to finish talking."

"Sho' you right, girlfriend. Get on back in here whenever you ready. Here baby, don't forget the shampoo."

"What is it you two have to talk about?" Jessie asked with a smile.

"You!" Terri and Pumpkin answered in unison.

Walking through the salon, Terri looked back at his hanging portrait again. That was a pleasant surprise. Jessie knew how to make a girl smile. Terri didn't even have to ask him. When they got in the car Jessie rolled down the windows before he pulled the BMW into the flow of traffic.

"Did you like Pumpkin?"

"Yes, a lot." Terri slid the shampoo under the passenger seat and adjusted himself so the airflow would blow through his thick, shoulder-length hair.

"Why?"

"Because she's honest, trusting and really in touch with her feelings. I like her. You don't meet people like her everyday."

The sidewalk of Chicago's gold coast area was busy with pedestrian shoppers. Terri wondered how many were actually rich and could afford the expensive boutiques and salons, and how many were pretenders and hopefuls. He was a hopeful. What was Jessie?

"You're right about that, and you certainly won't meet them being around Don. That's for damn sure."

"I met you around Don." Terri fluffed his hair in the air that was rushing through the window.

"That was destiny."

"Tssst, please."

Destiny. The word sounded nice. He stopped fluffing his hair.

"Fat Nancy! That's who Pumpkin reminds me of."

"Fat Nancy? Who's Fat Nancy?" Jessie asked.

"He was a good friend. He died of pneumonia."

Fat Nancy was more than a friend. He was Terri's mentor of sorts. Terri stopped himself from drifting into deep thought and became of aware of Jessie turning south onto Michigan Avenue. The afternoon traffic was slightly heavy.

"I'm sorry to hear that, but tell me, were you surprised about the shop?"

"About what?" Terri decided to play dumb and looked down at his fingernails. Of course he was surprised. More than surprised he was pleased. He was glad there was more to Jessie than what he saw.

"The salon you just left."

"Oh yeah, I was surprised it was Black."

Terri looked out the passenger window so Jessie couldn't see the grin on his face.

"Did anything else about it surprise you?"

"No. Not really."

"Okay, well maybe the rest of the day will surprise you."

"I got my hair done. I was really thinking about going home," he lied. Wild horses couldn't pull him away from Jessie that afternoon. Jessie was a mystery unraveling and he was a sucker for a mystery, or as Madear said, just plain nosy.

"Oh no, we got the whole day together."

Jessie really sounded like he wanted to spend the day with him. Terri wanted to rest his head against Jessie's shoulder as he drove, but he didn't.

"Well, what else are we going to do?" Terri asked, trying to play the part of the pouting brat.

"Don't worry. It will surprise you."

Terri wanted to see where Jessie really lived. He did not share Pumpkin's acceptance of the unknown. Unanswered questions circled Jessie—one big one in particular.

"Are you gay?"

Terri hoped he would say yes. He didn't want another Payton, not even as a friendly screw.

"No."

"Tssst."

That was it. They were never going out again. A man as old as Jessie didn't even know he was gay. What was it with black men and denial? White men were running down the streets shouting it out for all the world to hear and a black man wouldn't even admit it in the privacy of his own car. Maybe Jessie needed the facts laid out for him.

"You screw men."

"I slept with a couple of queens, but I'm not gay. I don't find masculinity attractive at all."

"You're in the closet and you don't even know it."

"No, Terri, I'm not in the closet."

"Does Pumpkin know I'm a man?"

"Are you a man?"

Touché. That question caused Terri to pause. He didn't consider himself a man, but that was a private dilemma, one he hadn't truly sorted out yet. He decided to ignore the question.

"If your friends don't know you have sex with men, then you're in the closet. If you can't admit that you find men attractive, then you're in the closet from yourself."

"Who says?"

"I say."

"Terri, you're what, eighteen years old? You probably just heard the term *closet*. You are not an expert on who is and who is not gay."

"Don was the first man you fucked?"

"Yep."

"And you fucked him for money?"

159

"That's how I see it."

"What about the queens at the Jeffery Pub? They pay you too?"

"Yep."

"Tssst. So you're a whore?"

They were stopped at the light on Michigan and Huron.

"I do a lot of things for money, most of which you're going to experience today."

"Where do you live?"

Terri decided to change the subject. Somehow Jessie was squirming out of acknowledging his homosexuality, and Terri wasn't quite sure how.

"I'll show you when I'm sure you're going to be part of my life."

"Part of your life? I thought all you wanted was sex." Terri wanted clarification.

"I want more than that."

Terri put off asking what the more was and asked. "Why is my picture in that shop?"

"Because."

"Because is not an answer, and why did you tell Pumpkin I was your girlfriend?"

"Because."

"Tssst. Because what? And why are you still bothered with Don if you got your own money?"

"Baby, you are full of questions."

Jessie pulled to the right on Michigan Avenue and brought the BMW to a stop in a cab stand zone. Terri liked the fact that Jessie stopped driving to talk to him.

"Look, Terri, when I met Don I was working two jobs and breaking bones part-time. Don opened my eyes to easy money. It's a lot of white men that want their ass beat by a big, black man. I run an ad in the *Reader* newspaper. They call; I get the money. But I want more. What I get from them is crumbs. I know that now. Successful white men make millions of dollars before they're forty. I know at least six.

"I'm going to make my first million any way I can before I'm thirty. I'm twenty-four now. I got a hundred and eighty thousand in the South Chicago Bank. That leaves nine hundred and twenty thousand to go. And in ten minutes you're going to watch me make thirty-five hundred."

"How? Is it dangerous? Could I get in trouble?"

"No, you can't get in trouble. The how is for me to know and you to watch. Don't you wonder why I'm showing you all this?"

"Let me guess." Terri put his slender index finger to his temple and acted as if he were in deep thought. "Because you want me to be your lover?"

"Not just that. I also want you to let me be your manager. I can get you there."

"Where?"

"To the top." Jessie pulled back into traffic.

"Tssst. I don't know how to do it on top. We tried it this morning. Don't you remember? You said I had to practice. Now you want me on top. Niggas, they don't never know what they want."

Terri didn't want to talk about business; he wanted to find out about Jessie.

"Why do you give stuff to kids in the Audy Home?"

"I spent some time there when I was a kid, and when I was there we hardly went anywhere and the toys we got was bullshit. Look, I really don't like talking about my past. Matter of fact, I never talk about it. Let's talk about you leaving Don and coming with me."

"Leave Don?"

Leave Don, the only person who showed any real interest in his career? Leave the person who told him he could have a career? Leave a man who spent money on training him and paid him? No, it would take more than a good fuck and some fancy frozen Kool-Aid for that to happen.

"Yeah. Leave Don."

"Why?" Terri asked.

"Because he's not doing anything for Terri! Look, do you agree that doing the *Oprah* show will help your career?"

They hadn't made it a block before Jessie pulled into another cabstand to talk.

"Of course."

"Can you think of any logical reason not to do it?"

"Not really."

"Then ask Don to let you do it. If he says yes, then fine, I'll leave the managing of your career to him and I'll only chase your heart."

"I'll ask him Sunday."

"Good. Now I got a couple of questions."

"Go ahead, ask."

A yellow cab pulled behind them and honked. Jessie pulled in front of the hotel and blocked the fire hydrant. Terri surmised he really wanted to talk to him.

"You ever have sex with a woman?" Jessie asked.

"Please. No, never. Well, not really sex. When I was in high school I had a real brainy friend, Ruthy. She was the valedictorian of our class. Really the only female student I spent any time with. Anyway, I told her I was gay. We were sophomores. I told her I had a lover and I was certain of my homosexuality. She decided we should research it before I accepted it.

"We went to the library and looked up homosexuality in *Everything You Wanted to Know About Sex but Were Afraid to Ask.* At the time I was completely happy with the definition they offered. She was not, so we looked through encyclopedias and dictionaries. All the definitions were about the same: someone attracted to another of the same sex. She didn't

162

believe it was possible. She said men were just horny and would have sex with anything.

"To prove her point she took me to an empty classroom, stripped and offered herself to me. I didn't get hard; I couldn't get hard. I got sick and threw up on her. That was enough to convince her and me."

"That doesn't prove you wouldn't like it if you actually did it."

"Tssst, please! I like men. I'm not even curious about women."

"Could you do it for money?"

"I don't think I could. I might, though. Money does motivate me."

"Then you might be heterosexual because you might have sex with a woman."

"I might turn a trick with a woman. That don't make me straight."

"That's exactly my point! My turning a trick with a queen doesn't make me gay."

"Tssst. You are so deep in the closet a Mack truck couldn't haul you out."

"Did you have a sweet sixteen party?"

"What kind of question is that?"

A mounted police officer came up beside the BMW and waved Jessie away from the fire hydrant. Jessie ignored him.

"I thought you were asking personal sexual stuff," Terri said.

"I'm asking the questions. Did you have one?"

"You better move this car. These mounted police don't play."

Jessie pulled up slowly.

"Yeah, I did have a sweet sixteen party. Matter of fact, that's when I first met Fat Nancy. She helped me dress for my first night out in drag. I went to Fun Town."

"That was the amusement park located at Ninety-fifth on Stony Island, right?"

"Yep. That's the one. For my birthday Madear sent me to Fat Nancy to learn about man loving, as she called it. She was worried about me hurting my body. As I'm sure a smart man like you has guessed, Fat Nancy was huge. He was the fattest person I'd seen in my life. At first I doubted that he could teach me anything worth knowing.

"He was so big. His house was loaded with king-sized everything: chairs big enough for three people to sit in and a restaurant size refrigerator. His bathtub was an indoor swimming pool. His whole house was extra large. The doorways had been customized for extra space. He made that house fit him. He made the world fit him. Some of his tricks didn't even know he was a man. He had huge titties and the prettiest, longest hair I'd ever seen.

"He bathed about three times a day. He couldn't stand having any type of body odor. When I first met him he was in the bathtub. At any given time he had about six or seven young queens living with him. They did his bidding lovingly. He didn't screw them or anything because he loved manly men. They just liked being part of Fat Nancy's life. Like me, I guess they were learning from him.

"He told me his men just loved fat. They would fuck him in the folds of his arms, his thighs, between his titties; he had more places to please a man than a man could dream of. Baby oil, sweet words and his meat was all he said he needed for most of them. He took care of most of his tricks in that swimming pool-sized bathtub.

"What I learned from him wasn't only about wearing a gaff and lubricating—although I learned those things from him. It was more about changing not just your physical self but the way you feel about yourself. Here was an obese man who could have been a sideshow freak, but instead he was a desired temptress.

164

"I saw men waiting hours for their turn to be with him. He was what they wanted. He very seldom left his home. He brought the things he wanted to him. He controlled his environment. He exposed himself only to those who desired him. No negative energy. He changed his world."

"No. I disagree," Jessie said sternly, driving with the flow of traffic. "He hid from the world. That's not reality. True, he found some people who like fat, but he only dealt with them. Life is about adapting to situations. He adapted by hiding. I don't admire that. A person has to go out into the world and make changes. The world is too big to bring to you.

"You grow by taking the good with the bad, not by running from what you don't like. Growth is changing, and you change by experiencing new situations. If you control everything around you, you don't experience anything new and you don't grow, you don't develop. Fat Nancy might not have been in a circus, but he was still a sideshow attraction."

"What do you mean?"

"People stand in line to see freaks at a circus. They sat and waited in his house to see a sideshow attraction. He didn't deal with reality; he only dealt with the good. A person needs the bad too. It's a balance: the yin and the yang, the passive and the active, the positive and the negative, the good and the evil. You have to have both to see the truth. The truth is reality. He didn't have both. He wasn't living in reality. He was living in the world he created. Just like a sideshow freak behind the glass, except he was in his own home."

"Tssst. That's a mean thing to say."

"No, it's truthful. But anyway, you were telling me about your first night out."

"I might not feel like talking now." Jessie was doing something to him, causing him to think differently. Terri wasn't sure he liked it.

Jessie made a right turn off of Michigan Avenue. "It's up to you." They were parked in front of Lawry's Prime Rib restaurant.

"Recognize that guy?" Jessie pointed to a white man twice his size.

"Yes. He used to play for the Bears. He does the car commercials now."

"Car insurance commercials. It's kind of ironic because the motherfucker didn't take no insurance out on his own ass. He owes his old bookie thirty-five thousand dollars. The parking valet here is his new bookie. He hit yesterday with his new bookie.

"Real lucky that he hit for forty grand, unlucky because his new bookie told his old bookie. His old bookie called him yesterday and the big star told him to fuck off. And since he's a big star, his old bookie didn't want to be associated with his ass beating, so he called me. I have no known affiliations. I'll beat anybody's ass."

"You're going to beat him now? In broad daylight?"

"No, not now. I'm going to give him a minute to get the money. If I retrieve the money, ten percent is mine—four thousand dollars. Oh yeah, there we go! Look at the bastard counting it. Be right back."

Terri watched the man who Pumpkin had said couldn't hurt a fly beat the big man like he was filming a karate movie. He kicked him, punched him, jumped in the air and kicked, flipped him and stomped on his head once he hit ground. He went into the big man's jacket and calmly took the money. When he got back in the car he wasn't even sweating. Terri's mouth was hanging open.

"That's it, baby. Let's go get the money."

Jessie U-turned back onto Michigan Avenue.

"I thought you just took the money."

"This ain't my money; this Manny's money. I get my money from Manny."

"Where is Manny?" Terri asked.

"It's a little after one, right?"

"One thirty-eight by your BMW clock"

"He's at Berghoff's."

"The restaurant?"

"Yeah, you hungry?"

"A little."

"Good, because I'm starved."

What kind of man was Jessie? What kind of man could beat a man, stomp his head then act as if nothing unusual had happened? He was a good fighter and Terri had to admit it was kind of sexy watching him in action. That man was a professional football player and his baby wiped his ass. Wait! Did he think of Jessie as his baby? *Slow down,* Terri told himself.

The air conditioning was on full blast in Berghoff's. The lunchtime crowd had dwindled. Only four tables were occupied, one by Manny, who waved Jessie over to his table in the back. It was covered with sports pages from five different newspapers.

"Not too long ago I was reading about you in these papers, huh, Jessie? Sit, you and your pretty lady.

"She must be special. I never seen you with a lady. You bring her here, so she must be smart. Sit, pretty lady. Manny don't bite. Forget what Jessie told you."

Terri smiled sweetly and nodded his head, hoping he wouldn't have to speak too much; as always, his voice was a concern when meeting new people. Terri tried not to stare, but he couldn't stop looking in the big man's face. It was a familiar face, but he knew he didn't know the man.

Jessie sat next to Manny and stared directly across to Terri.

"I'll be finished with the papers in a second, then I'll buy you lunch. Okay, Jessie? Can I buy you and your pretty lady lunch?"

The smile on Terri's face grew. He loved the way the fat man kept referring to him as a pretty lady.

"Why not?" Jessie answered Manny but his eyes remained on Terri.

Terri avoided Jessie's direct look and glanced around the restaurant. The decor was too dark for his taste. He preferred bright restaurants where he could really see his food.

"You have something for me, Jessie?"

Terri's attention returned to the table with Manny's question. He noticed Jessie slide the money under the papers. Manny grabbed it and wrapped it in the *New York Times* sports page. He stood.

"Tell the waiter to clean off the table and fold the papers up for me. Order what you want. I want a Rueben sandwich and a big glass of ice water. I'm going to get rid of breakfast."

"Tssst!" Terri made the sound without caring how the others would react to it. Manny needed a manners coach worse than he did.

"Do I know that man?" he asked once Manny was far enough away.

"Why do you ask?" Jessie said in a serious, dry tone.

"He just looks so familiar, and you were looking at me as if I should know him."

"Open your eyes, Terri. Really open them and you'll know why he looks familiar."

Terri was not at all pleased with Jessie's dry tone. He thought of going out to the car and waiting for him there, but he wanted to find out who the man was. He shrugged off Jessie's attitude to doing business. When the waiter arrived he asked Jessie to order his lunch.

"I don't know what you like."

"A gentleman always knows."

Terri hoped his comment would bring a smile to Jessie's solemn face. It did.

When Manny returned he squeezed into the chair next to Jessie. "You did good, Jessie. You got the whole forty grand. You never let me down, even when you played ball. You didn't know I bet on you, did you? Damn, I was so proud of you. Did he tell you about his glory days, pretty lady? My boy threw the little round ball harder than any man alive, and he was in high school.

"The biggest pitcher I ever seen in my life, and he was good too. But he inherited his old man's temper." Manny put his arm around Jessie and hugged him. "He's got a temper, young lady, and he don't like white people telling him what to do. He lets me get away with it because I'm an old Jew, and I ask him. I never tell him.

"That coach, what a schmuck. You knocked all his teeth out, didn't you? City championships and you knock the coach's teeth out. A temper. This man has a temper, lady. Be careful with him."

Manny winked to Terri.

"Here's forty-five hundred. The extra five is for kicking his fat Irish ass like I know you did. Eat my Rueben. I got to go. My bowels are all locked up. I eat like shit. I haven't eaten good since your mother died. I got some work for you in Vegas. Stop by the office Sunday night. The ticket and traveling cash will be in the safe."

"Make it two tickets. My fiancée will be going with me."

"Fiancée?"

Terri watched a smile crack open Manny's whole face, showing his worn-down teeth.

"Very good. Maybe you will be the one to give me a grandson."

He patted Jessie heavily on the back. Terri didn't see Jessie return Manny's smile; instead he gave Manny a sneer.

"Why not? I'm the one that does everything else. But tell me, Manny, will he be able to come to your house as your grandson? I just want to know, should I teach him to call you

Manny or Papa? It's a big question, Manny. You don't have to answer it today."

The smile left Manny's face as quickly as it came, and a sneer matching Jessie's took its place.

"Always with the wise mouth, this one! Black skin, my face, my brain, my temper. Okay, I tell you what, smart mouth. You make me a white, Jewish grandson, and then he can call me Papa. It's not me, Jessie. It's just the way of the world."

Terri watched as both pairs of eyes remained locked on each other. The sneer left Jessie's face first.

"Hey, I never said it was you, Manny . . . Don't forget— two tickets and maybe a little extra spending cash since Terri will be traveling with me."

"No problem." Manny paused and looked again to Jessie. He shook his head once from side to side then cast his eyes down and back up to Jessie's.

"I put the stone on your mama's grave. I'm sorry I didn't think about it last year. I do as much as I can, Jessie." When Manny stood to leave he almost toppled the table.

Holding the table down, Jessie said, "You never hear me complain, Manny." Jessie stood and embraced him. "Goodbye, Manny."

"Goodbye, Jessie. It was nice meeting you, miss." Manny nodded his fat head, sent another wink in Terri's direction, and left.

Terri waited until Manny was out of earshot.

"Tssst. Damn! You got a white daddy! You're the blackest man I ever seen in my life and you got a white daddy! When he came back from the bathroom and sat next to you I knew it. I don't know why I didn't catch it at first sight. You look just like him! Damn.

"He's cold-hearted man, and that was some ornery shit to say: make him a white grandson. No, a white, Jewish grandson. Tssst. I can understand why you never talk about your past. I wouldn't talk about it either." Terri said it all without taking a breath. His words shot out in rapid succession.

"It's really not that bad."

"What?"

"It's really not. I just found out he was my father about a year ago. I can't miss what I never had. He was never my daddy. I never had a daddy and I don't now. I use that daddy shit to get what I want, and he knows it. He feels a little guilt, but if I pushed him too far, he would have no remorse in killing me.

"The real money is for him and his legitimate kids. I accept it because with the crumbs I get from him and all the others I'll sneak up on them and excel past them. I have more than his brain; I have my mother's brain, too, and she milked his ass for years. Until I get ready, the crumbs are fine.

"I knew him most of my life from a distance. My mother cleaned his office. After my mother died I was going through her stuff and I found this letter addressed to me. You see, I was raised to believe that my mother was my foster mother, not my biological mother. She got me from the Audy Home when I was seven, so it was easy for me to believe that she wasn't my mother. Are you following me?"

"Tssst. Yes, I'm not stupid, just . . . shocked. No, not shocked, surprised."

"Okay. Well, the letter basically told me that she was my mother and Manny was my father. Her and Manny had a thing going. She not only cleaned his office; she cleaned his pipes and cooked his meals. It couldn't have been a bad arrangement. He paid her seven hundred a week under the table to run the vacuum cleaner and throw out the trash.

"After my mother died, I went to him with the letter. He asked me what I wanted, I told him a job. I had two, but I wanted to see what he would offer. He told me to clean the office for five hundred a week. It's a one-room office, so I took it. He asked me was I still playing baseball. I told him no, I got into karate.

"I invited him to a tournament. After he saw me fight he offered me other work. I did a couple of jobs for him, then other people started calling me. No one mentioned Manny's name, but I knew he was sending the business."

"I'm sorry to hear about your mother. Was she sick?"

"Only in the head, Terri. She got drunk and fell down the basement steps. Broke her stupid-ass neck."

"What?"

Terri's face went blank and his bottom jaw dropped open. He'd never heard anyone speak so ill of the dead, especially his own mother.

"I cared very little for my mother, Terri. Once I read the letter, I figured out why she got me out of the Audy Home. She was milking him for more money. I remember the day she picked me up from the home. I was so happy. The social worker told me I had a placement. That was the magic word in that place. That meant you was leaving, you was going to live with the Brady Bunch.

"I sat in the back seat of a cab by myself, choking on the reefer smoke from her and the cab driver. My bed was in the kitchen where the table was supposed to be. I slept in that kitchen 'til I was nine years old, then all of a sudden we had a house.

"A big house in South Holland. We were the only Blacks in the area. She loved that. She kept a house full of white people. When we first moved out there a lot of white families came to visit us. I guess they were welcoming us to the neighborhood, but as time moved on, only the men came.

"Eventually the kids in the neighborhood got over the novelty of my black skin and I made some friends. I stopped thinking about being the only black kid until school started and we took a field trip to the Museum of Science and Industry.

"The place blew me away. I spent most of my time watching the baby chicks hatch. Me and a couple of kids from the school was in line buying our souvenirs when two black kids jumped on one of my little white friends. I don't even remember his name. He was my friend so I pulled the two black kids off of him.

"I put it out my mind, right. No big deal. The little white boy was happy; I was happy. We go to get on the bus and about six of them little niggas pull me out of the line and whip my ass. They called me all kinds of Uncle Toms. My little white friend ran on the bus and watched me get my ass whipped.

"A black security guard pulled me from the ass-whipping and walked me to the bus. I'm crying about the beating and the betrayal. The guard picks me up and shakes me hard. 'Boy,' he says, 'black people got enough battles to be fighting. Don't go volunteering for no white man's fight. You a raisin in the sugar bowl; when the water comes, all the sugar gonna run together and the raisin be left.'

"I was ten years old and knew exactly what that motherfucker was talking about. When I went home and told my mama, she whipped me because I made a scene. She said if I got in any more trouble she was going to send me to school in the city with the niggas. I got in trouble every day and she sent me. I couldn't have been happier.

"All she and I had in common was her black-ass skin and height. I was always in her drunk-ass way. You know how many black people was at her funeral? Two: me and the nigga that dug the hole. Me telling Manny to buy her a headstone was just something I thought of to fuck with him. I could have bought her a headstone. She had insurance up the ass, but I needed more crumbs for my pile. Fuck her."

Terri didn't know what to say, so he said nothing. The waiter brought two broiled half-chickens and the Rueben sandwich to the table. Terri was no longer hungry. He watched

Jessie devour both chicken orders and the sandwich. He didn't suck the marrow from the bones, but there was no meat left on them.

Pumpkin was right; he was raised poor, but what was lacking had nothing to do with money. Terri didn't know why, but he felt a deep sorrow. He thought about his own mother. Then he thought about Madear and knew he was blessed. He hadn't seen Madear in a while. He was ready to leave. He wanted to go see Madear.

Jessie let go of a loud, deep, guttural belch. Despite the black skin, the full, wavy head of hair, and the muscular body, all Terri saw was Manny.

"Tssst. Let's go!" Terri stood, turned, and walked for the door. He didn't want to hear any objections.

Inside the BMW Terri was quiet. He slurped the remainder of his Italian ice and thought about Jessie's relationship with his mother. It was the way Jessie said fuck her. True, he had no good feelings to speak of for his own mother, but if she died, he doubted that he would say fuck her. To use her death to benefit his own gain seemed cruel. Jessie was nothing Terri expected.

On the surface Jessie was a hustler, playing for the thousand-dollar date. Terri could deal with that, but this deeper Jessie; this in-the-closet Jessie; this white-man-beating Jessie; this salon-owning Jessie; this hanger-of-pictures Jessie; this illegitimate Jewish son Jessie; this dark-skinned, thigh-stroking, cheek-kissing, good-loving Jessie was a strange man.

"Don't get quiet on me now. Tell me what you're thinking."

Jessie was driving on Lake Shore Drive heading south.

"I was thinking about Madear, my grandmother. I haven't seen her in a while. If you have nothing else to reveal to me—and I hope you don't, at least not for an hour or so—I'd like to go see her."

"Don't tell me I overwhelmed you."

"Tssst. Of course you overwhelmed me, and that was your intention."

"No, I wasn't planning on overwhelming you, just impressing you. I want you to know that I got my own money, and I am not Don's property. I do have something else to show you, but it can wait an hour or so. Where does your grandmother live?"

"She lives on Fifty-first and Princeton."

"I know the area. It's a little rough to grow a sweet little thing like you, isn't it? Were you raised there?"

"I'm not raised yet. I have some growing to do. Aren't you the man who keeps reminding me that I'm only eighteen? But yes, other than with Don that's the only place I ever lived. It wasn't always rough. We used to sleep with our windows open and no security bars. But as Madear says, times change."

"Will I get to meet your grandmother, or do you want me to drop you off and pick you up later?"

"Of course you'll meet her. I'm not the one in the closet."

"You have to be gay to be in the closet. I'm not gay."

"I'm not a woman. I ain't paying you. We made love. You act like you're attracted to me, but you're not gay?"

"Do you want to be a woman?"

"Yes, and one day it will happen. I'll be more than a woman; I'll be a lady."

"I rest my case."

"I don't understand."

"I'm attracted to the lady inside of you; the one that's growing, developing and preparing for me. I see what you don't think I see. I see the softness, the caring heart, the gentle ways. I see the lady. When I first saw your face, Terri, I knew you was the one for me. We're soulmates. That's why our lovemaking is so good. You're mine. You don't know it yet, but the lady inside you knows. She's growing for me."

Terri wanted to wrap his arms around Jessie and kiss him forever. Instead he said, "Tssst. That was good! I bet the

175

queens at the Jeffery Pub die over that shit." If they didn't, Terri knew he was ready to. Jessie's words were softly caressing his heart and his brain.

"Whatever, baby. It might not happen now, it might not happen this year, it might not happen in ten years, but you're mine. That's it and that's all."

"You want to hear about my first night out?"

Terri was ready to talk and not think about Jessie's comforting and satisfying words. Jessie put too much on his mind and he did it too fast. Terri wanted to get on familiar ground: his own memories

"Yes I do."

"Well, Fat Nancy didn't go with me. He sent two of the queens that was living with him. They couldn't have been much older than me. I don't remember their names, but I remember we had fun. I was dressed in a pair of white short-shorts. And Jessie, they was tight—skin tight.

"Fat Nancy gave me my first gaff and showed me how to wear it. I was so happy with it on. It looked like I had camel lips, you know, a beaver print. Jessie, you couldn't tell me a thing. I was fine.

"I had this string-tied halter complete with stuffed cups. A small B-cup. Fat Nancy corn-rolled my hair with white and yellow beads. Jessie, when I saw myself in the mirror I cried. I knew that was how I was born to look. Like a girl.

"We rode all the rides except the roller coaster. We laughed and even flirted with the boys. No one could tell I wasn't a girl. I can't explain the freedom I felt. I felt whole. I skipped around Fun Town like the little girl I wanted to be. Then this man that was selling snapshots asked to take my picture for free. He said I was the prettiest girl he'd seen all day. That did so much for me. I couldn't stop smiling after that. Madear has that picture on her mantle now.

"We was getting ready to leave when this older boy, almost a man, came up to me and asked me for my phone number. I didn't know what to do. I was so flattered but I was a boy, and he thought I was a girl. He asked me to go on the roller coaster with him. I was scared of that roller coaster, but he took my hand and we went. When that thing dipped I hugged him tight.

"I had been with Payton before, but this was different. This was a boy who thought I was a girl. This was way better. When we got off he asked me if I was okay and he kept his arm around me. If I would've died then, it would've been okay with me. I was a girl, and a boy liked me. He kissed me goodbye and I gave him a phone number. It was perfect."

"Yeah, but you gave him the wrong phone number. HUdson3-2700 was a carpet store." Jessie winked over one of his hazel-colored contacts and smiled at Terri.

"How do you know that's the number I gave him?" Terri asked, smiling about the memory. "Yeah, we thought that was cute, giving him the wrong number. I didn't know what else to do. I certainly couldn't tell him I was a boy. How did you guess I gave him that number?"

"How do you think?"

"Yeah, it was a popular wrong number back then. A couple girls gave it to you, huh?" Terri teased.

"Only one, and she gave it to me at Fun Town, standing at the bus stop with her two cousins. She had on yellow shorts, a white halter, yellow daisy earrings, clear plastic sandals, and she smelled like lemons and had the prettiest dimples when she smiled."

"Damn, I forgot about the earrings and the lemon cologne. How did you—No! It wasn't. You are a liar. No!"

"Girl, I told you it was a special memory. I told you we soulmates!"

"Unh-uh, this is way too freaky. It couldn't have been you!" Terri was staring hard into Jessie's face, trying to force the memory clear.

"You might as well stop fighting it, baby. We belong together."

"Tssst. That is Madear's house. You can park right in front of it." Terri was shirking it off on the outside—no big deal—but on the inside he was turning flips. Damn, maybe Jessie was special.

"Wow! That's a big house. Does she rent rooms?"

"Not anymore. She used to a long time ago. Before I was born. You'll like her, but be warned; she sees through bullshit."

"Will I meet your mother and father too?"

"I don't think so."

"Why?"

"Because my father's dead. When I was a kid I wondered about him for minute. I asked Madear about him once. She told me he was drunk Indian who my mother thought the sun rose and set for. I don't think Madear liked him too much, so I never asked about him again. And my mother, she's a bitch. I hardly see her and never miss her."

When Terri and Jessie entered Madear's living room they found her sitting in the new LaZBoy chair, watching the new floor model Zenith color television Terri bought her. Terri smelled the Ben Gay and spotted the electric blanket across Madear's legs. Instantly he felt he was shirking his responsibilities with Madear. He would visit her more.

"Hey, Madear."

"Terri! Baby, I had you on my mind. I knew you were coming today. I'm not going to get up because getting in and out this new chair you bought me is more than a notion. Come on over and give me a kiss."

Terri walked over to Madear with moist eyes and a big smile. He bent to the chair and kissed her half on the cheek and half on the mouth.

"I missed you, Madear."

"I missed you too, T.T., but it's your fault. You're the one that's going all the time. I'm right here. You know where to find me. And I know that manager of yours don't tell you when I call. I can hear it in his snake voice."

Jessie broke in out laughter. Madear looked to him.

"Now, who is this bit of sweet midnight you brought in my house, T.T.?"

"This is Jessie, Madear. He wants to be my new manager."

"Well, do tell. Well, Mr. Jessie, are you qualified for the job?" Madear asked, sitting upright in the chair.

"Terri would be my first client." Jessie took steps toward Madear.

"A rookie, huh? Well, he's honest. That's better than what you have now." Madear looked Jessie up and down.

"Now, Madear, Don isn't that bad." Terri was tightening Madear's salt-and-pepper-colored braids.

"He's not that good either," Jessie interjected.

"Oh, child, I like you already. Sit down on the couch and talk us into letting you manage T.T."

Jessie sat on the couch. Terri saw his gaze land on the picture from Fun Town and saw ease and remembrance cross his face.

"I really don't have much to say along the lines of convincing you," Jessie began. "I know I'll work hard for Terri and get the best gigs available, all top dollar. I think—no, I know Terri's got what it takes to make it. Terri just has to see the real Don. To see that the only interest Don has is his own."

"Child, you have never lied. That white man is up to no good. He keeps Terri away from me on purpose and there is no good that comes from staying away from your family. That I know. So tell me, Mr. Jessie, are you on sweet on T.T.?"

"Yes, ma'am, I am."

"That's good. How do you make your money now?"

"I own a beauty shop and I do a little consulting from time to time."

Madear stretched her neck to see out the front window. "Is that your pretty car parked in front of my house?"

"Yes, ma'am, it is."

179

Terri sat on the arm of Madear's chair. He enjoyed Jessie being on the hot seat.

"If you have never managed anyone before, how do you expect to get T. T. top dollar?"

"Well, ma'am, I'm not managing Terri now, but I got him a spot on the *Oprah* show."

"The Oprah Winfrey show?"

"Yes, ma'am."

"Are you going, Terri?"

"It depends on what Don says, Madear. He is my manager."

"Well you be sure and tell me what that snake says. If he says no, I like to hear his reason. Now, Mr. Jessie, this isn't a hard house to figure out. In the kitchen there is a fresh caramel cake that I baked this morning. You be a dear while I talk to T.T for a minute, and go get us a couple of slices. Everything in the kitchen is where you think it should be. There's no mystery to it."

"Okay." Jessie stood and left.

"That is a pretty black man, T.T. I didn't think you like them that dark."

"He's nothing special, Madear. Not yet anyway."

"You think he can do the job? Managing, I'm talking about."

"I don't know. I don't know what the job really is. I don't know what it takes, but I do know if Don says no to *Oprah*, things might change between us."

"Good. So Mr. Jessie got some money?"

"Yeah, he does. He's his own man, but he's a little scary, Madear. He makes me nervous."

"That's good. It's good to be a little scared of your man."

"He's not my man, Madear, just a friend."

"Well he is the first friend you brought by here, so I can't help but to think he's a little special."

"Maybe a little."

Sunday found Terri sore, anxious and guilty. He and Jessie spent all day Saturday doing it like houseflies. They buzzed through the kitchen, through the living room, through Don's room and finally on the back porch. They slept outside naked, wrapped in one of Don's sleeping bags until first light.

"You want me to stay while you talk to Don about *Oprah*?" Jessie pulled him closer and tightened the sleeping bag around them. There was a brisk morning breeze blowing across the porch.

"No. I want him to know that it's me wanting to do it and not you influencing me." Terri was outlining Jessie ear with his index finger. To be such a big man he had tiny ears. "I thought Jews had big ears and noses." Terri giggled.

"You trying to start a fight? Don't be calling me a Jew. I'm Jewish." Jessie chuckled.

"Oh, *excuse* me!"

"That's all right. Just don't make that mistake again. Now, you sure you don't want me to stay?" Jessie kissed him on the cheek.

"I'm sure."

"Okay. Page me if you need me. You know how to send a page, don't you?"

"Nigga, you ain't all that. It's just a beeper."

Alone in Don's house, Terri felt like a hustler. Don had given him a dream when he had none. Don trained him, paid him, and made him more than the coach's little black friend. And how did he repay him? He slept with Don's boyfriend— his rented boyfriend. He hoped his guilt wouldn't affect his decision if Don said no to *Oprah*.

They were in the kitchen and Don was standing over the counter preparing a veggie juice. Terri watched his blond ponytail bounce across his shoulders. Maybe Jessie and

181

Madear were wrong.

"You're going to love this, Terri. I know you been cheating this weekend, so you got to drink it."

"Cheating?"

"On your diet. Child, you worse than I was. I've been finding those Hershey wrappers."

Terri was sitting at the table with his head down.

"What's wrong, girl?"

"Don, do I have a spot on the *Oprah* show?"

"Ooh! I knew I should have told him to keep his black ass away this weekend. Yes, my child, there is a possible spot for you on *Oprah*."

"Jessie said I had it."

"Jessie is not a manager. He does not know the ins and outs of the business. He called them and they said they might have an interest. It's nothing to get worked up about. Believe me; when you're ready, *Oprah* will be small potatoes."

"So I don't have a spot?" Terri knew somebody was lying.

"No, just an audition, and that's a waste of time right now. We're going to win this city first, then move national."

"I want to do *Oprah*."

Please Don, Terri thought, *let me do* Oprah. *Don't lie. Don't be the snake Jessie and Madear say you are.*

"It's just an audition, not a spot."

"Jessie said—"

"Jessie is not a manager! Jessie is a two-bit hustler with visions of grandeur. I am your manager. Now drink your veggie juice!" He slammed the glass down in front of Terri.

What he said was *Drink your veggie juice* but what Terri heard was *Nigger, do what I tell you to do.*

"I do three shows a week, Don. How much do you get for each show?"

"Enough."

"I need a figure, Don, a dollar amount."

"Not according to your contract." Don was standing over Terri.

"What?"

"Listen, baby." Don placed his hand on Terri's shoulder. "I don't know what Jessie's been filling your head with or whatever else he's been filling, but we have a contract, a three-year contract with two more years to go. When that time is over, you can ask me how much I make. Now drink your damn juice." He bent to kiss Terri on the cheek. Terri jerked his head away.

"Fuck you! I got a spot on *Oprah*! I'm going. Jessie sent my tape. And as far as that contract is concerned, I was seventeen when I signed it, and I signed Terri Parish. My name is Terrance. My grandmother has lawyers. If you want to go to court we will go. I trusted you, but you are a snake just like Madear said." He slung the drink in Don's face and ran from the kitchen.

"Get your ass out!" Don yelled at his back.

He ran from the house taking nothing. All he wanted was air. He ran for blocks; he ran until his legs crumbled to his knees. He thought Don believed in him. He trusted Don. Don told him he could be a star. Don lied to him.

Jessie believed in him. Jessie believed he already was a star. Jessie hung his picture in Denzel's spot. A phone booth was across the street. He stumbled to it and paged Jessie.

"He lied to me, Jessie. He said it was only an audition."

"Where are you, Terri?"

"I'm on Wilson and Broadway by the Burger King. Why did he lie?"

"Because he wants to control you, baby."

"He said I could be a star. Was he lying about that?"

"What do you think, Terri?"

"I don't know. I don't know what to think."

"I'll be there. I'm not too far from you."

It seemed like Jessie was there before Terri hung up the phone.

"You want me to take you to Madear's?"

"No. Not really." Terri was not up to explaining things to Madear.

"Where do you want to go?"

"Take me where you want me to go."

Terri didn't want to make any more decisions. He didn't want to argue, debate, figure out, manipulate or think. He wanted to surrender. He wanted Jessie to pick him up in his arms and take him to his home, lay him in a big, fluffy bed and pamper him. Nibble on his ears and neck and tell him everything was going to work out fine. Hug him tight and make him feel safe and cared for. That's what he wanted Jessie to do, and he wanted Jessie to do it without him asking.

Terri expected large columns, a circular driveway, a lighted path, manicured lawn and shrubbery. What Jessie's mother left him was a Georgian with a side driveway. Jessie flipped the wall switch and the beige, wooden-blade ceiling fan with brass lighting fixtures lit the living room, along with two lines of brass track lights, one on the east side of the room the other on the west. The room was freshly painted eggshell white.

Two-inch strips of metallic gold paint striped each corner, the floor moldings, window ledges and doorway moldings. What Terri guessed was previously exposed oak was now covered with the metallic gold. Terri hated it. Wood trim should never be painted over.

"I did the painting myself."

"Tssst. It shows."

The sofa and loveseat were French Provincial. Jessie's golden touch was upon their wood trim as well. The only wood besides the ceiling fan blades that was left unmarred by Jessie's golden stroke were the blond floorboards, and they were polished to brilliance.

184

"Why did you paint the sofa and loveseat? I know they were stained cherry wood."

"It was dark. I wanted this room bright. It only gets indirect sunlight. I wanted to brighten it up. I might have gone a bit too far with the furniture."

Way too far, was Terri's feeling.

"What do you mean dark?" Terri asked.

"Everything was dark rose and cherry wood. She had a cherry breakfront and purple carpet. All her prints were in cherry wood frames."

The walls were bare.

"What prints?"

"She had a bunch of roses on black backgrounds. Three large prints, one on each wall." Jessie pointed to where the prints once hung.

"They were five by five—huge. They swallowed the room."

"What happened to the breakfront?"

"I sold it and bought that coffee table and two end tables. It's not a big room, as you can see. I didn't think it needed all that."

The tables were teardrop-shaped glass with brass legs. Terri liked them.

"You could use a chair."

"Maybe. If you decide to stay awhile, feel free to make any changes you want."

"Did you do the floor yourself?"

"No. I had to pay for that. I love blond wood."

"Show me the rest."

"There's not much more." He put his arm around Terri. "Like Fun Town, huh?"

"I still don't believe that was you," Terri said, looking up into Jessie's eyes.

"Yes you do." Jessie kissed him on the forehead.

The purple shag carpet remained in the dining room. "This is spacious." Terry smiled.

"Yeah," Jessie answered solemnly. "I sold all the shit that was in here." Jessie's teeth were clenched. "I hated this room. This was where I was put on display for her guests. I would have to get dressed up and sit quietly at the table while she entertained the neighbors. I sold the shit that was in here first."

Terri noticed the fading in the carpet, the worn marks, the indentations. The walls were painted a dark rose. Terri saw the outlines of once-hung pictures, wall mounts, a China cabinet and credenza. It had been a well-furnished room at one time.

Against the far wall he saw a pallet made of comforters and couch cushions.

"Do you sleep in here now?" Terri had hopes of a big, fluffy bed in mind.

"Not often."

The kitchen was full—two blenders, three electric mixing bowls, two microwave ovens, a range stove, a double refrigerator with icemaker, and a meat freezer. A butcher-block counter surrounded the entire kitchen. The table was old. It had chrome legs and a Formica top with tiny, faded blue flowers and yellow butterflies. Cigarette burns and hot pot marks showed the usage the table withstood.

"Do you cook?" Terri asked Jessie. He wondered why he hadn't sold these things.

"No, but I like to eat. I figured my soul mate would love to cook. Do you cook?"

"I'm not saying."

Terri loved to cook. He spent hours in the kitchen with Madear, learning all she was willing to teach. What Madear didn't know Betty Crocker knew. Terri had never cooked for a man before. He never had a man besides Payton who he wanted to cook for.

Madear warned him that men took eating seriously. *"If you are not serious about a man, T.T., don't cook him a good meal.*

186

If you feed a man well, he'll never leave you alone. You could be finished with him and he'll still come around to eat. Be careful about who you feed."

When Jessie opened the door to his bedroom Terri was pleased. There was a big, fluffy bed with lots of pillows.

"This is where I—we sleep."

"For tonight?"

"For as long as you want."

"Is that your way of asking me to move in?"

"Yes."

"Are you sure you can manage the affairs of my heart and my career?"

"I'll try my best."

* * * * *

Terri woke from the doze comfortably. The comfort didn't last a second when he realized he was in the abandoned car. He quickly looked around. He saw no one. He was safe. He hadn't thought about Jessie in years. *"Good memories are like a cool breeze on a hot day."* He hadn't understood it when Madear said it. Now he understood.

He had to use the bathroom. Getting out of the car was not an option, and there was too much wine left in the bottle to waste. He thought about peeing on the floor, but smelling his own urine for hours was not high on his most desirable list.

The car door was too noisy, so he cranked the stiff window down as far as he dared. He didn't want it to get stuck. He got on his knees in the back seat, flipped up his leather miniskirt, pulled down his pantyhose and white silk panties, and flopped his thang out in the night air.

The air felt good upon his crotch. He aimed for the stubby weeds and dirt. He didn't want the noise of his water splattering on the curb. For a few seconds after he finished he left himself open to the air. It did feel good.

187

The window cranked more easily, but it wouldn't go all the way up. He sat back in the seat and adjusted himself. He was very tired. It would be ideal to sleep until early Saturday evening. He could just curl up on the floor of the car and sleep. No one would find him. No one looks in abandoned cars. He tried to shake the thought from his head and the sleep from his eyes. Mo-red would search the sewers for him. He had to stay awake and alert.

He told himself the easiest way to stay awake was to be high. Then he told himself the dumbest thing in the world to do would be to get high with Mo-red looking for him. No, he decided, the dumbest thing in the world to do was steal a hundred and thirty-five thousand dollars from Mo-red. Since that was done, he might as well get high.

He pulled the Ziploc bag of rocks from the white plastic bag. He pulled his pipe and lighter from his pocket. He slumped down in the seat and began.

"You are one sick-ass bitch," he said aloud after smoking three bags. "Every thug in the city is looking for your black ass and you sitting in the back of an abandoned car sucking on this glass dick."

He continued until the involuntary muscle twitching wouldn't allow him to hold the pipe or lighter in his hands. The pipe fell hot to the car seat, burning a small hole in it.

"Fuck it."

With eyes bucked and head jerking he looked around. He thought he saw someone standing on the corner behind the car. He reached for the razor but couldn't hold it.

"Damn, they coming!"

He dropped to the floor of the car.

"God, please don't let them see me. Please, please, please."

He felt ants crawling on his face and down his neck. He slapped at them but they were getting away. They were crawling down his back and biting him. No, they weren't ants, they were spiders, hundreds of them, and he felt each of their eight legs! They were biting him. Poisoning him!

He couldn't kill them; they were moving too fast. He tried to roll over and squash them, but they were on his stomach now. When he reached for them they shot down to his thighs. He had to get out of the car, but Mo-red was outside.

"Oh, sweet Jesus, help me!"

The tightness started at the sole of his left foot. His toes curled down and balled up tight in the red pumps. The cramp didn't shoot up his leg; it inched up, snapping his leg against his butt. When it got to the small of his back, he forced the driver's door open and crawled into the street, gasping for air.

The tightness was in his stomach. He tried to stand on one leg, but he fell hard to the pavement. He had to run. They surely saw him. He stretched the leg out against the tightening, and as suddenly as it came it was gone.

He didn't stand. He peeped under the car to the corner behind the car. No one was there. He looked to the sidewalk— empty. They didn't see him. He didn't want to stand. He slithered back into the car and closed the door. He sat back in the seat and searched for the smashed spiders. He found none.

"Damn, girl, you were tripping. Thank you, Jesus."

The end of the glass pipe had melted into the seat. He snatched it free and drew back to sling it out the window but stopped.

"Now you really trippin', ho." He put the pipe in his skirt pocket. "One is too many and a thousand is never enough. They ain't never lied."

He grabbed the Richards. "Fuck it. I'll get drunk and go to sleep. If they find me, fuck it! I've slept in cars before. If it's my time, it's my time."

He uncapped the Richards, turned it up and gulped continuously.

"Me and Payton used to sleep in abandoned cars all the time when we were kids. Camping out, we called it. Well, tonight I'm camping out."

He closed his eyes and tried to force sleep. He needed to relax. With eyes closed he gulped the alcohol. He capped the bottle and tried to remember what he was thinking about before he started tripping. *Jessie.*

* * * * *

They had a good thing for a while. Jessie was right about Don, but wrong about him. At eighteen he had no interest in finding his soul mate. Jessie proved to be a good manager. After *Oprah* he arranged five bookings in Vegas, two in Paris, ten in Miami, ten in San Francisco and hundreds of one-night shots all over the Midwest. The money was good, and after a year Terri had a following of fans who adored him.

Men were offering him Cadillacs, trips to the islands, apartments, diamonds and thousands and thousands of dollars. In the beginning he ignored the offers. The love he and Jessie shared held him—until Jessie stopped touring with him.

Terri had become comfortable on the road, and Jessie's business could no longer stand his absence. They came to the conclusion that Terri could finish the year out without Jessie traveling with him. In Jessie's absence the offers from fans got bigger and more appealing.

His admirers kept his dressing room filled with orchids and roses. When he performed on the stage his feet would be covered with twenties, fifties and hundred dollar bills that were tossed from the audience.

Terri began listening to the generous men who wanted him so badly that they pleaded. All they wanted was sex. They didn't talk about the developing lady and love. They didn't talk about him improving his poise. They didn't talk about contracts, bookings or building crumb piles. All he heard was their desire, and what they were willing to give to be with him.

The first one was a jeweler who gave him a three-carat diamond ring. The second was a plastic surgeon from Hollywood who gave him deeper dimples. The third was an entertainment lawyer who bought him a silver fox jacket. When it was established that Jessie would no longer be able to tour with him, Terri took advantage of the freedom. Each road trip brought a new lover.

Confident that Jessie had no knowledge of the affairs on the road, and acquiring a taste for new lovers and their gifts, Terri began to cheat when he was home. Afternoon rendezvous turned into nights out. When Jessie was out of town on business or gone to martial arts tournaments, Terri went out on the town. When Jessie was home, Terri would lie to go meet his new lovers.

After a while, the faces and names began to blur. They became their gifts. He had been gone a week with a diamond tiara. When he came home Jessie had all his belonging packed and waiting at the door.

Taped to the Louis Vuitton trunk was a large manila envelope. It contained a canceled management contract and the listing of upcoming shows, along with the amounts he was to be paid. He was booked for two years. A check for every cent Terri had earned from the shows Jessie arranged was also in the package. Jessie gave him back every dime.

"Tsst," was all Terri said. He picked up the phone and began dialing for a cab. He heard Jessie in the kitchen fixing breakfast. He thought of speaking to him, but he could think of nothing that needed to be said. The contract was canceled. His shows and his money were in order. He continued dialing for the cab.

When the cab arrived Jessie helped him load the bags. Neither spoke. Terri was sitting in back of the cab when Jessie told him goodbye through the window. Jessie handed him a laminated card with a phone number: 234-5678.

"It's easy to remember. It starts with two, not one. I paid extra for it. It's to a service that answers twenty-four hours a day. When you're ready to come back and be with only me, call me." He turned and walked away.

"Don't hold your breath." Terri threw the card at his back.

Jessie turned around.

"You silly little girl. You don't even know who I am. You don't know the power I have. We've been together for a year. It's been the best year of your life. You got enough money to go and do anything you want. You got two years of work in your hand and you know very little about the man who helped you get it.

"You're chasing something, Terri, something that you don't have to chase. What we got is better than what you're chasing. We got everything right here! We're both successful, we got money and I thought we had love. No, we *got* love. You just don't respect it yet. Love is not always a thrill a minute. It slows down like everything in life, but that doesn't mean you walk away from it. What you're chasing will never satisfy you because it's not real. What we were building was real. One day you'll know it, and we'll get back together.

"I didn't make you a star, Terri. I only helped. You were born to be the star you will become. And you were born to love me, not the bastards you been fucking. I know the name of every man you been with this year. It hurts, but I'll get over it, and when you're ready, Terri, I'll be there for you. Don't forget the number. I sold this house last week. That number is the only way you can reach me.

"Choose your lovers a little more wisely, Terri. Two tried to sell porno shots of you to the media. Both are dead. I won't be there to protect you anymore. Be careful. Parasites are everywhere. You're mine, and when you realize that, all will be right with your world. We are soulmates."

192

Terri saw the hurt in Jessie's eyes. It was like Pumpkin told him; his eyes couldn't lie. Terri closed his heart to the feeling that was trying to creep up to it. It was over. The love Jessie said would last didn't. Other men desired him and he desired them. What did Jessie mean he killed two of them? Which two?

"Jerome, take this silly slut where she wants to go, and be careful because I still love the ho."

"Yes sir, Mr. James," the cab driver answered, pulling out of the driveway.

"Who the fuck are you calling a slut and a ho? Stop this gotdamn cab!"

"No, ma'am."

"What?"

"I said no, ma'am. I work for Mr. James. He owns this cab company."

"That nigga don't own no cab company. He owns a beauty shop!"

"No, ma'am, he owns about sixteen beauty shops, twenty restaurants, three cab companies and half of South Holland."

"I lived with him for the past year; I know what that nigga owns. Stop the cab!"

"I cain't. I need my job."

"I'm telling you he don't own this cab company. Stop the cab!"

"Lady, that's Mr. James."

"He ain't nobody. Who do you think he is?"

"I know he's Mr. James, and the story goes he killed his own mama right there in that house. Took the insurance money and bought his first beauty shop. Then they say he killed his daddy that never claimed him and sued his estate as a rightful heir. But the trashy street folks say he made his real money killing people for gangsters. That's who I think he is."

"You're wrong."

"No, ma'am, I ain't."

"I live with him and I'm telling you, you got the wrong nigga."

"Here." The cab driver handed Terri a slip of paper. "That is my paycheck. Who signed it?"

"Jessie James." Terri recognized the signature. He handed the check back to the cab driver.

"That's the man. And ma'am, when a man like that says jump, I say how high. I spent ten years in the joint. I know a killer when I see one, and Mr. Jessie James is a stone cold killer. My wife works at the bank; she say he's worth eight million. That makes him even more dangerous."

"Eight million?"

"Yes, ma'am. They call that nigga Midas. Everything he touches turns to gold. You walking away from a rich nigga."

"I ain't walking, I'm running. You just said he killed his own mama and daddy for money. I mighta been next."

"Maybe."

"You heard him. He said he killed two men."

"I told you Mr. James signs my check. I told you I was a convict. Lady, I didn't hear a damn thing. Now, where you want to go?"

"Fifty-first and Princeton."

* * * * *

"The mistakes of youth," Terri said aloud to himself. He slumped down as low as possible in the back seat of the abandoned car. He didn't want to think about the mistakes of the past. He didn't want to get depressed. He was rich now; mistakes were in the past. He had to come up with a plan.

What was it the counselor at the detox center said? *"If you fail to plan, you plan to fail."* Failing was out. No more failures. The world would see there was more to him than getting high and sucking thangs. He wasn't always a ten-dollar ho. He would make them remember.

He would be smart with the money this time. The first thing would be the change, then a house—a small house, his own house. Then he would get a sensible car, maybe a Ford. Then drama classes; he would attend a university and get a degree in theater, learn how to act, practice a true trade. Madear would be proud. As a woman, new doors would open for him.

He'd start out doing small community plays, join a company like the one that came to the detox center. They were all clean addicts, a bunch of crackheads and dope fiends starting over. That's what he would do—start over.

After the change he'd stop getting high. No more low-life activity. No hoein'. The first thang he felt inside his new vagina would belong to the man he loved. He would be a good man who would insist that they wait until after marriage. He would be a respectable man, a professional man—no show biz types, no fans.

He'd pay for Charlene's operation too. They would be like two sisters. He owed Charlene a lot. No matter how many times he lied to Charlene about coming to Birmingham, he always sent Terri the money for a ticket. Charlene was his last friend and he knew it. All the other bridges were burnt.

Dr. Goody hung in a long time, but even a horny MD has his limits. *"It's tough love, Terri. I can't keep giving you money to kill yourself."* That's what Dr. Goody had said the last time Terri rode the bus to the clinic to beg for a couple of dollars. The clinic!

"The clinic is on a Hundred-nineteenth and Halsted. And their house was right behind it. There you go, bitch! Work that plan."

Terri sat up in the seat. He'd never gone to Dr. Goody's and his mother's home, mostly because of his mother. He didn't want her to see him broke and begging, but he wouldn't be begging now. He only needed a ride to the airport. Maybe he had a plan. He slumped back down in the seat. His eyes closed and sleep came, a fitful sleep full of memories.

He was thirteen years old, wearing a pair of sky blue shorts he'd sewn himself. They were as close to a pair of culottes as he would dare. The shirt was also a Terri original. It had three buttons down the back. For his birthday Madear said he could wear whatever he wanted.

He was on the sidewalk in front of Madear's house, barefooted and jumping double dutch. Linda and Brenda, the twin girls with buckteeth who always made him play the father when they played house, no matter how much he protested— "You're the only boy that plays house with us. You have to be the daddy."—were turning the rope. Jackie, the only girl on the block who had more Barbie dolls than him, and Sharon, the first person to call him a faggot to his face, were on the side singing and keeping score. The song they sang kept track of how good the jump was. The further along in the song he jumped, the better his score.

"Miss Mary Mack, Mack, Mack, all dressed in black, black, black, with silver buttons, buttons, buttons all down her back, back, back. She asked her mother, mother, mother for fifteen cents, cents, cents to see the elephant, elephant, elephant jump over the fence, fence, fence. She jumped so high, high, high she touched the sky, sky, sky, and she didn't come down, down, down 'til the fourth of July, ly, ly."

They were on the sixth chorus; none of the girls had made it past the fourth. Normally the twins would miss a beat while turning, causing him to mess up, but this day they were flowing smoothly. They wanted to see how far he could go. It was already established he could jump double dutch better than any girl on their block or any block in the neighborhood. It was one of those days when they wanted him to show off. And show off he did.

He was jumping, turning, spinning and grinning, first with both feet then with one foot; then he switched to the other foot, then both feet as one, then he touched the ground, spun around and spelled his name out loud.

"T. E. R. R. I. Terri! I touched the ground! I spun around! I jumped so high I touched the sky! Now spell my name out loud!"

All the girls joined in. "T.E.R.R.I, Terri! T.E.R.R.I, Terri! T.E.R.R.I., Terri!"

Chapter Eight
Mother Knows Best

Terri stepped out of the Chrysler and adjusted his clothes. He took a deep breath of the morning air. The clouds weren't letting the early morning sun through. It wasn't a great morning, but it was another morning. He would follow the plan from the night before. He was on 115th Street; the clinic was less than four blocks away. He reached back in the car for the plastic bag.

"I know that ass." Terri heard a voice right behind him. "Baby, you still got a girl's booty."

Terri knew it was Payton. Terri was bent over in the car to get the razor off the seat. Payton stood behind him holding his hips.

"Damn, I miss this. Do you?" Payton ran his hand down Terri's thigh. "We was good together. We used to fuck in cars like this." Terri felt Payton throbbing against his butt. "I could slide it to you right here. You want it?"

"Get off of me, Payton!"

"Naw, hell naw, I ain't getting off you!" Payton shoved Terri into the car. He climbed in behind him and closed the door. Terri retrieved the razor and spun around. Payton had the .32 cocked and pointed at Terri's head.

"Calm down, bitch. I'm here to help you."

"You have never helped nobody but yourself!" Terri spit out the words, sitting back in the seat. Payton made himself comfortable in the other seat.

"How did you find me, Payton?"

"I know you, Terri. I know how you think. I know where you feel comfortable. I saw you last night, trippin', but I didn't know if you had a gun or not. I had to wait until I could get the drop on you. Mo-red's telling all the soldiers you're armed. He wants you shot on sight. You got his ass good, Terri. Where's the dope?"

"In the bag." Terri watched Payton go through the bag like the greedy bastard he was.

"Damn, he didn't say shit about the cash, and Terri, this is three kilos of dope. No wonder he wants your ass dead. He said you stuck him up at gunpoint. Is that true?"

"No."

"I didn't think so. I couldn't see you doing it. Mo-red's ass is hanging out. He got to find you. The word is he got the coke from some crazy black mercenaries with Colombian connections.

"Their cocaine is the best quality and the price is cheap, but these dudes are dead serious about their money. When I say dead serious I mean dead serious. Money on time or death. They don't even want the cocaine back. You got to have the cash on the agreed-upon date or you die. Most hustlers stay the hell away from them, but not Mo-red. He figured with all the workers he had under him he could make their deadline, but you threw a wrench in the works.

"The gang will try to help him find you, but if they don't find you, it's Mo-red's ass, not the organization's problem. He fucked up and he's scared. Now his people know he's going outside of them for work. He got to make good. He got to find you. Damn, it's over a hundred grand here. You fucked him up good, Terri."

"How you know so much?" Terri asked.

"Baby, it's the talk of the streets. A drag queen stuck up Mo-red and set his ass on fire! He couldn't keep it quiet. I know he tried, but the ambulance and fire department was involved, and you know how the streets talk. Not to mention the police.

"Shit, niggas was talking about it ten minutes after they pulled his ass out the fire. Even if he finds you, Mo-red's going to lose rank. How it look, a chief getting stuck up by a fag? If the mercenaries don't kill his ass the organization might."

Payton pulled his own pipe from his pocket and loaded it with a rock. "Give me a lighter."

Terri handed it to him.

200

"Payton, it's daylight. People are going to see you."

When Payton took the hit Terri thought about attacking him, but he decided against it. Payton had information he needed.

"Remember when we used to camp out and fuck in abandoned cars like this? It was me and you against the world then." Payton blew the crack smoke in Terri's face. Terri reached for his own pipe but changed his mind. He needed a clear head, a working brain—not a crack-restricted one.

"We did more than fuck, Payton. We read a lot. You exposed me to what you called literary fiction. Remember? I was reading *True Confessions* and *Bronze Thrills*. You would get so angry. You told me I was filling my head with trash, so you started bringing your books. You don't remember the books. I do. *Native Son, The Man Who Cried I Am, The Spook Who Sat by the Door, I Know Why the Caged Bird Sings, The Invisible Man.* You started me reading in abandoned cars. Camping out was about more than fucking. Now, that's all the time I got for memory lane, Payton. I got to get the hell outta this city."

"Where you going, to *Birmingham* to get your thang cut off?"

"Fuck you, Payton. Okay, why the fuck are you here?"

"'Cause I knew how to find you. I knew you was going to try and get to your stepdaddy's clinic. I came out here looking in abandoned cars. Mo-red got every soldier in the city looking for you and he said you killed a man in a alley last night."

"That's a lie. Mo-red killed Andrew!"

Payton took another hit from his pipe, smiling sideways at Terri.

"Look, Terri, I know we had our problems, but I'll help you get out of this city. I'll drive you to Birmingham. My cab is parked around the corner."

"And what do you want?"

"Either we start over together or you give me half and I'm on my way."

"Will your cab make it to Birmingham?"

"Hell, yeah. Birmingham is only fourteen hours away."

"Half and you're out of my life?"

"If that's what you want."

"You got a deal. We leave now?"

"Right now."

Payton reached for the bag but Terri snatched it out of his reach.

"It's mine until we get to Birmingham," Terri said sternly.

"Fine. I just thought you might have wanted me to carry it for you."

"No. That's okay."

They exited the abandoned car. The early morning air was fresh. Terri's mind was clear he was grateful he hadn't given in to the temptation of smoking a rock with Payton.

Payton looked better than Terri had him look in quite awhile. He'd gained a little weight and was dressed rather nicely. He was wearing a pair of gray linen pants and a short-sleeved black silk dress shirt. His feet were partially covered by a pair of black Italian sandals.

"It looks like you been doing okay, Payton."

Terri was curious. Payton got just as high as he did, if not higher. How was he able to buy new clothes, especially handmade Italian sandals?

"You hit the lottery or something?"

"Naw, I just been doin' a little work here and there. Got a couple of new lovers. You know the routine."

Payton was nervously looking behind them and ahead as they walked down the block.

"I don't want to walk down Halsted," Payton said. "I'm parked on a hundred thirteen, half a block west of Halsted. Let's walk down Green. I think it will be safer. We don't want nobody to get lucky. "

Terri too began to look around. Maybe going with Payton wasn't such a good idea.

"Where did you go last night after you saw me?"

"You won't believe me."

"Try me."

Terri's reluctance to go with Payton grew. What was he thinking? Payton had proved untrustworthy in the past. Terri stopped walking.

Payton paused with him. "Up that tree." Payton pointed to the tree behind the car.

"You climbed the tree?" Terri laughed.

"Like a damn squirrel. I didn't know what was true and what wasn't. You might've shot me." Payton restarted his walk.

Terri followed but he continued to look around. He didn't trust Payton, but he trusted Payton's greed. Payton would help him if the payday was big enough, and it was.

"Yeah, I was tripping pretty bad."

Terri needed a shower and he needed to change his clothes. He didn't like Payton looking better than him, but it would all have to wait. He would have to arrive in Birmingham funky.

"I smoked so much crack last night I couldn't hold my pipe. I ain't been that high in months. I must have smoked an ounce of cocaine between what I did with Mo-red and what I did by myself."

"You and Mo-red got high together?"

They turned north down Green Street.

"We got high as hell! Then the bastard started tripping. You know we used to kick it in the joint. The mean dog hasn't changed a bit. Once a gorilla pimp, always a gorilla pimp."

"Yeah, he's a mean bastard."

"You know him?" Again Terri stopped walking.

"I really don't know him. I just did a little business with him, that's all. To tell the truth, Terri, I told him where he could find you."

203

"What?"

"I was over his place a week or so ago buying an ounce of cocaine from him and he started talking about Statesville. He almost sounded like he missed it. Anyway, he got to talking about you.

"He didn't know me and you used to kick it. He sounded like he really missed you, so to get a few points with him I told him where to find you. The mark was so happy he gave a free sixteenth. I didn't know it was going to lead to all of this, I swear. I figured I was sending you some business."

Terri remained silent and restarted his walk. What choice did he really have? If Payton was hooked up with Mo-red, Terri figured he was already found. If Payton was not with Mo-red, he would be his escape.

"It ain't my fault you ripped Mo-red off, Terri."

"I'm not saying it's your fault. I just didn't know you knew him, that's all."

"It ain't like we buddies. Just business. It smells fresh out here, don't it?"

"Yeah, it's the fresh air from the trees," Terri answered.

"Ain't too many trees on Division Street, huh?"

"Nope, not like these. These big boys look like they guarding the neighborhood, don't they?"

"Yeah, look like they guarding something. They were spooky last night. Shadows and shit moving all across the streets. If you catch one out the side of your eye, look like it be reaching for you. It's spooky out here when it's dark. The streetlights make it worse. In the country trees in the dark is trees; in the city with that damn light they change into all kinda shit."

"Were you high, Payton?"

"Yeah, but I wasn't *that* high. Them damn trees is spooky."

Neither spoke as they walked down the block filled with brick bungalow homes. The neighborhood was still asleep. A

few birds were chirping; their songs along with the clack of
Terri's heels were the only sound.

"There it is. A little dirty, but she'll get us there."

"Are you going to radio in?"

"No. I'm already over. When we get to Birmingham I'll
call them. Here you go, my once love." Payton opened the cab
door for Terri.

"Thank you, sir."

Terri sat in the front seat. He was impressed. The cab didn't
smell and it was clean. Payton sat beside him and turned on the
engine.

"It's clean in here, Payton! You really are changing."

"Sorta. You know I went to drug rehab for a couple weeks.
It slowed me down a little. When I got out I wanted to stay
drug-free, but I didn't. But after I got clean I saw how nasty I
really was. I still get high, but I try to keep myself up. You
know what I mean? Ain't no excuse for poor hygiene. And
besides, people don't like riding in a funky cab.

"Now I got people that actually request me. I sell more
cocaine than I smoke now, and it's cool. I buy either out here
on the south side or out west then sell the shit up north for
premium prices. I filled the cab up before I came out here, so
we can get straight on the expressway. You went to rehab,
didn't you?"

Payton pulled onto Halsted quickly.

"Why you taking Halsted?" The alarm was in Terri's voice.

"It's the only street I know that goes straight through. We'll
be okay," Patrick reassured him.

Terri quickly looked out the back, front and side windows.

"No, not rehab. I went to detox for three days. One of the
judges sent me. I wasn't thinking about stopping until I got
there and heard what they had to say.

"Most of the people there blamed drugs for fucking up their
lives. For me it was bad decisions. Using drugs was a bad
decision; smoking cocaine was definitely a bad decision. What

detox showed me was I could start over. I didn't have to stay a crackhead ho. I had a choice.

"At first I didn't buy that shit about addiction being a disease. I really didn't believe that mess about one hit is too many and thousand hits is not enough, but I buy it all now. Addiction is a disease and once a addict gets high, he unleashes it. There is no controlling it. I would have smoked up every bit of that shit last night if my body hadn't stopped me.

"It's like that every time. If I take one hit I'm off to the races. I hate what I've become, Payton. I hate being a addict, but if it wasn't for that detox center, I wouldn't know I was one. I knew I had a problem but not a disease."

"You ever gonna stop?"

"When I get to Birmingham. I'ma sell this shit—hopefully in one pop—and start over. I got to let it go. If not, it will keep me broke and hoein'. I want to rise up, and crack will only take me down."

"Not if you got enough. That's three kilos. You couldn't smoke that shit up if you wanted to. You ain't got to stop now. You got thousands of dollars and kilos of cocaine! Now ain't the time to stop; at least for me it ain't."

"I been around kilos and thousands of dollars before, Payton, and believe me, an addict like me will still fuck up. A monkey can't sell bananas. You can have this coke from here to Peru and still end up ass out. Addiction is not a game; its primary purpose is to take you out. Kill you. I know that, but I still keep fucking with it. That's why when I get to Birmingham I'm cutting drugs loose.

"Wow. I just thought about something. You a dope dealer now. How about I give you all the cocaine and we call it even?"

"You'll give me all three kilos?" Payton asked.

"Hell yes!"

"You got a deal!"

"You sure?" Terri asked.

"Hell yeah, Terri. Birmingham is your chance to start over. For me, three kilos will start me over just fine. When we get to Birmingham I'm on a plane to New York City, where the true players dwell. Here it is, baby, 57 south. Hold on!"

Payton floored the cab as they descended the ramp. There was no traffic. The windows were down and the wind ripped through the cab. It felt like freedom to Terri. He was on his way to a new life, a drug-free life, a Mo-red-free life, a hoeing-free life, a thang-free life.

"You know the first thing I'm going to do, Payton?"

"Yes I do." Payton settled in the seat for the long drive.

"What?"

"The change. It's what you wanted since I've known you."

"You got it. It's going to make me whole, complete."

"I know better than to argue with you about it. You want it too bad. I hope it makes you happy."

"It will. It's my destiny."

"And after that what?"

"I'm going to get a legal name change and go to school."

"School?"

"Yeah, drama classes. Start a acting career. I been acting a long time; I must be a natural."

"You ain't never lied about that. I believe all addicts are actors."

"It's more to me than being an addict, Payton, and it's time to let the world know it."

"Terri, what do you think the chances are of us getting back together?"

"Stick to business, Payton."

"I was just wondering, you know. It's been a while since we was together, you know, and it is a long drive, and it ain't like I don't want to get with you."

"It's not going to happen, Payton. We're finished in that area."

"Not even one last time?"

207

"We had our last time."

"Ain't no thing, Terri. Just askin'."

Payton pulled the .32 from his waistband and placed it on the seat.

"It's uncomfortable." He answered Terri's gaze.

"Remember when we used to come out here and work Dr. Goody?" Payton asked.

"Yeah. I thought about him last night. He was sweet."

"Sweet? I remember him as a sucker, a last resort when we needed a couple hundred."

"That's how you saw him," Terri said. "It wasn't like that. Every time I came to him I had to promise that it would be the last time. He watched me go down that spiral of addiction. It hurt him.

"He was always reminding me of the star I once was. He would have gave me the money even if we hadn't fucked. I had sex with him because he still really desired me. He saw me as that star on Caesar's stage. When he gave me that last hundred he cried.

"I couldn't go to him after that. He cared more about me than I did. That's what addiction does; it stops you from caring about yourself. It takes you low. After I tripped last night I couldn't even throw away my pipe. What kind of shit is that? I know something is hurting me, but I keep going to it. No, man; drugs, crack ain't shit, and I know it. Being drug-free is the only way for me to grow."

"Umph. It sounds like you serious. Tell me about last night. How did you get Mo-red's ass?"

"It was just a lick and I took it."

"But how?"

"He was dope drunk."

"Why did you burn him?"

"He hurt me. He beat me like a dog bitch and I was tired of being a dog bitch. It was weird because that was first time I can remember fighting back. I mean really fighting back. It was

208

like I got a little bit of myself back. Mo-red picked the wrong day to beat this bitch's ass. Since you say you know so much about me, what was special about yesterday?"

"I don't know."

"Think."

"I don't know, Terri!"

"September seventh, my birthday. My day to shine."

"Well, you shined alright. Damn! Is that who I think it is? Look out the back!"

The Blazer was bearing down on them, followed by one police car.

"Gotdammit, it's him, Payton! Go, go! Please go!"

Payton floored the cab, but the Blazer continued to gain.

"We can't outrun them! We got to give up! Maybe they'll let us go when you give him the shit back!"

"Are you out of your fucking mind? The bastard will kill us!"

Payton picked up the .32 and pointed it at Terri.

"I'm sorry, Terri, but it's you he wants to kill, not me." He pulled to side of the highway and stopped.

"Don't do this. We can get away. You can have it all," Terri pleaded.

"I don't need it all. Mo-red's offering twenty thousand for you. That's enough for me."

"If I ever meant anything to you, Payton, please let me go. Please."

"You meant something to me, Terri, but twenty grand means something now. Don't move a damn muscle!"

The Blazer pulled in front of them and the squad car was behind them. Mo-red got out of the Blazer with hands taped and death in his eyes. Cars zipped past him as he walked along the shoulder of the expressway.

"Get out!" Payton ordered Terri.

"No! I'm not going!"

Mo-red walked to Payton's window. He stuck his head in the cab and kissed Payton on the mouth.

"You did good, Patty boy."

Mo-red looked to Terri. "Hey, bitch. How's tricks?" The police officer snatched Terri from the cab. "Put him in the gotdamn truck! No, wait." Mo-red walked around to the passenger side of the cab and stood before Terri.

"You coulda had it all, but Patty boy told me you wasn't shit. He told me he could find your ass too. Come here, Patty boy."

Payton crawled out of the cab.

"You didn't know me and Patty was friends, didja, bitch? It was Patty who told me where to find your ass in the first place.

"It's just one thing I don't quite understand, Patty. What the fuck you doin' on 57 south? You was supposed to bring the bitch back to me."

"I had to get his trust, Mo-red. I had to get his guard down. I was going to call from the gas station."

"He's lying!" Terri began rapidly shouting over the passing cars. "He told me, 'Fuck Mo-red!' He said, 'Mo-red ain't shit but a faggot.' He said he was fucking you. He said you was his bitch. He said you was stupid and about to fall from power. He said the dope wasn't even yours and the people it belonged to was looking to kill you. He said you was probably dead already.

"I asked him to take me to you. I knew I couldn't get away, but he said we could. He told me the highway was just around the corner and he could get us out the city. I was tired of running, Mo-red. He made me do it. He said you as good as dead. He said you was stealing money from the gang. He said you was stupid, you was buying him clothes and giving him free drugs. He said you was a dumb faggo—"

There were five bangs; five explosions and Payton joined the club of the headless. Mo-red, with smoking gun in hand, turned to Terri.

CHASIN' IT

"It don't make a difference what you said he said. I got eyes. I know I'm on 57 south. He was dead anyway, so don't think you talked me into it. Where's my fuckin' shit?"

Despite the ringing in Terri's ears, he heard the question, but his eyes were on Payton's twitching body, which lay at his feet along with the .32 that was still in Payton's hand.

"Did you hear me, bitch? Where is my shit?"

Terri faked convulsions; the officer relaxed his grip. Terri fell to his knees, imitating dry heaves. He fell across Payton's bloody body. What was left of Payton's face filled Terri's eyes. He no longer faked the dry heaves.

He had to do it. He had no choice. He had to think past the fear. He took the gun from Payton's hand then stood up shooting. A red dot appeared on the policeman's forehead and one on Mo-red's chin. They both fell back.

Terri jumped in the cab and threw it in gear. He drove up a hill and through a fence. He didn't look back. The cab spun when the tires grabbed the pavement. He drove against the flow of traffic. He U-turned and floored the cab. The engine stalled for a second then shot him forward.

The street was a blur. All he could do was drive. He ran lights; he drove on the sidewalk; he hit parked cars; he sped through alleys, parking lots and side streets. When he stopped, when his vision cleared, when his heart returned to beating as opposed to rushing, and when his body uncoiled, he was parked at the back gate of a cemetery. He'd been to this one before.

He grabbed the plastic bag and pushed the door open. He left the keys in the ignition; he wanted someone to steal it. The further away from him the better. He reached into the glove compartment and released the trunk latch.

Payton usually kept some sort of backpack in his trunk. Terri found a shoulder bag in there. It was stuffed with shorts, T-shirts, gym socks and toiletries. Terri emptied the bag of the clothing; the toiletries he needed. He stuffed the plastic bag on

211

top of the toiletries. Under the shoulder bag Terri found one of his old deck shoes. He rifled through the trunk and found the other one.

He reached down to pull off one of the pumps and his hand was filled with flesh. The heel of his shoe had punctured through a piece of Payton's cheek. That slowed him down. He slid to the ground.

The front of his red nylon top was covered with blood. It was all over his hands and his arms. He began to cry. He didn't want to cry; he didn't have time to cry, but he couldn't stop. He moved beyond crying to wailing. He kicked off his shoes; he tore off his top; he yanked the fishnets from his legs and he continued to wail. He rolled over in the grass and beat the earth. He lay facedown in the grass and sobbed.

"God, please let it end soon. If You don't want me to have the money, I don't care. I'll leave it here. Just end it, Lord, please. Don't You understand? I can't take it, Lord. It's too much. I don't want to see nobody else die, Lord. I don't want to die, Lord. I'll leave the money and the drugs. Just get me out of this city, Lord. Please."

Terri pressed his face into the grass. He hadn't prayed since Statesville. There he prayed for death; now he prayed for life.

He felt something in his ear. He was uncertain about what he felt. It was wet, warm, and probing his ear. He opened his eyes. It was a puppy. A little brown puppy with a stubby tail and black, droopy ears, and a big puppy smile on his face.

Terri tried to push him away, but the puppy was not to be denied. He gave Terri a bigger smile and licked the tears from his face.

"Stop it!"

Terri sat up; the puppy yelped and jumped in his lap.

"Look, puppy, I'm not the one this morning. Go on home." Terri told the puppy to leave, but he didn't push him away.

"What are you doing out here anyway?"

The puppy snuggled under Terri's chin and licked his neck.

"Oh! I know you a boy dog because you think you slick. You see a girl crying so you come over and try to put your moves on her."

Terri hugged the puppy. The puppy whimpered happily and beat his stubby tail against Terri's breast.

"Damn!" Terri realized he was sitting half-nude behind the cemetery. He pulled the puppy to his chest, stood and walked to the trunk of the cab. He pulled out a white T-shirt with a black Nike swoosh on the front.

"This will do. What do you think, little fella?"

The puppy yelped and beat his tail against Terri.

"I think so too." Terri placed the puppy in the trunk and slid on the T-shirt.

"You are a friendly little fella, aren't you? What's your name? You don't have a collar. You are nobody's dog, huh? Well, you my dog now. It's me and you, puppy, against the world."

Terri put the puppy on the ground.

"If you follow me you're mine. I'm not going to call you. I'ma just walk away."

Terri walked toward the opening in the back gate. The puppy yelped.

"I'm going this way, puppy. Madear is in here. I got to tell her goodbye."

The puppy yelped again. Terri turned and saw the puppy trying to follow him, pulling the shoulder bag.

"Well, I'll be blessed. We suppose to take that with us, huh, puppy?" The puppy yelped and circled the bag.

"Okay, fine. We on!"

Terri slung the blue canvas shoulder bag over his right shoulder and he scooped up the puppy with his left arm.

"I hope you like action, little fella."

When Terri passed the cab he saw the gun on the dashboard. "We might need that."

213

He reached in and took it with him. He placed it in the small of his back. He squeezed himself and the puppy through the opening caused by the slack in the chain that locked the back gate of the cemetery. Terri guessed it was about six-thirty in the morning.

"If Payton thought the trees on those blocks were spooky, these boys would scare the shit out of him, huh, little fella? Big old trees. I bet most of them over a hundred years old. Madear is in the Weeping Willow section up on a hill. That's the only tree I can name because they look like they're weeping. These big boys might be Oaks or Maples. I don't know.

"Trees die quiet, little fella—no bangs. They die a little at a time. They don't bleed; they stay in the same place their whole life. That's probably why they live so long."

The ground was dry and hard. Terri walked, snuggling the puppy against his cheek. He walked in no particular direction. He didn't look for a hill. He didn't look for Weeping Willows. He walked until he knew was there.

"Hello, Madear. This here is Lil' Fella. God sent him to me, but you know that."

He sat next to her stone, which was placed in the earth. The stone simply read: *Florence Parish is with us.* No birth date, no death date because he didn't know her actual date of birth, and he didn't consider her dead. Since Clyde paid for the stone, Terri put on it what he wanted, despite Diane's protests.

It was two months after the funeral when Terri had Clyde bring him to the cemetery. He couldn't locate her because there was no stone. His mother refused to talk to him about it, so he told Clyde to buy it then put his own words on it.

Whenever someone asked Madear when her birthday was, she'd ask theirs then she'd tell them hers was the next day. *"The day after yours, baby, so I know you won't be forgetting it."* When he was growing up, Madear and Terri shared birthday celebrations.

"Happy birthday, Madear. It's your day to shine."

214

CHASIN' IT

No sooner than the words left his lips the thick, gray clouds were gone and the sun shone brilliantly.

"You go, Madear! This is your day to shine!"

The tears started again.

"That's right, Madear. We don't take no mess on our birthdays. Push those clouds out your way. It's a Parish birthday celebration!"

Terri wanted to stand up and shout, dance in the sun, clap his hands, shake his butt and act a fool dancing for Madear the way he did when he was a child, but all he could do was cry and hug Lil' Fella.

"I don't have a party in me today, Madear. My heart is heavy. I didn't love him anymore, but I swear I didn't want to see him dead. I was mad and I said a bunch of stuff to cause confusion, but I didn't want him dead—not Payton, not dead.

"I made Mo-red kill him, and that's the truth. I killed him. I killed Payton, Madear. And this is Lil' Fella. He's kind of cute. He's my puppy now. I know you was a cat person, but you can put up with him while we here, can't you?

"I wasn't trying to kill him, Madear. I was mad. I tried to kill Mo-red. I tried, but he's not dead. I can feel him.

"Madear, if you can kill him, kill him! Please. Ask God to kill him. He deserves it, Madear. I swear he does. You know he does. God knows he does. Tell God to kill him, Madear. In detox they told me I could have a God of my understanding. I can understand God killing him.

"I think I killed a cop—a crooked cop. I shot him in the head. I think this puppy is going to be a big dog. Look at how big his feet are. He's kind of cute. I'ma sit for a minute, Madear. Get my head together. We had some good birthday parties.

"I don't know if Payton will make it up there, but if he does, tell him I'm sorry. And that cop, too, if he's dead."

Terri put Lil' Fella down and lay out in the grass next to Madear's grave.

"You sure did brighten it up out here. Did you know Payton was scared of trees? I love trees, the bigger the better.

"Tell God He doesn't have to kill Mo-red. Just keep him away from me. But I could use His help with getting out this city. I asked Him a short while ago, but you can ask Him again for me, Madear. Do you like Heaven?"

Lil' Fella found his way to a waterspout. Terri watched him drink from the puddle formed by the drip. Terri opened the shoulder bag and pulled out a bar of soap and toothbrush. Someone else's toothbrush was better than none; but he thought about Payton's teeth and decided against it.

He glanced around. The cemetery was empty except for him and Lil' Fella. He reached to his head to pull off his wig and discovered he wasn't wearing it.

"I musta left it in the abandoned car. Payton remembered camping out, Madear."

Terri slid off the deck shoes, stood and walked to the spout.

Lil' Fella darted back and forth between his ankles, yelping to be picked up.

"Don't tell me you spoiled. Now I know you a boy dog."

Terri knelt down to the faucet and turned it on. The water gushed out, rusty in color. The force of the water excited Lil' Fella. He barked his best puppy bark at it and whimpered more than growled. Terri let the water run hard until the rust cleared. He reduced the force and rinsed his mouth with the soap. He placed his head under the stream.

The water was colder than he expected; it caused him to shiver, but he kept his head under. He let the water run through until his hair felt soaked. He peeled the T-shirt over his wet head and allowed the water to run over his upper torso. He worked the soap into a thick lather, washing his hair and upper torso. The suds were sliding down his skirt.

"Fuck it."

He wiggled out of it and his white silk panties and stooped directly under the flow. The water was splashing the top of his head and running down his body.

He thought of Pumpkin and her short stature, but this would have been a tight fit even for her. He bent his head forward out of the stream and offered it his back and buttocks. He soaped and rinsed his lower torso twice. When he stood from the makeshift shower he saw Lil' Fella entangled in his silk panties.

"There is no doubt about it. You are a boy dog."

He slid the skirt and T-shirt back on. The panties belonged to Lil' Fella.

He couldn't remember ever taking a cold shower. He liked his showers hot, but there was something to be said for cold showers. He was alert, refreshed, and had a little pep in his step. And thanks to Lil' Fella he was swinging free between his legs. He actually felt kind of good.

He walked up the small hill to Madear. He sat next to her and pulled the other toiletries from the shoulder bag. Lil' Fella hopped in his lap with the panties hanging from his mouth. Terri rinsed his mouth with Payton's Plax and rolled on Payton's deodorant. He powdered his back and chest with Payton's Johnson's baby powder. He didn't use Payton's Brute. He found a large-toothed comb and a jar of Vaseline. He checked the Vaseline to make sure it was free of debris then began braiding his hair.

"I wish you was here to do this for me, Madear. I miss you." The puppy yelped. "I'm not talking to you. I'm talking to Madear. I can tell he's going to be a mess, Madear; spoiled rotten already. I didn't mean I miss you because of the things you did for me. I just miss you. I know you're with me, but I miss hearing you and seeing you. I miss shopping with you. I know the stores miss us. I haven't done much shopping lately. Remember how we used to shop when I moved back in with you after me and Jessie broke up? We hit all the stores.

217

"The money was really good then. All I had to do was follow the plan Jessie laid out. Two years of good money and then—what did you call it? The big head sickness.

"I can accept that now, but then I thought you were against me too. None of the managers or owners would book me after Jessie's arranged bookings ended. I had fans, a strong following, but they all said the same thing: I was more trouble than what I was worth.

"I didn't see it as my fault back then, Madear. Sure, I came to work tipsy sometimes, but I still gave them a damn good show. And yes, I fucked my fans and that did cause confusion. They all wanted to claim me as theirs, but I wanted to be no one's. I wanted to be with who I wanted, when I wanted. Sometimes that was in the dressing rooms, the club bathrooms, club parking lots—whenever the mood hit me. No discretion. That was the problem, and the owners wasn't having it.

"And the fights, I know they had a lot to do with it. To be honest, Madear, I liked the men fighting over me. It was exciting to see them come to blows right there in the clubs. Madear, I felt so desired, so wanted.

"I brought more men out the closet than a Frisco gay parade. It was important to me that they admitted they were gay. I don't know what kind of soapbox I was standing on then, but each one had to tell me he was gay. I didn't want a confused lover or one waiting for the lady inside of me to develop.

"I was so arrogant, when a club owner would tell me to be more discreet with my affairs I'd tell him to kiss my ass. I was the star. Youth, Madear; there is nothing like it. I never thought the money would run out. It seemed endless.

"I didn't understand fans. You got to be a star to keep their admiration, and a star needs a place to shine, a stage. I didn't know that when my bookings dwindled down to nothing, so would my fans.

"They are fickle and have short memories. They forgot their promises to love me forever, to want me for eternity. They wanted me as long as I was in the stage lights, something held up as special, something greater than them, something that allowed them to be part of the greatness, the stardom. I didn't think about the bragging rights they acquired by fucking a star. I was a thing to them, a star, just as they were things to me—fans.

"But you knew it all along, Madear. Fair weather friends, you called them. Lord, how I loved that lifestyle: shopping, being desired, being kept, being spoiled. I loved it all and got used to it pretty quick. When I saw it ending—once-desperate fans not returning my calls, club owners refusing single night engagements, no orchids or roses being shipped to me—I wanted to keep it. I lost it all so fast. I wasn't ready to give up, but it gave me up.

"Then I got the idea about the credit cards. Why not? I was used to getting free stuff anyway. Oh, the mistakes of youth. I was so spoiled and selfish. You want to hear something funny? Once I got to prison, I was a star again. That's some sick mess, I know, but it's the truth. I had more than most. In that system, that world, I got back what I couldn't hold on the outside. I was Queen Bitch, a star. Until Mo-red.

"He brought me down, Madear. And it wasn't like I let him. He took my joy, Madear. Took it! And wasn't a thing I could do about it. I was so afraid of him. He was bigger than life. He was life. He told me once he was my god on earth and I believed him. But on the outside, Madear, he's just a man—a man who bleeds and burns. He's not going to win, Madear. I know that now. I forgot I wasn't alone. I forgot I had you on my side."

Terri was finished with his hair. It was in four braids; one on the top that he connected to the one in back, and one on each side. Lil' Fella was sleeping comfortably in his lap.

"I don't have a plan, Madear, so I guess I'll leave it up to you and God."

He was putting the toiletries back in the shoulder bag when he heard a car on the gravel road. It was a white Lincoln Town Car. It stopped at the foot of Madear's hill. A man and woman were inside. Terri smiled.

"Thank you, Madear."

Dr. Goody and Terri's mother walked up Madear's hill. Dr. Goody spoke first.

"Good to see you, Terri."

"You too, doctor. How are you? How are the kids doing?"

Terri hadn't seen him in months, since his words about tough love at the clinic office.

"I'm okay, Terri, and the kids are fine. They're away for the summer."

Terri heard the edginess in his voice. This was the first time the two were together with his mother present. Terri could think of nothing to say that would ease his edginess. He wanted to, because Dr. Goody had been good to him.

Lil' Fella woke up and growled his puppy growl at Dr. Goody.

"It's Madear's birthday. I wanted to say goodbye before I left."

Terri and his mother met eyes; neither looked away as each expected the other to do.

"It ain't really her birthday," his mother said. "She didn't know when her birthday was. She picked the day after yours so she could celebrate with you. She loved you, Terrance, more than she loved anything or anybody on this earth. It's good you came to say goodbye."

"I don't need you to tell me what's good between me and Madear."

They were still staring in each other's eyes.

"Terrance, I know you don't need me to tell you anything, especially about you and Madear. You took care of her when I

220

wouldn't, but I took care of her, Terrance, when you couldn't. Despite the problems she and I had, I was the one that was there while you were in jail. I was the one she took her anger out on about dying and you not being there. She didn't understand you leaving. That's how she saw your going to prison: leaving her.

"I wouldn't take care of her anymore, but she didn't *want* me to take care of her. She wanted you to take care of her, but she was too hurt by your leaving to ask you. I had to put you two together and leave you together. It was the only way she was going to get better. She was my mother, Terrance, before she was your Madear, and I loved her too."

Terri saw the tears forming in Diane's eyes. He looked away. He didn't want to see her crying. He didn't want any new emotions where she was concerned. She was a bitch and that was all there was to it.

"Well, I've said goodbye. I'll leave you two alone with her. But if you don't mind, I could use a lift to the airport," Terri said, looking to Dr. Goody.

"Sure, Terri." Dr. Goody's eyes were on the ground.

Terri stood with Lil' Fella in his arms. He hoisted the shoulder bag.

"I'll meet you both by the car." Terri walked down Madear's hill, trying not to think about his mother and trying harder not to think about the last thing Madear said about her.

"It's not all her fault, Terri. Your mother and I experienced hard times. We lived through them, but we are both scarred. I could tell you about them, but you would only hear my side. You need to hear how it was from your mother, to understand your mother. She spent her young years raised in a whorehouse, Terri.

"I didn't think about her much until it was too late. It's my fault, I guess, but I can't make it right and I'm too set in my ways to try, but you and her have time. Work it out, T. T. Promise me you will work on it. It will only be you two left."

Terri tried to put his mind on getting out of the city, but the forgotten promise made to Madear demanded his thoughts. *"It will only be you two left."*

He preferred thinking about Mo-red wanting his death than settling whatever there was between him and the bitch. What was it Jessie said? *"You can't miss what you never had."* He never had a mother; he had Madear, and she was better than a mother. At least she was better than his mother.

Terri stood against the white Lincoln Town Car and looked up the hill to Diane. She'd gained weight and grayed. Her hair was in two braids parted down the middle like Madear wore hers. Standing atop the hill he noticed how much she looked like Madear, with the same lean face and the same deeply set eyes. She was wearing a flowered housedress not unlike the ones Madear wore. Maybe just a short talk on the way to the airport. He kissed the puppy on the top of his head. "What could it hurt?"

"You want us to take you straight to the airport?" Dr. Goody asked, looking in the rearview mirror to Terri.

Terri gave him a warm smile and answered, "Yes, please."

"Are you in trouble, Terrance? I had an awful dream last night," Terri's mother said.

"I'm fine, Diane."

"I don't believe you. Madear woke me up this morning and told me to come here. Something's wrong, Terrance. I know it."

"It's nothing you can change or help with, Diane. The lift to the airport is really all I need."

"Why don't you come home with us for a while? We can talk a little and give you time to rest. You look tired. What time is your flight?"

"You want to talk, Diane?"

"I think we need to."

"What would we talk about, Diane?"

"I'm sure we'll find something, Terrance."

"Is that okay with you, Doctor?"

"Terri, I've always wanted you and your mother to spend a little time together, and if you're leaving . . . y'all might not get this chance for a while, so it's fine with me."

"I don't know if you still like them, Terrance, but I baked a caramel cake using Madear's recipe. Give yourself time to think before your flight. And like it or not we are family. Your problems should be ours."

"What?" Terri clapped his hands and exhaled heavily. "Diane, my problems have never been yours. We don't know each other."

"We should know each other, Terrance. It's only you and I left."

Dr. Goody cleared his throat. "It's settled. Terri, we're taking you home."

Terri liked the sound of the word *home*: a safe place, a place to rest, a place to eat Madear's caramel cake, and a place to talk to Diane. Sitting in the plush leather seats of the air-conditioned, freshly scented Lincoln Town Car, Terri gave in. Perhaps this was Madear's plan. "You got enough of that cake for Lil' Fella?"

"Sure, Terrance, it's enough."

"Diane, do you think you could call me Terri?"

"Do you think you can call me mother?"

"Terrance is fine."

* * * * *

It wasn't Madear's house but it could have been. Terri saw the same style of furniture—big country couches, and the same colors—brown, green, and gray. At first sight Terri was angry because he thought it was Madear's furniture, but he noticed it was newer.

It was a large house, but Diane had it cluttered with things, just like Madear. In a room where two lamps would do she had four. On the side of each chair and at each end of a couch was an end table. Doilies covered all armrests.

"It looks like—"

"I know. I tried not to, but it came out like hers anyway. I bet yours will too."

"I doubt it. I can't stand doilies."

"We'll see. Let's go to the kitchen. I think I did better there."

She hadn't. It was Madear's kitchen, complete with mixing bowl, grill stove and cookie jar.

"You didn't do much better."

"Yes I did. I got a dishwasher. Madear would never buy a dishwasher."

"You're right about that. She said they was a waste of water and electricity."

Dr. Goody cleared his throat as he walked behind Terri and Diane into the kitchen.

"Well, I'ma leave you two alone for a while. I got some work to do." Dr. Goody kissed them both on the cheek. "Terri, the past is the past and we are family. Keep that in mind." He turned to Diane. "Don't waste time. You been waiting a long time for this chance. Say what you want to say." He left them sitting at the table.

"Whether you believe it or not, Terrance, I miss Madear too."

"That's not something for me to be concerned with. You and Madear had your relationship, she and I had ours, but—"

"But?"

"She wanted me to talk to you, get to know you a little better. It was one of the last things she asked me to do."

"Sounds like her. She and I went through hard times for a while, Terrance. I was young—sixteen or seventeen—and everything changed. Not saying that things were as they should

224

have been before, but that man changed Madear. Changed her for the worse, I believed then, but now I know it was for the best."

"Man? Madear never talked about a man."

"She wouldn't. I believe she pushed it out her mind. His name was Roman. He was a no-good bastard. He ran Madear and her business into the ground. He got her strung out on heroin. Like I said, I was young, so I don't know all the details. I remember him and Madear fighting like cats and dogs and always about money.

"The women who had been with Madear for years left her. He brought in new women, women who stuck that needle in their arms. He started selling heroin out of the house. He changed it from a brothel to a shooting den. If they made more money it wasn't showing. All the money I made Madear took. The maid stopped working because nobody was paying her. All I remember was filth, needles, people sleeping in chairs, cigarette stench and no food.

"The way I remember it, when Roman got all he could out of Madear, he left and took his addicted hoes with him. Madear stayed in her room for weeks. I cooked what I could and tried to feed her, but she wouldn't eat. All she wanted me to do was run down the street and get those little packages. I did it for weeks; I was afraid she would die without it. I wanted things to change. I wanted her to wake up, so I did something she told me never to do. I went and got the police. I brought the police into her home.

"After they took her away, I ran away that night and never lived with her again. I heard the police kept her about a month. When she got out she started renting rooms."

"That's who Willie was talking about?"

"Willie? Willie Jones?"

"Yeah, I met him last night."

"I saw him at Madear's funeral. He's gotten old. When I was a kid he kept a pocket full of candy for me. He and Madear was sweet on each other for a minute. I used to think he was my daddy because he was the only man Madear let in the kitchen. But then I remembered seeing him give Madear some money. Madear had told me my daddy was a broke, no-good nigga, so I knew it wasn't Willie."

"What about my father?"

"Your daddy was a pimp and a junkie. A full-blooded Cherokee, more nigga than any black man I'd ever done. Cooked pig feet, greens and cornbread better than Madear. I'd see him sniffing around Madear's house trying to pick up one of her girls or steer a customer to one of his street girls. He was the finest man I'd ever seen. Wore his hair in two ponytails and dressed as slick as a snake. When I ran away that night, I ran to him.

"Every dime I made went to him. He started me shooting dope, told me all hoes shoot dope. I let him put the first spike in my arm. When I got pregnant with you, I didn't want to shoot up, but he told me it would be alright. He said we had strong blood and nothing could hurt our baby. So he kept me doped up and working the streets. I was eight months pregnant, stomach sitting out a yard, and men was still buying me; and Two Moons was still working me. He drove me to the hospital when my water broke, and that was the last time I saw him."

"Madear said he was a drunk."

"Madear remembered the world as she wanted. She'd gotten old; she shaped her memories to suit her. Terrance, please don't get offended by this . . . but I have to tell you something. I do volunteer work at the Cabrini Green children's center. I saw you on Division Street, Terrance. I damn near tore up Albert's Lincoln the first time I saw you. You was my son and you looked so bad, and I was too far away from you in my mind to help you.

"From the day you was born you was Madear's child. I was so strung out on heroin all I could do was give you to her. My girlfriend Denise—she's dead now—she was strung out like me. Her baby was born with no arms or legs. When you came out with all your parts and yelling to beat the band, I knew I wanted you to stay alive, and you would've died with me. Madear took you without saying a word. I didn't come back to see you until you was three years old. You cried when I held you.

"I didn't know how to be a mama. I was a ho and a junkie, and that's all I wanted to be. When I saw you on Division it was like looking in the mirror of the past. I had tried so hard to forget my past, but you brought it back; you brought it back clear. I wanted to snatch you off the damn street, but who was I? Certainly not your mama.

"I watched you jump in and out of cars, knowing what you were doing. I watched you stand under those elevated train tracks and suck on that pipe. You would get out of a car and run straight to one of them niggas and give them the money for that shit, then run under the tracks and smoke it.

"It was the same for me, but you was my baby. It was supposed to be different for you. That life wasn't supposed to be yours, but I did nothing to stop it from being yours. Madear raised me and I turned into a ho; she raised you and you turned into a ho."

Terri snapped erect from the kitchen chair. "Don't you dare! Don't you dare blame Madear for your fucked-up life or mine! You left me with her and she did the best she could by me. I chose to be a ho."

Terri's trembling index finger was in his mother's face.

"No you didn't. She raised you to be ho, just like she did me. She saw nothing wrong with prostituting. Trading her body for money was second nature to her. As long as they paid top dollar it was alright. Damn, she named me after a ho! Madear was sick, Terrance, and it took me a long time to know it."

"You're the one that's sick!"

Terri sat back in his chair and Lil' Fella yelped at Diane.

227

"Yes, I was, for a very long time. I was raised in a ho-house. All I knew was hoeing. My first time was with a trick Madear sent to my room. I was fourteen. The white bastard paid Madear three hundred and fifty dollars, and I was so proud.

"I was working for my money, and my mother was proud. Every ho in the gotdamn house was proud of me! It was a ho-house; of course they was proud of me! Except one. Fran.

"She told me to run away. She told me little girls didn't have to be hoes. Hoes were women who didn't have husbands and families. Hoes were bad, she told me. She told me to run away. I told Madear what Fran told me, then Fran was gone and only hoes that liked being hoes was left. And I was a ho that liked being a ho. A fourteen-year-old ho."

"Madear's not here. She can't speak for herself."

"Yes, she can. Remember, Terrance. Remember the things she used to tell you. I know it wasn't any different than what she told me. 'Always be pick of the litter; expect the best; the value one puts in one's work should always be reflected in the price; don't sell it cheap.'

"Why sell it at all, Terrance? The world didn't make us hoes; our environment made us hoes. I don't really blame Madear for my life because that was all she knew at the time, but with you, Terrance, she could've did better."

"You could've did better! If you was so motherfucking concerned about me being fucked up, you should've raised me. Madear taught me to value myself."

"Yes. So you would know the value of what you were selling."

"No, that was my decision."

"Did she try to talk you out of it? No! You were programmed from the beginning just like me. She bred what she was. She didn't see anything wrong with prostitution. She was sick.

228

"Selling yourself is not what is expected, Terrance. It is an exception to the norm."

"What, some counselor told you that?"

"Yes, a lot of counselors, Terrance, and a lot of priests, a lot of social workers, a lot of therapists and God. I had to get a lot of help to change what was imbedded in my brain. I am forty-six years old and the only man that didn't pay to sleep with me was Albert. Terrance, you share the same sickness."

"I'm not sick, at least not like that. I'm a addict. My problem is with drugs!"

"No, it's deeper, much deeper. Drugs are on the surface. We got the wrong message from the beginning. We traded ourselves for money. Where there should have been love, we took money, gifts and things. When we were faced with love we turned our backs on it, looking for what we were accustomed to—things, money and gifts. She taught us the value of money, not the value of love or the value of self. She taught us to sell ourselves."

"No. She taught me more than that. She loved me."

"Yes. And she loved me, too, but she was sick and she made us sick."

"Where's the bathroom?"

"Out that door make a left. I'll cut the cake while you're gone."

Terri left Lil' Fella and took the shoulder bag to the bathroom. He tore into the plastic bag, fumbling for the cocaine rocks. "The bitch is crazy."

He stuffed the pipe and lit it. Madear was not sick. Madear was the only thing real in his life. She did not train him to be a ho; she accepted it. He lit the pipe again and again until Diane's words were no longer in his mind.

He walked back to the kitchen and sat at the table. A slice of caramel cake was in front of him. He pushed it aside.

229

"You high now, ain't cha? The truth sent you running to your drugs. Dropped your poor little dog on the floor and ran in there to that gotdamn pipe, your real friend, right?"

"Fuck you, okay? You don't know shit."

"I know you're high. I know the truth hurts, but I also know it will set you free. You're trapped, Terrance, in a vicious cycle, and I know you know it because I knew it but I couldn't find a way out as long as I kept that spike in my arm.

"I only been clean for two years, Terrance. You ain't got to wait as long as I did, baby. I did that time for you. You ain't got to suffer anymore. I know the cause."

"I'm not suffering."

"Oh, you like sucking dicks for a living? You like failing at everything you try to do? You like being a ho?"

"I'm not going to be a ho anymore. I'm going to Birmingham to start over." Terri heard his voice but the words sounded like those of a child.

"You gonna leave the addict here, right?"

"That's right."

"Wrong. He's gonna always be with you, waiting for you to slip. Waiting for the truth to hurt you so bad you run to the drugs. You know how you stop the truth from hurting you?"

"No."

"You accept it. I wanted to keep blaming myself for my life. It was easier. I did it to myself, so fuck it. But I didn't do it to myself; my environment, my mother did it to me. The mother that I loved. The mother that cried when she saw me on the streets. The mother that taught me to value myself based on the money men gave me. That's what fucked me up! Madear fucked me up! Accept it and you can move on."

"No, you put those needles in your arm."

"True, but why?"

"'Cause you wanted to get high."

"Why?"

"'Cause you liked it."

230

"Why the first time?"

"'Cause you was looking for something different."

"Yeah—love, acceptance, guidance, nurturing, and someone to depend on. All the things a good mother gives you. I was looking for them. You ain't ready for Birmingham, Terrance. Stay here. Let me pay for your treatment. Let's work together on getting you clean."

"It's too late for that good mama shi—"

Terri stopped in mid-sentence, his eyes fixed beyond his mother.

"Don't no motherfucker move!" Mo-red was standing in the doorway with a gun to Dr. Goody's head.

"I thought you said they was gone. I can't stand a lying-ass nigga!"

"No! Don't shoot him, please. Here it is. It's all here. Just don't shoot him. Please."

Terri took the bag to Mo-red. Mo-red took it and shoved Dr. Goody into the kitchen.

"Bitch, you shot me in my motherfuckin' chin. You burned down my house, you slashed my arm, burnt my hands, and ho, you askin' me not to kill somebody. I'ma kill every motherfucker in here! But bitch, you gonna be last."

They moved in silent quickness. Terri spotted one behind Mo-red. He thought they were Mo-red's soldiers, but they shot Mo-red. Terri tried to duck, but they shot him. It wasn't a bullet; it was dart, a big dart. They shot Diane with one. They shot Dr. Goody with one. They shot Lil' Fella with one and everybody was falling.

Terri counted six of them. They were moving slowly. Terri tried to reach for his gun but he had no arms. The intruders were dressed in black, like ninjas from a movie. They left Dr. Goody, Diane and Lil' Fella. They took Terri's gun from the small of his back then one of them picked him up. He was relived to see his arms dangling in front of him.

One of them took the shoulder bag. Two of them picked up Mo-red. They accidentally dropped Mo-red on the concrete steps of the front porch. His chin started bleeding through the bandage. Terri heard himself laughing in the distance.

It was a pizza delivery truck. Did Diane order pizza and didn't pay for it? They should be taking her; he ordered no pizza. He tried to tell them, but all he heard was his own laughter.

.

Chapter 9
Reunited

The dream was crazy. Madear was chasing him with a crack pipe and a needle. She chased him into a room full of naked white men. Terri had a three hundred and fifty-dollar price tag around his neck and they were all trying to fuck him.

Terri forced himself awake, but his eyelids were heavy and they wouldn't stay up. He turned his head and saw Jessie sitting in Madear's LaZBoy chair.

"Oh, fuck." He gave up and let his eyelids close.

In the next dream, Payton was chasing him with bits of his head falling all along Division Street. The trees bent down and picked up the pieces of Payton's head and ate them.

"Don't turn your back on our love, Terri! I love you."

Terri ran to safety in a group of Weeping Willows in the middle of Division Street. Madear was standing above her headstone, beckoning him closer. He reached for her but she moved farther away. He leaped for her but he fell down into her grave.

The swimming coach was there, begging for a blowjob. Jessie appeared above the grave and threw him a rope, but Clyde ran over him with his new Mercedes. Then big boulders of cocaine fell into the grave, burying him. He got his pipe and tried to smoke his way out. He stopped the dream and opened his eyes.

He woke up to a panoramic view of Lake Michigan. The red sun was setting beyond the edges of the lake. The sky was reddish gold, the color of autumn leaves. No boats could be seen on the gray water; only the water filtration plant was in the horizon.

Terri was lying on a day bed in front of the largest window he'd seen in his life. Pillows were placed under his head and the small of his back. He was not restrained and actually quite comfortable. He decided not to look around. If it was a dream, he wanted it to stay as it was.

By the color of the sun he figured it was late in the day. Wherever he was, it was better than sitting at that table hearing the foolishness coming out of Diane's mouth. If the ninjas were going to kill him, fine. He was tired of running. His shoulder ached from the dart. He stretched his arm and his hand brushed against something cold. It was a crystal goblet filled with chilled Chablis.

"Well, alright now!" He didn't hesitate to sip it. If it was poison, so what?

He always wondered why the water of the lake changed colors: blue, green, brown or gray. It would have been nice if it was blue now—that deep, rich blue, that bright, summer afternoon blue. He sipped the Chablis. What was Diane trying to make him think, talking against Madear like that?

"Bitch. I shoulda told her that the one man that didn't pay her did pay me."

What was she thinking? What did she hope to accomplish? It wasn't Madear's fault. No, she didn't stop him from going out with the coach, but he never expected her to. Madear never judged him. She never told him he was doing wrong, because he wasn't doing wrong. He was gettin' his money. She never asked for any of the money. And he was grown—well, almost grown before he ever knew she was a ho.

And who was to say prostitution was wrong? He was just tired of it. Madear didn't raise him to be a ho. If anything she raised him to be on the stage, an actress. She never sent any men to his room. Some people hoed their whole lives. There was nothing wrong with hoeing. Hoes knew love. Willie loved Madear.

"I'm more tired of getting high than I am of hoeing. I'm tripping about being a ho. I should be tripping about being a ten-dollar ho."

Terri recalled Diane's words. *"She taught us to value ourselves based on the money men gave us."*

Then he remembered Madear's. *"I didn't think much about her until it was too late . . . There are no perfect people in the world, T.T."*

"Damn." Terri gulped the Chablis and stood.

"Let's see what's going on." He turned around and saw a huge room, empty except for the daybed, the small table on the side of it and the chair that held Mo-red. He was beaten, bound and gagged. Not fear but pure delirium surged through Terri's veins. He couldn't help but laugh.

"They didn't give you any wine? Baby, it looks like they beat your ass some too. How's the chin, baby? Oh, Mo-red, this hasn't been your day, has it? Mo-red! Gorilla pimpin' Mo-red."

Terri approached with no fear. If death came, it came. He punched directly into the blood-soaked bandage that covered Mo-red's chin.

"I know that hurt. But you know what? It didn't hurt me a bit."

Mo-red tried to break free, but the binds held him.

"Tied your ass up good, didn't they?" Terri reached in his skirt pocket and pulled out his lighter.

"What did you tell me? You was gonna cut my thang off and burn it? Is that right?"

Terri flicked the lighter.

"Yes, that's what you said. Well, let's pull out that red motherfucker of yours and see if we can light it up!"

Mo-red squirmed in the chair. Terri unzipped his pants.

"You used to like me unzipping your pants, Mo-red. Remember when you used to make me sit under the cafeteria table and suck your thang while you ate? Well, just think about that. I tell you what—I'll even suck it for you a little bit. And I'll make you a deal; if it don't get hard, I won't burn it. But if it gets hard, we going to light it up!"

Terri dropped his head to Mo-red's lap.

"Well, would you look at that thang growing! Damn, it's getting big! Big enough to light!"

Terri held Mo-red's thang in his hand and stuck the head in the flame.

"It's bubbling like a marshmallow. Look at that, Mo-red! But the smell, what does that remind you of? Mmm, burning Vienna sausages! That's it, Mo-red!

"Mo-red, are you crying? Too bad Payton didn't have a chance to cry. You know what? It's only cooked on one side of the head. We have to do the other side!"

Terri turned up the lighter. "I think we need a little more flame."

Terri dug his nails into the burned side of Mo-red's thang and twisted it over into the flame.

"This side bubbling too, baby. Ooh! You got all kind of stuff oozing out of this side!"

A voice came from behind Terri. "Stop it! That's enough!"

Fuck whoever was talking to him. This had to be done. It had to be burned to a nub. It had to be destroyed. Payton was dead, the money was gone, Diane was crazy, Birmingham was out, he was a ten-dollar ho, Weeping Willows was on Division Street and Madear raised him to be a ho. He put the bubbling flesh in his mouth and bit clean through it. He brought his head up from Mo-red's lap and spit what was left into his face.

"Fuck you, Mo-red."

He shoved his thumbs into the soft pockets of Mo-red's eyes, forcing his thumbnails under each eyeball.

"Die blind, motherfucker!"

Terri felt the sting in his back; he knew the feeling. It was another damn dart. He didn't hear himself laugh and saw no one moving slowly. There was only the sudden darkness and dreamless sleep.

Terri woke groggier than the first time. He was stiff all over. The room appeared smoky. A full moon replaced the sun.

The moon was all there was; the sky and the water were one. Blackness and the moon.

Someone had cleaned him up. The Nike T-shirt and his leather skirt were gone. He was dressed in a long, black T-shirt. The Chablis was replaced with a bottle of Remy Martin and a shot glass. He downed two straight shots. He smelled a familiar fragrance.

To his left was the chair that once held Mo-red. Now a man was sitting in it, in the shadow of the moonlight. A cigarette glowed as he inhaled. The silhouette of the man was familiar. Terri knew at once whose company he was in.

"When did you start smoking?" Terri asked.

"About five years ago. I wouldn't stand if I were you. I shot you with a different tranquilizer than the first one. That shot was supposed to be for Maurice."

"Is he dead?"

"Yes. I killed him. I couldn't let him live dickless and blind. He begged me to kill him."

"It was your money?"

"No. My drugs."

"Oh. How is Pumpkin?"

"She's good. She's in Atlanta opening a new beauty shop."

"Lucky her."

"Yeah. Lucky her."

"What about me?"

"What about you?"

"Am I to die here?"

"Have I ever hurt you?"

"No."

"Then why ask?"

"My mind, it's not right."

"Maybe it's opening?"

"If this is what a open mind feels like, I want mine closed."

"Closed to what?"

"Everything—seeing people killed, wanting people killed, causes—every fucking thing!"

"Causes?"

"Causes!"

"I can understand seeing and wanting people dead, but causes?"

"Diane said she knew the cause of my fucked-up life."

"Diane?"

"Diane is my mother."

"Okay, you always referred to her as 'the bitch.' "

"Diane, the bitch, said Madear raised us both to be hoes."

"Madear? Your grandmother."

"Yes."

"And?"

"And . . . and . . . I'm starting to see her point. And I don't want to accept it."

"How are you seeing her point?"

"Dreams, and remembering she never told me not to do it. She never said don't be a ho. She never said be something more. I was hoein' before I got on stage. She took me to the theater but she never told me I could be a star. Don told me that. When I told her about the coach, she didn't tell me to go to the authorities and report him. She didn't tell me to stop. I thought it was her accepting me being gay, but it wasn't. It was her accepting me hoein'.

"If I had a child and he came to me at fourteen and told me a man gave him thirty dollars to let the man suck on him, I would tear down walls getting to his ass. But Madear didn't. I tried to give her the money; she told me to keep it. She said I was the one earning it. And like Diane, I felt proud.

"Diane was right; love is not what I want. Things, money, gifts—that's the shit I've chased my whole life. Chasin' it! Look how I fucked up our relationship. It's a perfect example. Chasin' things. Chasin' a good hit of a crack pipe, chasin' a trick with money. Been chasin' shit my whole life. Trees don't chase shit; they stay in place and take what comes to them and they live for hundreds of years.

"Diane's right; I need help. I can't stop chasin' crack. I can't stop chasin' tricks. I sell myself for five and ten-dollar rocks. I smoked up every gotdamn thing I owned and damn near every friend. I got to change."

"Into what?"

"I don't know."

"Into what?"

"I . . . don't . . . know. I just know I got to stop gettin' high."

"Then what?"

"I don't know. I need help."

"I'll help you."

"No. I need my mama to help me. She knows the cause."

When Jessie rose from the chair into the moonlight, Terri saw he hadn't changed much. The moonlight gave his dark skin a bluish tint.

"Will you help me up? I need to use your bathroom."

Jessie extended his hand, assisting Terri's slow rise. Once up, Terri anchored himself against Jessie.

"What kind of uniform is this you're wearing? You with the D.E.A. or something?" Terri's muscles, especially his legs, were sore and very stiff. He took small, unsteady steps. Jessie moved with him.

"No, this is nocturnal gear."

He stopped and let Terri steady himself.

"It's called Night Mesh. The D.E.A. might use it. I don't know."

"Why do you use it?"

"For nighttime situations."

Jessie placed his arm around Terri's back, giving him more support.

"Thank you."

"The bathroom is not much further. Just down the hall a bit."

"Is this your place?"

"Sort of."

"Did you really sell the house in South Holland?"

"Yes. I left the day after you."

"How did you find me?"

"When?"

"Today."

Terri reached the bathroom and stood in its doorway. He located the light switch on the inner wall and flipped it up. Damn! Jessie looked good to him. Not a scar or pimple on his smooth face, and the waves Pumpkin grew were still flowing. Terri turned away from Jessie, knowing he certainly didn't look as kept.

"I wasn't looking for you, Terri. Our business was with Maurice."

"Our business?"

"When you finish in the bathroom I'll explain. Can you manage?"

"Yes."

Terri didn't sit on the toilet to pee as he normally did. His legs were too stiff to bend. He stood and balanced himself with one hand against the wall over the toilet.

The mirror showed him that he looked better than he felt. His eyes weren't bloodshot as he had expected, nor were there bags under them. He noticed a couple of specks of dried blood on his chin. He cupped his mouth to muffle his own scream.

He hadn't forgotten what he did, but the blood put it in focus. He'd bit Mo-red's thang off. He'd scratched his eyes out. Mo-red was dead. Terri didn't expect it, but a smile appeared on his face in the mirror.

He thoroughly rinsed his mouth with hot water. He soaped his hands and washed what was left of Mo-red from his face. When he exited the bathroom, Jessie was waiting to assist him

241

back to the daybed. The blinds were closed and the moonlight was replaced by fluorescent light from overhead panels. They were in an office. Once Terri was in a reasonably comfortable position on the daybed, he asked Jessie, "So what business did you have with Mo-red?"

"Who?"

"Maurice."

"Oh, we were there because he was trying to steal the cocaine."

"You're a drug dealer now?"

"No, the cocaine wasn't really mine. It belongs to an associate."

"Still bullying people for money?"

"No, not at all. He's an associate I met through touring."

"Touring?"

"I still fight. I tour to different martial art tournaments throughout the country. Martial artists are very interesting people. You'd be surprised at what they are involved in."

"So you met Master Lee the cocaine dealer and he hired you to beat up Mo-red?"

"No, not quite. I tour with a group of six martial artists. Two are mercenaries. As mercenaries, they're approached with all types of propositions, and people don't always pay in cash. The group coordinator came into twelve kilos of cocaine, two of which he gave to Maurice on consignment. Maurice was a day late and avoiding his calls. We were tailing Maurice. Seeing you was totally unexpected."

"A pleasant surprise, I hope."

"Without a doubt. But tell me, how did you get involved in all this?"

"Life hasn't been sweet, Jessie. I've gotten into a lot of different things since we were together. Mo-red stole the drugs from your friends; I stole the drugs from him."

"I see. He was telling the truth."

"What?"

242

"He said you stole the cocaine from him and he'd been tracking you down for two days."

"That's a lie! I stole that cocaine from him yesterday."

"Calm down. It really doesn't make a difference. Maurice is dead and dumped and the drugs were recovered with a bonus kilo."

Terri resisted the impulse to ask about the money. He was alive, and that was good enough for him.

"You're not a cop or a dope dealer; you're a grown man playing soldier. Jessie, you could have gotten killed."

"Is that concern I hear?"

"A little."

"Well, it wasn't the first time I went along with them on one of their missions, and I hope it won't be the last. I need the action. Why did you attack Maurice?"

"He's been trying to kill me for years, bit by bit. I had to stop it."

"Well, you stopped it. But there is something you should know. He died calling your name."

"So."

"Were you lovers?"

"No. He was a sadistic rapist."

"He raped you?"

"Yes. He robbed me of myself. I attacked him because I hated him. I attacked him because he hurt me."

"I'll remember that."

Jessie no longer drove a BMW. Jessie no longer drove. Jerome, the cab driver who took Terri away from Jessie's house years ago, now drove the Silver Shadow Rolls Royce limousine as they cruised down Lake Shore Drive.

"You know that's not a summer fragrance."

Jessie laughed from his gut. "No shit."

"I haven't done much shopping lately, but I'm certain they've come out with some new scents."

"I don't change things I like."

243

"That makes sense. You were always a practical man. Can I ask you a question?"

"I'm not married."

"That wasn't my question."

"Okay. Ask."

"If you have all this, if you've made it, if your crumb pile is as high as it looks, why be bothered with low-life activity?"

"The truth?"

"Please."

"I could say it's the money, but it ain't. It's the sport, the rush, the danger, the power. The life-and-death action of the streets. True, my crumb pile is high—I got a couple of piles—but I got this hole inside of me, and sometimes the life-and-death action of the streets fills it, at least for a while."

"If the drugs don't get you, the lifestyle will."

"What?"

"It's a sayin' I heard in detox. If the drugs don't get you, the lifestyle will."

"What does that mean?"

"It means you're addicted."

"I seldom use drugs."

"It's not the drugs you're addicted to. It's the action of the lifestyle."

"Girl, you and your labels. Years ago you was trying to tell me I was gay. Now I'm a addict?"

"Yep. You're an addict; you're addicted to the action of the streets."

"No. I got a hole and it needs fillin'." He touched Terri in a way not offering support or assistance. He placed his hand on Terri's thigh.

Terri looked down at Jessie's hand and lightly placed his own on top of it.

"I'm so full of holes, Jessie, you'd leak more with me. The state I'm in now, I'm no good to myself. I would only hurt you."

"I'm a big boy."

"But I'm not a big girl. I got some growing to do, Jessie. I think I stopped at fourteen, but I'm not the only one sitting back here that needs help. There is a cause for your hole, and it ain't missing me."

The Silver Shadow parked in front of Dr. Goody's house. Jessie placed the blue nylon shoulder bag in Terri's lap. "The money has no owner."

"I can keep it?"

"Have I ever let you leave me broke?"

"No."

"The phone number is still on. It starts with two."

"After all these years, Jessie?"

Terri avoided looking into Jessie's face, Jessie's eyes. Pumpkin had told him years ago that Jessie's eyes didn't lie. Terri didn't want to see that Jessie pitied him. He didn't want to see that Jessie found him repulsive, scared, worn-out and drugged-out. He didn't want to see that Jessie saw he'd become a ten-dollar crackhead ho.

"I told you a long time ago, Terri, we are soulmates. That number has never been turned off."

When Terri looked into Jessie's eyes, he was thrown back in time. He saw the same honest desire in Jessie's face that was there the first time Jessie saw him nude. They were in Don's shower. Jessie placed his hand to Terri's cheek and pulled him close. He gave him more than a kiss. It was more than a promise. It was more than forgiveness. It was more than desire.

"Soulmates," they both said after what was more than a kiss ended.

Dr. Goody opened the front door as the limousine pulled away.

"Terri! Dear Lord, thank you! We thought you were dead." He pulled Terri into an embrace the likes of which Terri had never felt from Dr. Goody—one with no lust. Dr. Goody

245

wasn't pressing his crotch into him. He held him snugly around the back.

"No. I'm not dead. I'm still hanging in. Where's my mother?" Terri stepped free of the embrace.

"Who?"

Terri breathed out a short laugh. "My mother?"

"She's in the kitchen."

If there was a bigger smile in existence Terri hadn't seen it. Dr. Goody was showing teeth from ear to ear.

Diane was standing over the sink washing dishes. Lil' Fella was eating chicken livers out of a bowl on the floor in front of the dishwasher.

"What sense does it make having a dishwasher if you don't use it?"

"Terrance! Oh my God! Baby, I didn't know what to do. Albert wouldn't let me call the police, and we woke up all dopey, and your little dog had the shits, and you wasn't here, and that man had that gun! Oh, sweet Jesus, thank you!"

They embraced. Terri whispered in his mother's ear. "I need your help. I can't keep chasin' it. There is no catching it. I'm not ready for Birmingham. I need you. I'm not ready for no place alone. I need your help. Will you help, Diane, please?"

"Yes, baby, with the all strength the Lord gives me. You are my child."

The next morning he woke in his mother and stepfather's guest bedroom. The night before they had agreed on an eighteen-month treatment program, the one from which his mother had graduated. She told him it wouldn't be easy. That was fine with him; he wasn't looking for easy, just better.

The bed was comfortable, filled with huge, fluffy pillows. His mother wouldn't allow Lil' Fella to sleep in the house. Terri heard him yelping in the backyard. He threw the sheets back, freeing himself to go the window and see Lil' Fella, but stopped when he saw the blue nylon shoulder bag. It was sitting to the side of the bed in an armchair.

He hadn't told his mother or Dr. Goody about the money. He wasn't keeping it a secret from them; it just never came up in the conversation. They talked mostly about Diane's recovery and the treatment center.

Terri hadn't looked in the bag because he was afraid there might have been some cocaine left in it. Diane had told him the night before that if he was serious about quitting, he'd already had his last time. She told him his addiction would tell him he needed a last hurrah. There was never a last hurrah with addiction, she told him. It would always find a reason for him to get high one last time.

Diane had been right. He found himself regretting not asking Jessie for his pipe. He could use one last blast. Diane had told him an addict wants to get high; the most natural thing in the world for an addict is to think about getting high. She told him not to beat up on himself if he woke up wanting a hit.

Terri had thought she was wrong. He felt certain that after last night the desire to get high would be behind him, but he was wrong. He wanted a hit badly. One last hit.

Maybe he could take a couple hundred out of the bag, sneak out and find somebody to get high with one last time. Nobody would know, and so what if they did find out? He was going to treatment anyway.

The thought was growing into a plan. He went to the bag. He was standing over it, looking down at the zipper when his mind flashed back to the young boy under the El tracks—the one who called him a ho, the one who gave him a ten-dollar rock to swallow his cum.

"No! No more!" he screamed. "Diane! Diane! Diane!"

His mother burst into the room, housecoat flying behind her. "Terrance! Oh my God, what's wrong?"

Terri stood trembling over the bag. "I got money in this bag—a lot of money—and I'm scared I'm going to get high with it. Take it out of here!" Terri screamed at the bag.

Terri looked to Diane, who was smiling.

"Look in the bag, Terri."

"I don't want to see the money, Diane, and it might be some rocks in there. I can't," he said, pleading.

"Look in the bag, son." Her tone was stern but warm.

Terri unzipped the bag and found it emptied of the money. All the bag held was a picture of Madear, which he pulled to his breast.

"I been where you going, Terrance. I emptied the bag last night while you slept. I had Albert put the money in the safe at the clinic.

"It's not going to be easy, Terrance, but you did the right thing. You called for help. You're going to have to keep doing that, son. I'm here to help you."

Terri stood silently looking at the picture of Madear while the trembling subsided.

"She's with you, Terrance. Believe that. We are family, and we're here for you, always."